THE COLOR OF
RAIN

THE COLOR OF
RAIN

CORI McCARTHY

RP TEENS
PHILADELPHIA · LONDON

Books published by Running Press are available at special discounts for bulk
purchases in the United States by corporations, institutions, and other organizations.
For more information, please contact the Special Markets Department at the
Perseus Books Group, 2300 Chestnut Street, Suite 200, Philadelphia, PA 19103, or
call (800) 810-4145, ext. 5000, or e-mail special.markets@perseusbooks.com.

ISBN 978-0-7624-4821-0

Library of Congress Control Number: 2012953353

E-book ISBN 978-0-7624-4846-3

9   8   7   6   5   4   3   2   1
Digit on the right indicates the number of this printing

Designed by Frances J. Soo Ping Chow
Edited by Lisa Cheng
Typography: Berthold Baskerville, Capture It, Dead Man's Hand, Frutiger,
Letter Gotic, Mr Moustache, PiS NeoPrintM319, and SS_Adec

Published by Running Press Teens
An Imprint of Running Press Book Publishers
A Member of the Perseus Books Group
2300 Chestnut Street
Philadelphia, PA 19103–4371

Visit us on the web!
www.runningpress.com/kids

To Mario,
for brazen honesty

Of all the directions to be looking, I stare up.

So I see her second foot leave the forty-something floor windowsill. Her dark form opens against the gray sky, her arms and legs out like a star falling—a falling star.

Akimbo.

Her hair splays brown. Her face coming clearer, so serene. She falls while I almost forget to pull my brother by his collar, to bring us out of her landing. I almost forget that there are really only two directions in this known universe: we accept it or we escape.

She falls, her eyes as open as mine, and I grip my brother and *run*, hearing the *flit flit flit* of her clothes beating the wind followed by the pavement moment when she

Hits.

PART 1

YELLOW

CHAPTER
1

The smoke sky is impenetrable. Gray billows against gray, but still I search for a glimpse of the stars beyond.

No luck.

With the sea and its aging docks at my back, I hurry downtown, into the labyrinth of decaying skyscrapers and tall shadows. It's been a long while since I haven't been glued to my little brother, and I dig my hands into my pockets to keep from reaching for him.

My shirt snags the wind, snapping against my chest like a worn-thin flag.

Lo picked it out for me—her lucky shirt, she calls it. The very shirt she wore when she sold her virginity, but then, I'm not sure that I need luck for what I'm about to do. Even if he is twice my age and decidedly nasty. The luck was finding him in the first place.

It won't be that hard, I chant through my thoughts. *It won't be. It won't be. It won't . . .*

But still, my feet grow heavier and my body runs cold. I shouldn't be late, I know.

He's waiting.

His money is waiting, and yet unbelievably, beyond the towering buildings, a sole cloud throbs slightly whiter against the smog. It dares me to think about other things, about Simon, and *that* feels a little like luck.

I turn left instead of right, instead of going straight to him. Now jogging, I weave through a wave of factory workers until I reach the boarded-up windows of Dex's restaurant, the biggest one wearing the slapdash spray-painted words, WE'RE ALWAYS OPEN.

The only remaining window makes me pause; this was where I dreamed of the Void and its stars while scrubbing tables. And that day—hours before she fell over us—I was staring out that window when Simon caught me by my hips. He blew raspberries on my neck until I screamed and Dex roared *Shut it!* from the kitchen.

Was that really only weeks ago?

The window now glitters with a spiderweb of a smashed pane. Someone must have chucked a brick at it, and why not? For some hurts, there's nothing better than the sound of breaking glass, and there's not much glass left on Earth City.

Dex is probably still mad that I had to quit, so I head up the back alley, leaping over the piles of trash. After all, maybe this isn't the day I take a swan dive into the desperate world—maybe there is some hope here. Simon always thought of me as just a kid, but no kid would be on the edge of doing what I'm about to do.

I bang a fist against the screen door and wait, the wafting scents and sounds of frying food mix with an old rot smell. "Simon!" I yell. "Simon!"

My braid is coming loose, and I untangle my hair. Has he ever even seen it down? I center the loose neck of Lo's shirt around my shoulders. It's a little too obvious that I'm not wearing a bra, but then, as Lo said, "That's the point."

Simon whacks the screen door against the brick. His hands are covered in bits of raw meat; he must have been working the sausage pump.

"Look at you, Rain White." His hair is sandy and frayed at the temples, and his skin is that never-seen-the-sun color like everyone on Earth City, but he wears it well. "I heard you were following Lo the Ho into the street-corner life, but I didn't believe it." He flashes a tricky sort of grin.

"I wanted to talk to you before I . . . just before."

"Sorry, Rain." He flicks his fingers and bits of meat go flying. "I already talked to Dex, and he can't give you the kind of raise you want. Even with the whole situation with your brother. He feels bad about it. We all do."

"That's not it." I shift in Lo's shirt, wishing I was wearing my own clothes.

"No one's going to report Walker to the cops, if that's what you're worried about. We'll all remember the scruffy little ginger at his best. But still, I wouldn't bring him near here."

"It's not that. Walker's . . . fine. I just I wanted to see you. See if you'd ever want to sometime . . ." I've never been so timid of tongue, and it annoys me. "If you want to be with me."

He grins. "I do miss that too-forward way of yours, but I don't have that kind of money. Can't afford you, Rainy day. But I guess . . . thanks?"

I sway on the spot. "You think I want you to pay?"

"If this is your new business, you shouldn't be giving it away for free." He might be about to laugh, and heat claws up my neck like a hot hand. It closes around my throat and chokes my words.

"But I meant . . ." Lo was so right about him. "You're an ass, Simon."

"Kid, wait." He hasn't called me that in years, and maybe he realizes it. "Just hold on a second." His hands are still slimed with meat, and he shakes his fingers without loosing any of it. The globs are drying, clinging to his skin, and he smears them against his stained apron. "Now don't get all *crazy*."

I wince. He should know better than to use that word after what my brother is going through. "You'll need the hard lye soap to get that off," I say.

The alley blares with the sound of the changing shift bell.

"I'm late."

"All right." Simon's grin twitches, but it's somehow already not as cute as it was a few moments ago. "Don't be a ghost, Rain."

I hurry to the street, hearing the screen door slam behind him. The heat of my embarrassment leaves me in a hurry, and now I feel the swish of my empty pockets. I picture my brother below the spacedocks with Lo, locked in his distorted mind. But above it all, I feel the spiky place in my chest where my childhood crush just fractured like Dex's front window.

What was I thinking? I'm no kid anymore.

But now, at least, I can go to *him*.

⁓⁓⁓⁓⁓

A decrepit skyscraper slants against the smog, leaning over me. Its black windows spot like cavities—a grin with broken teeth. It seems to sneer:

You are here. This is happening.

His name is Hallisy, and he squeezes my hips, each of his jagged nails biting in. His breath comes in rapid grunts: animal sounds. I'm trying so hard not to hyperventilate that I may not be breathing at all.

I grip a ridge in the alley wall and begin to slip into some fantasy about the stars, but then I blink hard instead. We will break from this planet for real. That's why I took his money. No more daydreams. No more . . . Simons. I go over Lo's advice: *Be soft. He'll do the rest.*

The rest of what? I had asked. But now I know it. Little bit at a time, he does what he wants with my clothes. My neck. My belt.

Be soft.

But I can't, and I know that I'm as supple as the brick I'm pressed against. Hallisy seems to like it, though. He snorts into my hair, his body all rods and twisted wires. Still, he's taking too long to get to It. He's *playing.* And time is running out for Walker.

"Go on." I bite my tongue.

He peels his pants down and grinds his steel coil of a torso against mine. I feel too much—so *much* of him—and I lose my hold on the wall.

"LEAVE HER ALONE!" My little brother streaks like a bald bird up the alley, the flaps of his too-big jacket flying up like wings. "GET BACK!" He swings a piece of broken pipe at Hallisy who falls, caught up in his own pants.

"What the shit!" Hallisy scrambles to stand, to yank the pipe from Walker and to hold his belt up. Walker makes another solid loop with the pipe, but Hallisy wrenches it out of his grasp.

I refasten my pants and get between the rusty weapon and my small brother. "Don't be stupid. He's just a kid!"

"I'm more man than him!" Walker yells from behind me. He has a death grip on my shirt and is already tugging me backward. "Come *on*, Rain!"

Hallisy sneers. "That ain't even a kid." His pants are tented with a misdirecting arrow that makes a horrible taste rise in my mouth. "Looks to me like he's got a bit of the crazy touch."

I close my hand around my brother's wrist. I don't know how he knows about Walker, but if he knows . . .

He points the pipe at me. "Now you—"

"Sweet freakin' mess, Hallisy. You going to keep her all night?" Lo's lithe body slips around the corner. My best friend leans against the Dumpster, her hip bones jutting through her stretchy skirt like concealed guns.

"I'm on my business, Lo." Hallisy tosses the pipe behind him, causing a racket. "Moneys been exchanged. So you take *that*"—he says, jabbing a finger at Walker—"somewhere else while I finish."

Lo swings her stringy blonde hair behind her shoulders, revealing the dyed pink underneath. "Finish? You haven't even got going." She shakes her head at me. "I've changed my mind, Rain. He ain't worth it. I was down a bottle when I told you he'd do."

I touch the thick fold of bills through my pocket. "Moneys were exchanged, Lo."

"I'll finish him." She shimmies her shoulders out of her wide-necked top with a speed that would impress a Void captain. "He'll agree. He probably doesn't want his work buds finding out that he's a sweet freakin' mess with a taste for cherry popping."

"I don't want some used bag." Hallisy hooks his belt. "I'll have my moneys back, or I'll call *that* in." He points to my brother again, and I want to spit.

I dig out most of the bills and toss them at his feet. "I'm taking ten for what you already got." I sound more sure of myself than I am, but then, that's always been my superpower.

"I didn't get ten worth. And you were late."

"Not *that* late. And you're the one who took your bleeding time!" I scrub the spot where he sucked my neck. The pile of wadded-up notes jeers from the cracked pavement louder than any leering skyscraper. I pull my brother into my arms, the stubble of his shaved head pricking my chin. We were so close to having enough to buy passage off this planet.

Now we're not.

"Rain." Walker's voice shakes along with his hands. I clasp his arms together as though I can stop the tremors by sheer will, but the symptoms come on too fast, and I feel his fear like it's my own. *"Rain?"*

Lo steps close and fixes her elastic top over her bony shoulders. "There're cops down the way. How do you want to play this?"

"He'll make it to the pier." I eye my brother with a dare. His mouth seals in a firm line, nodding through his fear. I lead Walker down the alley.

"Where you think you're going?" Hallisy yells.

"You missed your chance," I toss back.

Hallisy charges, his steps echoing like gunshots through the alley, and I duck to cover Walker as he almost rips my shirt off. Lo shoves him with her whole body, and he bangs into the Dumpster, driving it against the wall to the tune of rippling, crashing steel on brick.

We hustle onto the main street, elbowing against a new wave of workers. I glance back, but the mouth of the alley is clear. No sign of Hallisy. Lo gets hung up in the crowd behind us, waving us on. I hate to leave her, but a squat woman with a metal hook through her earlobe scowls at Walker's trembling frame.

"Run with me, Walk," I whisper. "Run!" His feet stumble as we duck onto a side street and break into a sprint. Anyone could snatch us. Start a panic. And the cops would be here in a blink with their restraints, ready to take away the mentally diseased, the people we call *Touched.*

People like my little brother.

CHAPTER
2

By the time we reach the pier, I want to scream. Gone! That chance—maybe our only one—and it's gone. The neck of my ripped shirt slips down to my elbow, and I drag Walker's now rubbery frame. "Do you have any idea how much money we just lost?"

His shaking has stopped, but now his eyes are blank. Empty. "Who are you?" he asks. "Am I home?"

"No, Walker. We're not home." The wind whips off the oily ocean, and I maneuver us around the broken planks of the ancient pier. "We have to wait for Lo."

"What's a Walker?" he asks, and I swallow my irritation and pain. My brother is now the shell of the person who just stormed the alley to fight a man three times his age.

And that shell is cracked.

High above us, silver starships hang in invisible parking spots like stars lured too close to earth. Some are as large as skyscrapers while others are only big enough for a captain and crew, but they all gleam with blue light, the pulsing proof of their mighty engines. Engines that can break through the smoke sky. . . . Engines that run the Void and weave between the stars.

I've always been drawn to that blue. The color is so much more vivid than the monochrome ash and age of Earth City, and it's long since been my hope for our escape.

At the end of the pier, the hull of a small, abandoned starship rots. I guide Walker through the missing passenger door, situate him on the ratty covering of the old captain's chair and climb up on the stripped control panel. He gazes through the rusted-out ceiling, and the sapphire lights of the spacedocks reflect over his green eyes, shading the emptiness.

"Do bugs . . . like ships . . . forgotten wings," he murmurs.

"That's right, Walker. They're just forgotten." I try not to imagine the day when he doesn't come back from the fogs or what might happen if the disease takes me as well. Who would keep the cops from taking us then?

Lo drops into the passenger seat, making the ship's metal carcass groan. She's out of breath. "You didn't have to keep running. Hallisy wasn't chasing anything with that bobbing thingy between his legs."

"A woman was looking at us weird. Maybe a reward chaser." I wipe spit from Walker's lip with my sleeve before I remember that it's Lo's shirt. I finger the now ripped neck. "I'm sorry, Lo. Your lucky shirt . . ."

She sighs. "Well, it used to be my lucky dress." She points to the ripped hem at my hips. "Suppose it'll turn into my lucky headband. No biggie."

"Still . . ." We don't have much, and what we have we share. After all, she's helped take care of Walker like he's her own brother. She hasn't called him in even though the reward would be enough to put a roof over her head for months.

I can't help but remember the money at Hallisy's feet. The bulge of it. "What happened back there?"

She kicks her legs up on the dashboard. "I was sitting with Walker, and he just kind of blinked and woke up. He knew what you were up to, but I swear I said nothing. He's pretty smart for a kid, when he's not . . . you know."

"I thought he'd be out of it all day. He's been out of it for full days lately."

"He's getting to the end fast, Rain. You can't hide him from the cops forever."

I glare up at the starships. "I should have done it. All that money . . ."

"Hallisy said you were late. Why?" Lo knows me too well. "Rain, you didn't . . . not Simon! Didn't we talk about this?"

"It was stupid."

"Yep," she agrees. "He's the wrong sort of boy for anyone to love, let alone you. He's got just enough coin to make it to tonight."

"I don't love him. I just liked him . . . a lot. And I wasn't think-ing about his pockets."

"You were thinking about the way he always flirted with you and made you feel like you weren't on the most forgotten planet in the universe."

"Little good it did. You were right about him."

She nudges me with her foot. "Wish I wasn't, Rain. Really."

"Yeah, I know. You're far wiser than me."

"Only when it comes to the opposite sex." Lo crosses her thin legs beneath her and sifts through a pile of coins from the previous night's work. She sells herself cheap these days, and the more she sells herself, the cheaper she gets. Walker wanders through the missing door, and she leans out to watch him round the side of the ship. "He's just staring off into nowhere."

"Tell me if he moves." I dig out Hallisy's ten-credit note and hold it out to her. "For looking after him."

She shakes her head. "Did a zero job, didn't I? Besides, I was the one who said Hallisy would be fine and that one is clearly not fine. And how're you supposed to save up enough to jump planet if you give away what you earn?"

Earn. I remember Hallisy sucking on my collarbone and crumple the note in my fist.

"Don't worry. You'll find another. With your looks and clean record, someone will spill their banks to have you. You just got to find the right guy with the right offer."

I shove the wadded money in my pocket. "Walker's only got a few months before he slips away for good. Maybe less." I try to see around Lo. "What's he doing?"

"Told you, he's just staring." Lo shines her biggest coin on the edge of her skirt. "You know I love you gingers like my adopted family, but you're blind to the facts. He's a goner. If you wanted to jump planet, live your dreams, I'd take care of him here and—"

"If I get him to the Edge, the Mecs could cure him."

She sits up. "You don't know that freak Mecs could sort him. And I still think they eat their dead's brains. It's what gives them freak intelligence." I don't have to tell her that she's being ridiculous; my grimace says it all. "Well, you do only know rumors about a cure. So, don't go putting store in stories." She pauses to grin. "Hey, that sounded clever, didn't it?"

Lo makes me smile, but even rumors have hope if you let them. And hope isn't something that I'm ready to trade in. Not yet. Not ever. Just the thought of that distant planet—a technological paradise, people say—is enough to keep me going.

"We're getting out of here, Lo. I won't lose him like I lost the rest of my family."

Lo sighs. "Okay, Rain. If that's what you want, I'll say . . . okay."

I give her a smile, but it fades fast. "You don't think Hallisy will call the cops on Walker, do you?"

"Nah, he'll want another shot, and he won't have it if he gets the kid hauled away with the rest of the nutsos." Her shoulders sag. "Sorry, I'm a tad nasty today."

"Only today?" I tease. Most people, like Simon, wouldn't give Lo a second thought. Her body has that worn-through look that doesn't match her twenty years, and she drowns herself in drink a little too often. But she's real. And she found me on this very pier when I was on the edge of jumping into the rocks and waves with Walker. She was like an angel. An angel in pink spandex.

Lo pulls a rolled-up scrap of paper from her cleavage, gazing at a photo of her mom. Lo spent years trying to hide her from the cops, but then one day, the Touched woman wandered out of their apartment and was never seen again.

At least I got to say good-bye before they took my mother.

"What are you thinking about? You're looking weird," Lo says.

"Just when I met you out here. When I first saw you. I bet you thought I was nuts."

"I'd seen you lots before. Did I never tell you that?" She had, but I want to hear it again. "You used to come out here with that whole lot of a family. And I used to watch you with your dad and your brothers. Looking at stuff in the surf. Pointing out trash."

"Fish," I correct. "My dad gave us biology lessons. He was always trying to get us to look at things, but my brothers and me just wound up looking at the starships. We used to pretend to be Runners. Even Jeremy did, until he got old and cranky."

"Yeah, well, I ain't never seen something like your matching-head family. All together and looking like you loved each other. You just don't see that. Not on Earth City, anyway."

"Yeah." The memory fractures into little, lost pieces, just like my family. My mom and Jeremy taken. My dad murdered. Walker and me, the last of the Whites.

"You know what?" She scoots forward, her gray eyes growing sharp. "A guy I banged last week heard some space Runners say that the Touched are sold off planet and sacrificed to some kind of Void god. A black hole or something."

"Don't be gullible. There's no such thing."

"They go somewhere, don't they? And it's not to an asylum in the south or whatever the cops say." She pokes her photo back into her cleavage. "Don't get itchy. I'm just saying."

But I am itchy, and I have been since that girl almost fell on us all those weeks ago. I slip off the command panel, fixing the torn part of my shirt toward the back. I'd rather think about being in that alley with Hallisy than the whereabouts of thousands of missing Touched people, my mother and older brother among them. "I can't worry about what happens to the rest, Lo. I've got my hands full with just the one," I say. "Speaking of, what's he doing?"

"He's *fine*." She leans out the window. "Wait, I take that back. He's made a run for it."

--------~~~~~~~~~~~--------

I sprint from the ship, almost losing my footing on the pier's loose boards. I scan the walkway, but Walker isn't where I thought he'd be.

He's dangling over the edge.

A man in a black suit holds his small body by his jacket while his feet jerk in the air. I run faster, screaming, "STOP! Don't hurt him!" I yank his arms, bringing my brother's struggling torso against mine.

"The boy was trying to jump. I stopped him," the man says. He's lean and striking, and his flinty eyes examine me chest to face. Face to feet.

"Well, I've got him now, and I'd thank you if it weren't for the blatant ogle." I pin Walker's squirming wrists in my hand. "You can go your way."

"He's Touched."

"He's my brother!" I wrestle Walker farther from the edge. "And he still has lucid periods, so if you were going to call him in, you can save your breath."

The man's laugh is slick. "I don't bother with this earth's laws."

This earth?

Walker twists free, sprinting toward the ship where Lo tackles him. I turn back to the man and pull at the windblown hair criss-crossing my cheek. He's younger than I thought. Simon's age—and with the same sort of wave to his hair. But he's better looking than Simon by far.

"You're a Void traveler?" I force my stare away from the spot where his throat slides beneath the unbuttoned V of his collar. "You're a Runner?"

"Yes." He picks at a curl on my forehead, and I'm mesmerized enough to let him. "And you're a redhead. A *true* red."

His fingers skim my bare shoulder, and I lean away. The rip in my shirt was tossed to the front when I dashed to Walker and now reveals more side-cleavage than I thought possible.

I straighten it. "You've never seen a redhead before?"

"Natural red is considered extinct in the known universe." The slightest scowl twists his lips. "It's less of a flame color than I imagined . . . more of a perfect rust. No one's told you that before?"

"Extinct? I've never heard that one before, but I don't know many Runners." I fold my arms over my chest to keep them from twitching through my hair. "Not many of you wandering these parts of Earth City." We glance around at the rundown pier and the horizon of chipped skyscrapers as though we're sharing a thought. What *is* he doing here?

"True," he says. "I'm a little lost. Maybe you can help me." His hand slips into his pocket, bringing his jacket away from his trim waist. I wish that the move didn't make me glance at his belt . . . and a little lower. But it does.

25

"Do you know the Blackstar Bar?"

"Huh?" I'm too distracted by the warm color of his skin to follow. "Wait, how can you live in the black of space and have more color than me?"

"Excuse me?"

"I just meant—" I feel heat in my cheeks and speak fast. "I don't have a door between my brain and my teeth, at least that's what my dad used to say. Everything just kinda falls out."

His smile is the open kind, revealing rows of polished teeth. "What's your name?"

"Rain. . . . Who are you?"

"I let my friends call me Johnny."

"Johnny." The name slips from my tongue to my thoughts and back again before I remember the original question. "Well, the Blackstar is up on Trade Runners Row." I point to the street beyond the pier. "That way about three blocks, but don't pass through the alley with the wire mesh. That's where the Bashers set up camp, and you'd be a rich surprise. And keep clear of the girls on the corner of Downer and Glam Streets. They're not prostitutes; they're bait, if you catch my meaning."

His eyes are on me intensely. "Why don't you show me? I'll buy you a drink and tell you about my skin."

For a second, he's so tempting that I almost forget where I am. Simon could do that to me, too—make me forget everything—and that embarrassment is still fresh enough to sting.

"I have to take care of my brother. And if you're looking for a date, I'm not interes—" I stop and take a leveling breath as I reassess him. A *Void traveler*. "I'm not cheap."

"I wouldn't guess so," he says without missing a step. The darkness of his eyes reveals a deep brown, and I swear he's suppressing a pleased smile. "And I bet you're just desperate to jump planet."

I fight to hold my shirt together as the wind picks up. "How do you . . ."

"You're not the only one who can throw the truth out there. Besides, everyone on Earth City would love to leave, wouldn't they?" He brings a stone-handled knife from his pocket and snaps it open. In a flash, he's cut tabs in my ripped shirt and ties the pieces together. He flips the knife closed and returns it to his pocket. "Better?"

I adjust the now mended neck of my shirt but can't keep the question out of my voice. "Thanks?"

He points above himself to the starships in the sky. "Rain, that is my ship, *Imreas*. I take passengers of all sorts. Think it over and bring your deal to me by tomorrow."

"My deal? What kind of deal?"

His lips twitch with a frown. "Whatever you have for whatever you need. You'll find that I'm open to all sorts of *worthwhile* trades." He lifts his sleeve and glances at a strange silver communicator on his wrist. The metal gleams like a shining mirror. "But now I'm late. I hope to see you before tomorrow. Remember, the Blackstar Bar."

I find myself nodding. I've dragged a drunken Lo out of that seedy joint more than a few times.

"And Rain." He says my name like he's already paid for it. "Remember, I have whatever you need."

I open my mouth, but he's turned, his black outfit cutting against the pale cityscape. I glance at the ship he pointed to; it's shaped like the head of an arrow with three of the largest blue thrusters that I've ever seen. A fast ship, no doubt, but *his* ship?

"Who was that tasty tower?" Lo tugs Walker along behind her by the front of his jacket.

"He said"—my tongue feels thick as I watch Johnny turn a corner and disappear—"he's a Void captain."

"No shit," Lo swears. "Wouldn't that be freakin' sweet!"

I wet my lips. "I think he made me a kind of offer. He said, 'I have whatever you need.'"

"Screw Hallisy"—she says with a laugh—"*that's* the right guy for you."

I glance over my brother's vacant face. "I don't know, Lo. A young, rich guy like that doesn't need to bargain for a girl, does he? And how would he have his own ship?" I finger the knotted tabs of my shirt, the proof that he was just here. That he chose to touch me. "People don't just run into you and happen to offer what you've been dreaming about."

"Rich people do. They can have anything." The wind picks up, and Lo and I grip each other's shoulders while Walker stands immobile. "Don't overthink this one, Rain. Work what you want from him." Her voice is twisted high with emotion, and the sudden thought that she will miss me, should I escape, makes me cold.

I slip off Walker's too-big jacket—Jeremy's old bomber—and pull it on. Then I tuck my brother against me and fold the material over him as well. Lo is right. Can I really afford to doubt whether I should bargain with a Void captain? A *sexy* Void captain, no less . . . even if he was a little . . . off?

"Lo, he looked at me like he'd already bought me."

"They all do that." She licks her chapped lips. "Besides, what if you were being tricked into something? Isn't any trick worth jumping planet?"

CHAPTER
3

The rain is acidic on Earth City. It appears without warning, without lightning, biting into the skin on my forehead and leaving the backs of my hands itching and red. I lead Walker through it, trying to get him home before he goes completely catatonic.

All the while, Lo's words circle through me: *Isn't any trick worth jumping planet?*

I steer Walker around the spot on the square where that Touched girl almost fell on us, her blood halo already bleached into a pale stain by the rain. She was the exploding sun that made me see Walker's headaches for what they really were: the first symptom of the disease. Somehow I had deluded myself into believing that it couldn't happen to us because we were all we had left.

I turn a corner and, like a thunderclap, run into the angry block letters on the streets' endless graffiti of water-damaged billpostings.

KNOW THE TOUCHED!

Symptoms:
1. HEADACHES
2. SHAKES
3. MENTAL FOG

**If you see an afflicted, call 999. Abettors are criminals.
Do not sorrow. Fear the infection.**

My dad used to scribble the word "feel" between the "DO NOT" and "SORROW." *If they're going to tell us how to think, they might as well use words we understand,* he'd say. This always made my brothers and me laugh, but looking back, I'm not sure why.

Still, I shouldn't have missed Walker's first symptom. We were working at Dex's then, making enough money to fill our bellies, and I thought he was just not used to the long hours. Had it come on the same way for my mom? I couldn't say. I was barely seven when the cops came for her, Walker clinging to my knee, and all I remembered was that when I tried to hug her good-bye, her eyes were empty.

But I'll never forget when they came for Jeremy.

He wasn't afflicted but had been caught hiding a Touched man in the basement of our apartment building. I was twelve then. Old enough to do something when they locked him in a belted jacket and hauled him away. Old enough to do something when my dad threw himself at the cops and they beat him to death in our stairwell—the sounds echoing up the flights. Crashing, screams, and pounding.

Echoing, still.

Still.

I tighten my hold on the back of my little brother's neck and rush past a crowd of sketchy men who yell slimy words.

That night in the stairwell, Walker became my only family, and like hell will I give him up. There's always hope. There's always *some* chance. To forget that is to become one of the factory worker drones, and I won't bow to that life.

My dad didn't lose hope when my mom became sick. He read poetry to her, and he held on long after she was taken, working wicked nightshifts and then still staying up all day to take us on history walks through what he called old Manhattan.

"Dad would be doing exactly what we're doing. He'd get you to the Edge, to your cure, Walker," I whisper. My dad was the one who told me about the Edge, that settlement on the other side of the known universe. And he told me about Mecs, the evolved people who live there. I remember the shining silver communicator on Johnny the Runner's wrist. What I wouldn't give to touch it . . . to know how and where he got it. . . .

The Blackstar Bar is several blocks away, and getting farther with each step, but I have to see Walker home and settled first. And then, I will go to Johnny. But what will I say?

I lead Walker around a corner—and right into a trap.

"No moving, missy," a squat woman says. She's the same one with the hook through her ear from earlier. Two muscle-backed men creep to surround me on either side.

I was right: reward chasers.

"No fussing, missy. It's got to go before it infects the rest."

It. She means Walker.

I force my hand between my brother's stiff fingers, my pulse pounding against my ears. The men get closer. They're going to take him for the reward, and then Walker will disappear forever like the rest of the Touched.

No way.

I bring my brother's thumb from between our clenched hands and wrench it back. His body stiffens with pain, but I pull harder and harder until the tendons are about to snap. Finally, my brother's body shakes like a chill is rippling through him, but then he lifts his head. He arches his neck and then launches it forward, shooting a huge glob of saliva right into the woman's eye. She yowls.

"Just cuz he's here and now doesn't mean he ain't infected," she says as she scrubs at her cheeks.

"Yeah, but you can't prove he's Touched, so let us pass. Besides, shouldn't you worry about being infected now?"

Horror squashes her pudgy face, and the men step back, not just from Walker and me, but from her now as well. And I don't miss the moment. I grab my brother's hand and jerk us into a sprint.

———————

We're on the next street before I slow. "You were great, Walk."

A crooked smile gives life to his pale lips. "I'm the greatest. So said Dad. Remember?"

"I remember."

He touches his chest and arms like he just found them, still disoriented. "Those chasers been after us for a while?"

33

"'*Have* those chasers been after us?'" I correct. "And I don't know. I only noticed them this morning." It was a close one, but Walker is here now, and I bring out Hallisy's ten-credit note. "What do you want to do? We can do anything."

He snatches it. "How'd you get this?"

"I earned it." Walker frowns for a moment, and I worry that he's remembering how I earned that money. I clear my throat. "How about some eats? You hungry?"

My brother's great smile is worth five hundred credits. "I'm always hungry."

We swing by our favorite meat-on-sticks place, and it almost feels like old times, at least it would if I wasn't counting down the seconds until his clarity fades. We pick out a shish kebab for each hand and wander through the rain-washed streets toward our makeshift home.

Walker strips a piece of tough meat and makes a pleased groaning sound. "Rain, what happened before?"

"I met a Runner. A Void captain, Walk. I'm going to trade with him to get us passage." I look over my dinner but can't force another bite. "Maybe next time you wake, you'll be better. We'll be on the Edge."

"And you'll be the captain of your own starship, and Mom and Jeremy will be back, and Dad will be up from the dead like he was taking a nap?" He spits a bit of cartilage out on the sidewalk. "You're full of dreaming, Rain. If you really want a shot, you'd let them take me."

"Don't be such a depressing old man." I wiggle my kebab in his face. He bats it away with his skewer, and we swordfight until I de-stick him and claim arms-raised victory.

We reach an old fire escape, climbing to the roof. Our home is glass-paneled: a rooftop greenhouse from back in the eco days. People grew gardens here once, and someone even put a swimming pool in the center of it. Of course it's all gone to hell now. Many of the panes are cracked or missing, and the green plants have long since disintegrated into piles of ashy soil.

Walker sits on blankets in the shallow corner of the empty pool, and I grab my favorite tatty book from the stack that I rescued from our old apartment. The bindings have been glued and reglued. Some of them have grown mold, but I can't part with them. They were my dad's.

"Read from this one tonight." I gently toss the book to Walker, but he doesn't catch it. It scatters on the tile, losing pages. "Watch it!"

He scoops it up. "We've already read this one. *And* I don't like poetry."

"Too bad. Read."

Walker tugs the book open. He starts to read a poem, struggling with the rhythm and so many of the words. My dad would have taught him to taste the words as he reads them just like he taught Jeremy and me, but I've proven to be a bad teacher. Maybe I'm not trying hard enough.

" 'I pass death with the dying, and birth with the new-wash'd babe . . . and am not contain'd between my hat and boots.'" Walker's voice is lazy and heartless.

"Don't you feel it? 'Not contain'd between my hat and boots.' Do you get that?"

"I'm not wearing a hat."

"Don't be literal. It means that you're more than your body. Your mind goes outward. You know?" I close my eyes and finish the poem by memory, " 'And peruse manifold objects, no two alike, and every one good; The earth good, and the stars good . . .' "

"I guess it sounds nice." He shuts the book.

"That's a start." I lie back on the old diving board, my legs swinging off the sides. "We'll do more when you're better," I add to myself. "Much more." A brown-skinned vine grows along the rusted beams that crisscross the glass walls and ceiling. I admire that plant. The sun hasn't broken through the smog in over two years, but still it grows. A survivor. And somehow it's snaked through cracks in the glass without cutting itself.

How do you do what's wrong without losing yourself in the process? Is there a way to do what Lo does without becoming like Lo?

I push past the memory of Hallisy and rethink this Johnny. *Deal*, he said, *what you have for what you need*. Well, what I have is me. And what I need is passage.

Walker's voice breaks into my thinking. "What'll you try to trade this Runner?"

"Whatever he wants."

"Whatever?" Walker sits. He remembers the alley now. I can see it in his reddening cheeks. "*Rain*. Earlier you were . . . you were going to let that man . . ."

I leap from the wobbling board, landing in a crouch on the tile that shoots pain from my ankles to my knees. "I need to make money fast, Walk. You have to trust me."

"There are honest ways!"

"You don't think I've tried?" I pace. "Factory work. Mine work. *Sewer* work. You know what they all have in common? They pay nothing. And I can't wait around and watch you disappear."

He covers his eyes with his thin hands. "You could save up without me. You could save up in just a few years."

"Shut up." I hug him hard, my chin covering his head.

"You'll get hurt," he says. "Hurt bad. Remember when Jeremy said you couldn't jump from the fire escape?"

I hold him a little tighter. "Yes. And I did it."

"But you broke your ankle."

"But I did it."

He shakes his head, pricking the underside of my jaw. "You think you can do anything and no one can touch you, but it's like what Dad used to say. 'You can't run between the raindrops.'"

I can see our father through Walker's words—the phrasing he only remembers because I've told him it so many times. Some days I wonder just how much Walker truly recalls about our dad. I remember too much . . . his ginger hair. His coarse beard and green eyes. And I miss him too much. Sometimes I admit it out loud to remind myself that the pain in my chest isn't a cancer or my body going Touched.

It's just the missing.

The last time I saw my dad, the cops were dragging his body facedown into the street. Then they flew away in a hover cab, stealing Jeremy. My dad's beard had left scratch lines in the trail of blood leaving our apartment building, and I still see those lines in my nightmares . . . an endless rusted trail that I chase and chase without ever finding the place where I lost him.

Walker pulls out of my arms to curl up on the blankets, and we trade small smiles that have nothing to do with happiness. "Rub my thumb, will you? Feels like it almost ripped off or something," he says. I massage his bony hand and watch him fall asleep until violent shakes take him somewhere even farther away.

I run my finger down his cheek, feeling the first fuzz of soft stubble. He's been waiting for years to grow his scruff like Jeremy and our dad, waiting forever to be a man. Well, he will get his chance. I'll trade anything in the universe for it.

High above the glass panels, the smoke sky glows. It could be coming on morning or evening, but I can't hardly tell. On this planet, the day is always the same color as the night.

I wake with a start. My brother is not next to me. "Walker?" I get to my feet and check the gray room.

"Rain." His voice comes from above—from the diving board. He stands at the very edge, minutely bouncing on the old fiber plank. "You should go without me. You should save up and do it right." He stops bouncing. "Run the Void, and then if you do it, I'll have done it as well. Like a spirit or something." He opens his arms wide. "Remember when Dad used to call me Night Bird?"

"Walker, don't be—"

He springs on the board and dives, his head careening straight toward the tile. A scream breaks my throat, crashing echoes through the empty pool like waves against rock.

Waves that do nothing to stop the spray of his blood.

CHAPTER
4

Crimson neon lights bear down on the crowd at the Blackstar Bar like a demented oven. I push through arms and drinks and groping hands toward a table at the back of the room.

And he is there: Johnny.

I have whatever you need.

He fingers a drink, his legs jutting out from a slouch that brings all attention to his waist. When his eyes meet mine, he grins smugly and leans toward a guy beside him. I catch the end of his words: ". . . and you doubted me."

Johnny taps something into the silver band on his wrist and speaks without looking up. "Rain, let me guess: you'd like to see the stars. It's always been your dream."

I place my hand over his.

"I need . . ." My voice leaves me. Johnny pulls away, and my fingers streak blood down his tan skin.

He brings a handkerchief from his pocket and wipes at the red. Then he takes my hands and does the same. He turns each of them over, inspecting them. "You need what?"

What do I need? What could he possibly do?

Johnny's fingers wrap around my chin while he dabs at my face, the white cloth coming away scarlet. "I don't think you're the one who is injured," he concludes.

"My brother," I say. "I need your help. He fell."

"Show me." Johnny pushes me away to stand. He tosses a few coins on the table and snaps his fingers at the guy beside him. "We're going. Bring your toys."

The guy slips out of the seat behind Johnny. He's not as tall or as old—I might even call him a boy—but his shoulders are broad. His plain shirt and green cargo pants remind me of a military recruit but not from any service that I know.

Something about him begs a second look, but my mind buzzes with Walker.

We take their hover cab, the kind that can soar up into the thinnest atmosphere and maybe beyond for short distances. I sit in the back beside Johnny, squeezing the plush seat as the gliding sensation does weird things to my stomach. I keep turning from the strange guy in the corner, his face cast in shadow, to the back of the driver's shaggy head.

Faster. We should be going faster.

And yet, as the hover cab lets down on my rooftop, it's only been minutes since we left the bar. But even that might have been too long. . . .

There was so much blood.

I rush into the greenhouse, dragging Johnny behind me. Walker is curled in the deep end of the pool. His head is at the center of a great red puddle, and the sound of air leaving his body is a constant wheeze.

Johnny holds me against him as the other guy leaps into the pool. His boots slide down the blood-slick tile, but he comes to a skillful stop beside my brother and peels back the strips of blankets I tied around Walker's skull.

It hadn't been a long enough fall. He probably thought that he'd break his neck, but his head hit and just split. Then he screamed and screamed and screamed. . . .

"I couldn't go to anyone else. They'd take him away or put him out of his misery. But what can you even do?" I squirm in Johnny's hold, but his arms grow tighter, somewhat comforting but mostly restraining.

"How is it, Ben?"

The boy called Ben takes a metal disc from one of the many pants pockets. It pulses with the same sapphire light as the engines hanging over the spacedocks, and he passes it over Walker's cracked scalp.

"I asked you a question," Johnny snaps.

"It's bad." Ben pushes his light brown hair out of his eyes, but even as his words spear me, Walker's wound transforms under the blue light. Within breaths, the whole gash has sealed into a long, white scar.

"How in the hell?" I struggle out of Johnny's arms and drop into the pool. I run my hand over Walker's scalp. "How did you do that?" I ask Ben.

"Amazing what you can do with Mec toys," Johnny says.

"Where did you get Mec toys?"

"They usually come with the Mec." Johnny's tone is black. "Stars forbid they let anyone else have them."

"Mec?" I glance at the blue disc as Ben slips it into his pocket. "You're Mec?"

Ben looks away in a hurry, but I swear I see beneath his wild hair for a moment. I swear I see blue eyes that glint like something slightly metallic.

"Come, Rain. We need to discuss what happens next." Johnny beckons for me, but I stare at my brother's drooping eyelids and slow, slipping breath.

I look to Ben. "He's better?"

"On the outside," he says. "He's in a coma. They could do more for him on—"

"The Edge!" I almost yell. "I knew it!"

"Rain," Johnny commands. I climb out of the pool but keep trying to look back at Walker's still form. *They* could *do more for him.* A sharp sound brings me back as Johnny kicks the glass from one of the greenhouse panes, and I follow him out onto the rooftop with growing unease.

Below, people clog the street with their unhurried passage: the passionless procession to the next factory shift. "I don't understand this planet." Johnny motions to the workers. "Like insects with one purpose. No wonder your minds have been whittled down to a corruptibly thin wavelength." He spits over the edge, no doubt hitting someone in the head.

I look over my brother's savior in the numb daylight, my words leaking before I can stop them. "You're an angry sort."

He turns at me a little fast, and I take a step back. He puts a hand up that may have wanted to grab me but only shows his palm instead. "Don't be afraid of me. Do me that favor."

"All right." I lick my lips and stand close to him again. Close to the edge of the building where he could give me the lightest shove and send me over. "Should we deal now?"

"Deal." He sets his teeth on the word. "Let's."

I take a deep breath. "Well, you want me. Clearly."

He chuckles. "Clearly." He touches the curly ends of my hair at my elbow. "You're a rare beauty, but you know that. And up there"—he says, glancing into the smog like it isn't there, like he can imagine every detail of the stars beyond—"things get a little lonely."

"I'll go with you. I'll be your friend. More, even."

"More?"

"You want it in writing? I'll give you my virginity. Whatever."

"So you'll be my girl."

It isn't a question, so I don't know how to answer. I look over his profile, striking against the height of the fall just before us. His eyes seem to bleed with brown, but it only makes me want to know more. Who created this haunted sort of guy? How did he become a Void captain? And what else lies beneath this polished surface?

Maybe he's not what he seems. Maybe there are unimaginable diamonds in his deep places. That's what my dad had said about my mother when he first met her. She was homeless and starving, and yet he saw "sparks and stars."

"I'll be your girl. And you'll get me to the Edge with my brother," I say in a rush. "Deal?"

He frowns. "Your brother, of course." His gaze slips past me, narrowing like he's suddenly not so sure that I'm worth it. And I have to show him that I am.

I lick my lips as I reach for his collar, standing on the very edge of my tiptoes to bring his mouth to mine. I'm surprised to find him yielding and the slightest bit hungry before I lean away, embarrassed. He's the first person I've ever really kissed, and my heart pounds with nerves.

He touches his mouth with the back of his hand, making me think that I did something wrong, but his eyes glint in an encouraging way. "I've heard stories about redheads. Aren't you supposed to be fiery?"

I smirk. "My dad used to say that gingers are capable of all kinds of mischief."

"All kinds," he repeats. "It has been a while since I've had a challenge." A sudden grin strikes his face like a spark. "We have a deal." He spins, reenters the greenhouse, and I jog to keep up.

"So you'll take me and my brother all the way to the Edge? You promise."

"Cross my heart," he says with a laugh. "Now, we're in a hurry."

"You mean leave this minute?" I ask. "What about Walker? He's in a coma!"

Johnny stops by the edge of the pool, and I collide with his back. Ben stands in the center of the tile, holding my brother like a baby. Walker's head is against the Mec's chest and blood smears his white shirt. The sight is strange, but I can't put my finger on why. . . .

"So what do we do with him . . . ," Johnny says, and I don't like his tone. "What say we freeze him?"

"Freeze him?"

He frowns. "We can't have a Touched boy wandering around my ship, and this way you can get him treatment as soon as we set down at the Edge." He pockets his hands. "And he won't interrupt the business of the run. Yes, we'll freeze him. Those are my terms."

Ben is watching us. He adjusts my brother's weight in his arms, and his hair has parted enough to reveal that it wasn't my imagination: his blue irises really are rimmed with steel.

"He'll be fine if he is frozen?" I look to the Mec.

"Better than fine. He'd be preserved," Johnny says. "And no babysitting required."

Ben gives me the smallest nod.

I don't like the idea of freezing my brother, but no babysitting . . . I can't deny that I'm more than tempted by a reprieve of watching his every moment. "As long as he'll be safe."

"Have it done." Johnny inputs something on his wrist communicator and leaves Ben and me to stare at each other. On closer inspection, the Mec could be my age. Maybe we could be friends. He's got to at least know the ins and outs of the starship and this Johnny.

But Ben's voice stops my scheming midstream. "Now you've done it." He shifts my brother in his arms and steps toward the shallow end, his hair falling over his expression.

"Done what?" I ask.

"Made your bed with the devil."

<hr />

I don't like the Mec. His words bang around my thoughts. *Devil?* Johnny's clearly no angel, but *the devil*? I doubt that Mec has ever had to dodge the police or the Bashers . . . or worked so many factory shifts that his mind kinked up like an old wire.

He can't know what a real devil looks like. The kind of devil that comes through your own skin and makes you do things. Horrible things. Like stealing a pair of shoes from a dying old lady because your brother's feet are bleeding.

Or agreeing to sell yourself to the likes of Hallisy.

That Mec probably just doesn't like being ordered around; I could be wrong, but I think Ben is Johnny's servant. Well, no servant likes his or her master.

The morning shift horn ricochets across the crumbling skyscrapers, making the loose glass panels in our greenhouse tinkle. "That's the last time we'll ever have to hear that," I tell Walker. I touch the new scar on his scalp. "Maybe I wasn't dreaming. Maybe the next time you wake, you'll be better. We'll be at the Edge."

I'm still not crazy about the idea of freezing him, but this way he won't know what I've agreed to. An invisible wind makes all the hair stand on my arms. At least this Johnny is a tenfold upgrade on the lecherous Hallisy, and we are getting off this planet for good.

The hover cab driver, an older man with silvery hair and beard to match, wedges a metal pod through the greenhouse doorway. He rubs his hip through a faded black flight suit as he hunkers down beside me. "Blasted bones," he mutters. He observes Walker through work goggles so fogged that he looks like he has opulent bug eyes.

Johnny returns with a deep scowl, pressing his thumb to a

scanner on the pod's control box. The lid releases, and I watch him say something into his silver wristband as he leaves. I zip Jeremy's jacket up to Walker's collar. What could Johnny be angry about all of a sudden?

"Magic fingers," the old man says, interrupting my thoughts. "Johnny's fingers open *everything* on his ship." He tucks Walker into the pod, placing my brother's legs and arms gingerly. The lid latches with an airtight sound. "What's this?" He picks up my dad's copy of *Leaves of Grass*, the book Walker had been reading from last night.

"Some old poetry." I look at the pile of books beside the pool. "Don't suppose I'll be able to bring these."

He sighs. "He won't let you bring the clothes on your back, most likely. So you'll be the new girl? What are you called?"

"Rain White. And this is my brother, Walker."

He presses a few buttons and the pod hums. "Ah, 'Into each life some rain must fall.'" When I don't respond, he adds, "Longfellow. Another long ago poet. Too forgotten, like every artist. Tell me, Rain, are you falling into our lives?"

"Not falling," I insist a little fast, remembering the suicidal Touched girl. "My dad used to sing, 'I am the Poem of the Earth, said the voice of the rain.'"

He slaps his knee. "An Earth Cityite who can read *and* recite! You're a surprising little sprite, aren't you?"

"My dad was self-educated. He taught us." I glance around again, this time at the dreary scenery of my home. "But I won't be an Earth Cityite after I jump planet. I'll be a Runner, right?"

"If that's how you want to be known." He holds his hand out, and I glance over his dirty glove. "I go by Samson."

Perhaps I have made a friend. I shake his hand and then peer through the palm-sized window at the top of the pod. Walker looks better through the glass than he did beside the pool. "He'll be fine in there?"

"Aye, Rain Runner. We've used it to preserve meat for years."

Meat? I grip the book a little tighter.

"Here," he holds his hand out for it, and I give the book to him slowly. He tucks it in his pocket. "I'll keep it safe for you." He touches his nose with one finger. "Just don't tell anyone."

Samson rolls the pod out, and I help him maneuver it into the trunk of the hover cab. Johnny still stands by the edge of the roof. I hear him whispering something about being his father's errand boy, and I back away to the hover cab.

"You ask permission to come with me?" Samson asks.

"Why?"

"Because you need permission." His tongue points out the corner of his mouth like he's stopping a laugh.

"I'm going with my brother."

"Samson," Johnny calls as though he was listening. "Take her to the ship. I'll finish here and send for you. And tell that Mec I know what he's up to!" His eyes have narrowed into sharp slits, and I'm happy to put even more distance between us.

"Is that permission?" I ask just loud enough for Samson to hear.

"That's dismissal," the old man returns just as low.

―――〜〜〜〜〜―――

Within a few minutes, we've left my rooftop forever. I sit in the back of the hover cab, watching Ben use a tiny screwdriver on the communicator clasped around his wrist. It reminds me of a simpler version of Johnny's.

"Captain says he knows what you're up to," Samson calls from the driver's seat.

Ben grins, and I'm not ready for it. His whole face turns boyish and rascally cute. "Thinks he's smarter than me?"

"He can dream," Samson says while pulling the vehicle over the rooftops. The climbing, gliding sensation is easier to stomach this time, and I look out as the ugliness of the city fades to chunks of dull color. All those skyscrapers can't look down on me now. . . . Lo will never believe this.

Lo!

"Can we make a stop?" I ask. Ben ignores me, forcing a panel open on his communicator. I lean into Samson's driving space. "Mind stopping just up there?" I point to the pier below the space-docks where I'm sure Lo is sleeping off her liquid dinner.

"He doesn't take orders from you," Ben says.

I glare back. "Good thing I'm asking and not ordering. I'll only be a few minutes. You can just keep tinkering with your bracelet there." Samson chuckles, and I touch the old man's shoulder. "Please?"

"It's not a bracelet," Ben retorts. "So you want to change or something? Don't want to go into space covered in your brother's blood?"

I twist to face him. "I want to say good-bye to my best friend, you jerk."

Ben blushes, and I can't tell if it's out of shame or irritation. But he's right; I rub at the black-red blooms across my pants and shirt. I *am* covered in my brother's blood. I hadn't even noticed, but then, so is the Mec.

His half-open jacket reveals the red streaks on his plain shirt, and I can't help but remember how fast he sealed Walker's wound and how strange he looked cradling my brother's body in the bottom of the pool. "Thanks," I say.

"Thanks?"

"Johnny took the credit, but it was you. You saved my brother's life." When he doesn't respond, I add, "I'm not afraid of you. Even if you're a cannibal."

"Are you *serious?*" He looks up angrily and finds me smiling. "Wait, you're joking?"

"Should I be afraid, oh scary Mec?"

"No. It's just . . . this is a first." He refocuses on his silver wristband. "Samson, put us down where she says." He glances up, and I swear something nice flashes through the intensity of his steely eyes. "You can have five minutes. That's all."

Samson parks the cab on the far end of the pier. I slip out the door, annoyed to find Ben following. "I'm not going to run away. You don't have to come," I say.

"I do have to come," he says. "Get used to it."

I cast a sideways look at him. "So you have to guard me now? And what did you mean by *sleeping with the devil* or whatever?"

"That was a warning," he says. "Johnny's not what he seems."

"He seems like a spoiled, handsome playboy. Am I off?"

Ben leaps around a broken space in the walkway, bumping into me. "Wait. You mean you're not in love with him?"

"What? I just met him."

"That's—well, that's different. No wonder he's bending over backward with this brother thing." He examines me like he doesn't believe me. "Then you really are different. Most of his girls are so . . ."

"What?"

"I'm not allowed to tell you Johnny's business," he says.

"You're just allowed to give cryptic warnings?"

He groans a little funnily like I've beaten something out of him. "Okay, think of it this way." He holds up his arm. "This isn't a bracelet. It's a communicator—a com. It keeps me in contact with Johnny at all times."

"How very impressive." I leap over a serious hole, the waves kicking below.

"Think of it as a tag. A tracker. I can't take it off." Ben is stopped on the other side of the gap. "He could even use a setting to zap my nervous system—kill me—if he wanted."

"So you're a slave?" I ask.

"Bound servant." The wind pushes his hair up into a curly mess.

"And I'll be the same? A bound servant?"

He shakes his head. "You'll be his girl, like you agreed."

The kiss on the rooftop comes back to me. It was nice. It could get even nicer. Of course, I'll sleep with him, but maybe it won't be like it almost was with Hallisy. Who knows . . . maybe we'll be perfect for each other in unknown ways.

I hold out my hand, but Ben leaps across the gap without touching me. "What does it mean to be his girl?" I ask. "Has he had many others?"

Ben turns away.

"Hey!" I jog after him. "I asked you something." He keeps going, messing with his com to keep from looking at me.

"If that com is so important, should you be messing with it?" Panic freezes Ben's expression, and I revel in my leg up. "So I shouldn't tell Johnny about your little experiments there? Or should I?"

"I was fixing it," he says unconvincingly. "It's none of your business."

"Oh, right. I'll try not to mention it to him then."

His mouth pauses midcomeback. "You know, none of the other passengers make eye contact with me, let alone try to blackmail me. You don't know what I could do to you."

I laugh. "No offense, Ben, but I've seen scarier girls in heels on the corner of Glam Street." I think he laughs, but it's hard to tell over the wind.

We reach the old ship, and I call out for Lo. Ben wanders around the rotting hull. "This was a Mec vessel," he declares. "A K-Force ship. One of the first Void-capable ones."

"Sure," I say, having no idea what he's talking about. "Wait here. I don't need you freaking her out. She'll probably think you've come to eat her brain."

"Ha ha," he fakes, making him seem like he's twelve instead of my age. He takes another turn around the old ship. I try not to watch him but fail. He reminds me of Simon in all the wrong ways—the flirting ways.

I duck inside, checking the command center and the old passenger section. I even glance into the back cargo area. "Lo?"

WHAM!

The side of my face grinds against the gritty rust of the wall.

Hallisy leans over my shoulder, pinning my wrists behind my back. "Knew I'd find you, stupid slut." Spit flecks my cheek, and my arms strain to pop out of my shoulders. "Where's that diseased brother?" he asks. "I put in a call to the cops. So they take him, and I take you."

CHAPTER 5

Hallisy slams his wiry hips against my back. "Won't dick over an honest guy again, huh?"

He slips a hand under the side of my shirt, reaching toward my breast, and I get my wrist free, finding his ear and pulling it as hard as I can. He twists—only to drop against the back of my legs.

I spin, kicking his ribs as he moans on the ground.

Ben holds up a silver syringe that he just jammed into Hallisy's back. "Didn't need me, huh?" He retracts the needle with a click.

"It freezes!" Hallisy clutches his crotch.

"What'd you inject him with?" I brush flakes of rust off my cheek, my hand shaking.

"A testosterone killer. Designed it myself." Ben leans over Hallisy. "That means it'll be years before you're standing *anything* up again. Understand me?"

Hallisy's shock paints his skin with ash. "Fuckin'—fuckin' Mec freak!" He makes it to his feet through a slew of curses and staggers out.

Ben laughs. "I've been dying to try that stuff. I call it

Limpicilin. Get it? Because it's like penicillin only it makes a guy
. . . you know. Limp."

"I get it." I'm breathing too hard and a little annoyed that he's
trying to find humor in this. "Was that a joke?"

"Hell. That stuff always sounds funnier in my head." He
drops the dose rod into the calf pocket of his cargo pants. "You're
welcome, by the way."

"I would have sorted him," I lie. That was a close one. I can
still feel Hallisy's wiry strength as he forced himself against me. I
drop to my knees. "He said he called the cops, so we have to
hurry. If they get all the way out here and don't find someone to
arrest, they'll take us as abettors." I smooth some sand that's collected in the back of the ship and write a message:

*Lo, Gone to Void with W. Going to Edge.
We'll miss you. Love, Rain*

I reread my note twice before adding: *P.S. Stop sell-
ing yourself cheap.*

Ben stands over me. "Maybe you should put: 'Wait until you
meet some sugar daddy Void captain and trade it all in.'"

I get up, wiping the grit from my hands. "Are we going to have
a serious problem with each other?"

"Hey, I just saved you."

"Told you, I had that sorted," I say. "And you can save me a
dozen times, but that doesn't mean I'll put up with your lip." I step
into his personal space—something Jeremy always did when he
wanted me to back down. "I don't have to like you just because
you're a special Mec."

Ben leans in instead of out.

"Good." His breath puffs my nose. "Because the last time one of Johnny's girls liked me, she ended up out the airlock."

I back down a few inches. "You're serious?"

"I'm trying to help you." The fierceness in his gaze is a little daunting. "You're not as damaged as the others, I can tell. Maybe there's still hope for you."

"So you want me to know that Johnny is bad news, but you don't want me to know why. You can't say anything, but you can't seem to keep your mouth closed. And what makes you think that I'm not just as bad as Johnny? I mean I'm the one trading . . ." *Myself.*

I'm trading *myself.*

"That's easy." He leans back to break our standoff. "People on this planet don't seem to think twice about giving up their family members when they go Touched."

I look away. "People swallow the propaganda that the Touched are contagious. If they were, everyone would have it. We don't know what causes the disease."

"Right, but most people don't fight back. And they certainly don't hide their loved ones in an old pool." His voice softens. "I doubt a *bad* person would bother."

"He's a smart kid. Worth saving." I pause. "He's all I have left."

Ben holds my gaze, and it dawns on me why it was so strange to see him holding Walker's limp body in the deep end: No one touches the Touched. Even the cops have nets and gloves. "You're not afraid of them," I say.

"They need medical attention. Not restraints." He steps back.

"It bothers me how they're corralled and locked away. I've been trying to find details about the disease, but there is so little known. Before the emigration, they called it Alzheimer's, and it only affected the old and came on slowly. But it's evolved somehow."

"It bothers me, too. Seeing them treated like animals." I have a sudden urge to push his hair out of his eyes, but another question is more pressing. "Will your people really help him on the Edge?"

"I don't know if they will, but they can. He'll definitely be better off there than staying here. But what you're trading isn't worth it. You don't know what it's like outside of this planet. What *he's* like."

"And you don't know what it's like on this planet." I walk away. "Trust me. I've dealt with worse. I can deal with him," I add over my shoulder.

"Keep telling yourself that."

Back on the hover cab, Samson flies us toward the spacedocks. I hum with excitement as the starships I've always dreamed about grow larger and more detailed through the window.

"Ready to leave?" Samson calls back. "Need a moment or something?"

"Nope." I don't even look down. "The only thing this place ever did was strip away the people I love one at a time." I look up to find Samson's fogged goggles as well as Ben's judging gaze, and I glance at the trunk where Walker's pod rests. "I'm bringing everything I need with me," I add.

"Every planet's got its fire pits and gold mines. Don't be too hard on yours." Samson pulls off his goggles and tosses them back. "Read the strap."

I turn the greasy rubber over until I find a very common stamp: MADE ON EARTH. "So what? Everything on Earth City has that stamp." I hand the goggles back, and he tugs them on.

"Yes, but I bought these at a street market on the Edge. You might be surprisingly proud when you find that stamp at all ends of the known universe. Your people don't toil for nothing—they produce. They keep the Runners in business along the Void."

"*Produce*," I repeat. "That's a nice word for it. Too nice for this dead place."

"This planet's not dead," Samson says. "Just veiled." He pulls the cab straight up, and I grip the seatback to keep from tumbling into Ben. We soar higher than the spacedocks, slamming into the smoke sky. For a few breaths we are swathed in gray, but then we come rocketing free . . .

And I'm blinded by yellow light.

I peer through my fingers as the cab pauses above the smog, squinting into a stretch of blue sky and a golden sun. The light strokes my skin with gentle heat, and I turn my hands over and over in the baking glow. What I wouldn't give to share this with Walker.

Through my daydream, I hear Ben ask, "Are we above the net?"

"Aye." Samson grunts as he clears his throat. "It's now or never, Ben."

I glance at Ben's narrowed eyes. "Well, don't mind me," I say. He makes a face like he's chewing the inside of his cheek and turns back to his com. A high-pitched buzz slices through my hearing, and I clasp my ears. "What was that?"

"Interference." Ben pulls his sleeve over his com, and his eyes catch mine in a kind of playful dare.

"All right." I uncover my ears. "Call us even . . . for the *Limpicilin*."

Ben smirks. He might dismiss the idea that we could be friends, but that doesn't mean I can't use him for information.

I point to his com. "That's what Johnny was yelling about when he said he knew what you were up to, wasn't it? He thinks you're doing something with that bracelet. And you're a Mec. You could be doing anything with that technology, am I right?"

"All right. What do you want from me?"

I turn back to the window. "Nothing yet."

"We could still let you go," he says. "Your brother, too."

"It'll be your head, Ben," Samson calls back.

"No," I say. The dried blood on my sleeves scratches. "I have to save him." Ben's steel eyes are as clear as the sky outside, and I don't shy from staring into them. "There's nothing for us here."

He glowers a little and twists the silver band on his wrist.

Samson adjusts his own grip on the steering drive. "To *Imreas* we go."

I take a last look at the golden sun, and we fall through the smog to where the starships are parked in the Earth City sky. The skyscrapers appear less decrepit from our height, and I let myself look down, whispering a good-bye that I don't want them to hear.

"How long will it take to get to the Edge?" I ask.

"A couple of months. The Edge is at the other end of the wormhole."

"Wormhole?"

"The Void is a wormhole—an accelerated tunnel of sorts. Otherwise it would take decades just to get to the next star system," Ben says. "And the Edge is about six thousand systems away. But how long it takes to get there will depend on how long we stay on Entra and spend in the Static Pass."

"The what and where?"

"Hell. I feel like I'm leading Alice down the rabbit hole."

I turn from the window. "How do you know that Earth City story?"

"It's an *Earth* story. And, if you haven't heard, we are all human." He twists his hand in his hair; now I know how it gets so wild. "Before the Mecs emigrated to the Edge, we were all the same. Before the genetic advancements, we were all exactly the same. And we still are, for the most part."

"Genetic advancements?"

"I'm as human as you."

"That's a weird thing to say. I didn't mean that you're not human."

"Ben's just sore from the looks he gets on account of him being Mec," Samson supplies.

"It's not like you're green-skinned or anything. Apart from your eyes, you look just like an Earth Cityite." I glance over his shoulders and the strong muscles of his neck. "Of course, you're a good deal healthier." I lean forward, my excitement getting the best of me. "I've heard that Mecs are geniuses. *Evolved.*"

The hint of a smile turns up his cheeks into that boyish look. "A real genius wouldn't admit to being one, would he?" he says.

Samson snorts a laugh and steers us through the spacedocks until we're facing the ship that Johnny called *Imreas*. We dip below the vessel, coming up from behind with a great view of the fiery blue thrusters. A small hatch opens in the side, and we swing around and in as though we're being swallowed whole.

We set down on a platform, and I reach for the door release, so excited to step foot inside my very first starship that my mouth is dry.

Ben stops me. "Wait for the airlock."

A whining *clank* rises into a sharp *clang*, and Ben pops the door open. I help Samson pull Walker's pod from the trunk, and something inside twists up a little too tight. I touch the stinging cold metal. Have I traded my brother for this chance to escape? What if he never wakes?

What if *this* is how I really lose him?

I follow Ben across a catwalk that spans the length of a massive docking bay. Crew members in black flight suits cross a network of intersecting catwalks under a ceiling cluttered with hanging crates. Below the grated walkway, the starship's cavernous belly stretches into deep shadow, issuing tendrils of steam from clanking, unseen machinery.

The crew clears from Ben's path even though most of them are twice his age. Their faces even turn away like they're afraid he might take notice of them. Apparently it's not only Earth Cityites who fear Mecs.

Samson leads Walker down a different walkway, and I stop. "Where will you put him?"

"Wherever there's room," the old man calls over his shoulder. "I'll let Ben know where, and he'll let you know when he's allowed." Samson turns a corner, disappearing with my little brother. I didn't even get to say good-bye.

"When he's allowed?" I repeat. I hurry into a cargo lift behind Ben. "What did he mean by—" A crew member forces himself through the closing lift doors, distracting me. We begin to rise as the short man holds out a huge wad of bills to Ben. "Send me a good one, will you?"

Ben doesn't take the money. "You know it doesn't work like that," he says tightly.

"What about her?" Gregg ogles my chest. "She won't mind. In fact, she'll do nice—"

"She's a red tag," Ben says.

"Apologies." Gregg glances all over the elevator like he's worried that he's been caught on camera. He slams the emergency stop, making the doors jerk open between levels, and he shimmies over the edge to the top floor. Ben smacks a button, and we begin to rise again.

"What was that about?" I ask.

"A desperate act by a desperate idiot."

"What'd you mean by 'red tag'?"

He twists his com like it's cutting off the circulation to his hand. "You'll see."

We exit on a dark, quiet level, and Ben's boots bang confidently as I follow him toward a door with a giant wheel lock.

He presses something on his com, and the lock spins until it jumps open.

We step inside. "This is the center of *Imreas*," he says. "The safest place on the ship during early space. You'll be freed once we hit the relative safety of the Void. Johnny's weird about his girls walking around before we reach traveling speed."

"Girls?" My eyes turn around a huge room with high ceilings and . . .

Girls.

Dozens of girls are strapped to the wall. Their heads hang forward like a demented rainbow of white-blonde to black hair colors. "What the—"

"They're not dead. They're knocked out. Just like you're about to be." He steps to the front of the line and picks up an empty harness. "Hurry up. I'm late."

I step closer even though I'd rather be running backward. "These are all *his girls*?"

Ben laughs hollowly. "Johnny calls them *his girls* because they work for him to keep their spots on the ship. He trades them."

"Trades?"

"Prostitutes." Ben loosens the harness, talking low. "He pimps them to the crew and other passengers."

"He's going to pimp me?"

Ben slips the harness over my shoulders. "I tried to warn you." I stare into his face, but he looks away, locking the straps around my hips. "Besides, you agreed to give him your body. You didn't tell him that he couldn't share it." He shakes his head. "I didn't mean . . . hell, I always say the wrong thing. I'm sorry, Rain."

Of all my rushing thoughts, the words that come are soft. "I didn't know you knew my name."

"It's a hard one to forget." He slips something papery through my half-open lips. "Do yourself a favor and dream of some-place else."

A minty taste spreads across my tongue and darkness crowds my vision.

"But the Void is my dream." I keep my eyes open past the moment when they can no longer see.

CHAPTER
6

I fall . . .

And slam face first into the floor. Bright spots pop across my vision.

"*Move, move, MOVE!*" someone shouts.

Groggy, I lift up on my elbows. My cheekbone aches as I squint around the cargo room. Someone unsnapped my harness. Someone let me drop to the floor. But I'm in the Void now—I jumped Earth City.

"*GET UP!*"

I peer at the voice, and a familiar thin frame and pink hair come into focus. "Lo? What're you doing here?"

"Tell you later." She gets under my arm and hauls me to my feet. "We're in one sweet freakin' mess, Rain."

Someone barks orders while Lo drags me to the center of the room. Beautiful girls with varying shades of skin and hair are arranged in a line like they're waiting for an inspection. "Can you stand?" she asks. "I've got yelled at twice, and I think we'll be in it deep if we don't do exactly like the others."

I plant my feet and push off her shoulder. "What's going on?"

The line of girls straightens as the wheel on the chamber door begins to spin, and by the time it opens, the girls are as silent as though they've been struck. Ben enters, his wild hair covering most of his expression, but he's not the one who sends shivers through me.

Johnny's smile is daring. He steps in behind the Mec, one hand in his pocket as he strolls up and down the length of the room. His clothes are as elegant as they were on Earth City, but in the new scene, it's something more . . . commanding? Threatening? He inspects the girls one at a time, while Ben works his way down the line, injecting each of them in the arm with the same needle instrument that he used on Hallisy.

I panic as Johnny approaches, but a girl with black, tightly curled hair takes his arm before he reaches me. Her skin is so dark that it reminds me of a cocoa bean. "Johnny, I haven't seen Shara. My cousin. Do you know if she . . ." Her voice trails off as he shakes his head. She lets go of his arm, and her eyes begin to redden.

What have I gotten myself into?

Dizziness makes me reach for the girl next to me, but she throws me off with an elbow to the ribs. I stumble forward and end up on one knee before Johnny's great height.

He takes my arm and lifts me back to my feet. A smile touches the corner of his mouth. "Welcome to the Void, Rain." His fingers skim my hair, and I can't help but notice the looks from every other girl in the room. Jealousy and heat.

Johnny spins on the spot to face Ben. "She needs a shower and some color. Get the others on their way." He leaves and the girls burst into hushed whispers.

"Some party, huh?" Lo chews on her thumbnail. "Never thought I'd be under a pimp again. Not after Bismark." She rubs the jagged scar that runs around her neck like a perverse necklace and laughs shrilly.

She's in shock. I'm in shock. What *is* going on?

Ben makes his way to me and slips my shirt off my shoulder without making eye contact. I was waiting for him to get down the line, but now I don't know what to ask. The shot jars me back to the starship. To outer space. To being a prostitute.

"What was that?" I rub my shoulder.

"Birth control and a resistant antibody for STDs." He moves on to Lo. "You're all set."

All set?

He tries to get a hold on Lo's arm, but she slaps him away.

"It's all right. He isn't going to hurt you," I try.

"But he's a . . . he's a . . ." I get a hold of Lo's arm and hold it still for him. Ben injects her, and I wait for him to say thank you. Instead, he calls for the attention of the room.

"Green tags to the Family Room. Blues to the passenger levels," he orders. "And yellows to the crew deck. That's it. Go on." The girls stream toward the door in a rush. Those with blue-rimmed bracelets find others with the same color. And the greens converge with the other greens. The white-blonde girl next to me whimpers as she stares at a yellow-rimmed bracelet. I look down at my own wrist, happy to find no bracelet—no bizarre identifier.

Lo is unbraceleted as well. "What do we do?"

"We ask the Mec." I touch my cheekbone where my face smacked the floor. It's hot and tender, bruising most likely.

"We don't have bracelets," Lo says in a mousy voice that I've never heard before.

"You two need to be cleaned up." He touches the arm of a green-braceleted girl with the longest, prettiest dark hair I've ever seen. "Kaya, take the new girls up to the Family Room and get them bathed and colored, will you? I'll be by to tag them."

Kaya nods, but withdraws from Ben's hand as though it burned her. She beckons us toward the door, and Lo grips my waist like she's forgotten how to walk.

We pause at the very end of the crowd of girls, waiting for our turn in the elevator. Kaya combs her fingers through her dark hair, staring at Lo. Her eyes are a stretched, almond shape that I've never seen before. "You're much uglier than most. Johnny recruit you personally?"

Lo picks at the pink streaks in her stringy hair. "Was just having a drink at the Blackstar, and this guy offers to get me off planet." She looks at me. "I thought he was that same captain guy that chatted you up, so I thought, why not?" She touches her neck scar, her whole body shaky. "Couldn't pass up the Void. Plus I wanted to be with you, Rainy. Then next thing, I'm waking up strapped to a wall like a freakin' nutso."

I rub her back. "You think you've been abducted like the Touched?"

She leans into me, fishing out the photo of her mom from her cleavage and rolling it between her palms. "Feels a bit that way, doesn't it? Like no one will ever see us again?"

I can't help but agree.

She stops fidgeting. "Where's Walker, Rain?"

"He's safe." I don't like the way Kaya watches us while we talk. Me in particular . . . and mostly my hair. "He had an accident, but I'm going to get him help when we reach the Edge. He's going to be all right."

Kaya laughs as the elevator opens. "You new girls," she says. "You always have your heads up hope's ass."

I yank Kaya's hair so that her whole body jerks back, and she yelps. "That's for calling Lo ugly," I add, stepping past her and into the elevator.

She's ready to fight, but the doors close and a siren blares: *SCHREECHEEENSCH! SCHREECHEEENSCH! SCHREE-CHEEENSCH!*

All three of us fall to our knees, covering our ears. The sound slices straight into my brain so that I can't think or move.

After a few moments, it cuts off, and we breathe into the now deafening silence.

"Let me outta here!" Lo beats fists against the elevator doors.

"No use," Kaya says. "You see that red light?" She points to the ceiling. "We're in lockdown."

"What the shit is lockdown?" I say, wiggling my finger in my ringing ear. "And what was that siren for?"

"An alarm. Means something's loose. We don't go anywhere until it's been collected."

"What'd ya mean by 'something'?" Lo turns, her tiny features all bunched up. "Like some kind of space demon?"

"You for real, girl?" Kaya snorts. "Something or someone set off the alarm. *Imreas* is a passenger ship, but there's also things down in the storage areas. Questionable things. People bringing animals to sell on Entra. Or some other nonsense. Who knows." She snorts again. "Alarms don't usually get tripped this early in a run. Bet that Mec is sprinting around like a fool to fix it for Johnny."

"I didn't think Mecs could be fools," I say, both heated by the fact that she'd dismiss Ben and the hint that I care.

"Yeah, well, most Mecs stay on the Edge where they belong. Only the idiot ones leave their paradise." Something about her words is strange. Not to mention that her skin is a warm, toasted color that I've never seen before.

"You're not from Earth City, are you?" I ask.

"Are you kidding?" She gets to her feet and swings her long hair behind her. "I was born on the Entra settlement, and I've been with Johnny since his early runs. Back before he owned this ship." She rubs the green bracelet. "Takes a lot to keep in his favor, so don't think you can pull anything over on me. No matter your stinking hair color."

I stand. "What *is it* with my hair?"

"Johnny's always wanted a true red." She squints at my roots just as the warning light clicks off and the elevator begins to rise. "Can't believe he finally found one."

Lo grips my hand, and I give her fingers a squeeze. Kaya leads us down hallways lined with glass ornaments and plush carpets to a large open room filled with couches and pillows and a variety of floor mats.

"This is the Family Room," she says. "This is where Johnny's faves sleep when they're not with clients." Girls with green bracelet tags lounge around, and a half-dozen well-dressed men stand at one corner as though they're about to take a survey.

"Not bad," Lo says, looking over the colored veils. They hang from the ceiling, creating secret-looking nooks around the room. "Better than I'm used to." Lo leans in to whisper. "So this is where the green girls go? How do we get a green tag? And what happens to the other colors?"

"I don't know," I whisper back. "But we need to find out." Before we left Earth City, Ben had called me a "red tag," but I don't see any other red tags, and like hell do I want to be the only one.

Kaya brings us into a shower room with a steamy atmosphere and tiled walls. Lo coughs, and I rub her back, as Kaya points to a huge tub sunk into the floor. "Get in," she says.

"With our clothes on?"

"If you call those clothes."

Lo places her mother's picture on a towel, sinks to the edge, and wades in. "It's not bad, Rain. It's warm."

"Your name's *really* Rain?" Kaya chirps. "You should change it to something more suitable. How about Ginger or Scarlet?"

"Just as soon as you change yours to Jerk." I squat by the tub to keep from lashing out further. My mom gave me my name, and it's all I have left from her. I drag my fingers through the warm water and though our pool was always empty, I can't help but picture it how I last saw it: blood smeared across the deep end and Walker's desperate cries. . . .

Kaya shoves me, and I topple headfirst into the tub with a violent splash. I resurface, kicking and spitting.

71

"Hey!" Lo yells. "We're on your side! What's wrong with you?"

"I'm fine, Lo." I hack up a mouthful of water and eye Kaya. "She's just playing the queen. No doubt it's been a long time since anyone wanted her." I pause. "I bet Johnny barely even looks at her anymore."

Kaya stomps across the room and riffles through a shelf of products.

"You need to do what I do," Lo says so quietly that I almost miss it.

"What?"

"Stop running your mouth." She squints angrily. "Don't think that these girls are on your side. They all want to make the pimp happy. They all want to be his favorite. That's how this works. Trust me. And *if* you're his favorite, they'll all want to take you down."

I start to argue, but she splashes me in the face.

"Just keep your mouth closed. I don't want you getting hurt!"

I want to say that she's wrong and to point out that it's always been me taking care of her. What does she know? But then I see her terrible neck scar—how Bismark strung her up with a wire when a guy complained about her service. Perhaps she does know a thing or two that I don't.

"Rain!" Lo points to the water where red leaches from my clothes, blooming in the water like blackened roses. "Is that *your* blood?"

"Walker's." I run my fingers through a cloud of red as though I can feel my brother through the color. I suddenly ache so bad that I can't breathe.

"Freakin' mess! What happened?"

"He fell." For the first time since my brother dove, huge tears drop from my eyes. "I had to get help. I had to trade Johnny something, and I wasn't thinking straight."

Lo wraps her skinny arms around my neck. "See, I knew I wasn't high outta my head for getting on this boat. You need me. I need you." She pulls away and runs her knuckles along my cheeks. "And we got each other."

Kaya returns, and I do my best to swallow my grief. She pauses above the tub like she's got something snappy to say, but she dumps a cup of powder into the water instead. "Don't breathe," she adds with a smirk.

The water bubbles and hisses and foams. I thrash, creating waves, waves that grow hot and sting like they're scalding the skin from my bones. Lo shrieks.

"What the—" I start.

"Don't breathe!" Kaya repeats before using her foot to dunk my head. The water roils in my ears, and I thrash, nearing the desperate moment when I will have to breathe, and Kaya releases me.

I suck air as the bubbling dies out. Lo grips the side like a half-drowned sewer rat, and we're both naked. My body is the angry, raw color of skin beneath a burn, and nothing is left of my bloody clothes except for a maroon foam marring the edges of the tub.

It's so bizarre that I almost laugh. "Well, I've finally done it, Lo. I've killed your lucky shirt."

She hiccups a little laugh through her whimpers.

"Bet you've never been so clean in your life." Kaya sits cross-legged on the floor. "I had to do it too, you know." I don't like her looking over my nakedness, but I'm not about to cower and cover myself up. She tosses a comb into the water. "For your hair."

"I know what a comb is for." Lo darts a look at me, and I grumble, "Thanks, Kaya." I pick up the comb and work it through my curls. It feels so clean that it's almost light, and the grease and ash, which usually cake my scalp, are miraculously gone.

I wade over to Lo and work the comb through her hair. It's even thinner when wet, and I push past the eerie feeling that I can see the shape of her skull beneath her tight skin. "Your hair looks pretty," I lie, and she makes a small sound.

"Time to get out. We've got to give you girls some color," Kaya commands.

I help Lo out of the tub before heaving myself up the ladder. Lo reclaims her mother's picture. "What do you mean by 'color'?"

Kaya doesn't respond but leads us into a tiny room with benches. It's small and warm, and when she flips a switch, the walls begin to hum.

"What's going on?" Lo won't sit down. "What're the walls doing?"

"It's a sun room. It'll liven up that ghostly white skin of yours. Johnny can't stand the sick pale of Earth Cityites." Kaya has taken her shirt off and bends over to paint her toes from a small pink bottle.

I sit, looking to the cotton white of my forearms and remembering the pier. Johnny had seemed so healthy-skinned, but it wasn't because he travels close to distant suns; it's because he sits in an electric room. What a letdown.

Still, the air turns pleasantly warm, and the light gives my skin the same kind of baking sensation that I felt when Samson took the hover cab above the smog. The only difference is that the room glows orange instead of that wondrous golden color.

In a few minutes, my skin is completely dry. Lo still won't sit down, and I can tell that she's on the very edge of her nerves. Kaya finishes her toes and caps the bottle. "Can I have some of that?" I ask.

Kaya tosses the bottle over, and I beckon for Lo to sit. I begin to paint her toes, ignoring her occasional jittery shake.

"My lucky color," Lo says.

"I know," I tell her and wink. I check Kaya, happy to find that she isn't glaring for once. Perhaps I can appeal to her human side. "You said you were from Entra. Is that a spacedock?"

"It's the only other planet with a settlement between Earth City and the Edge. It's mostly farming, outside of the Runner out-posts." Kaya faces the orange ceiling as though she's looking at something I can't see. "We have two suns and two moons. That's *twice* as good as that ridiculous Earth."

"I don't doubt it." I force a kind tone. She fidgets with her bracelet, and the green light makes the skin on her wrist appear alien.

"What are the bracelets about?"

"To keep track of us." She twirls the band on her wrist. "Johnny can't watch over all of us all the time. He's got other busi-ness. More lucrative business. We're his head servant's job, though he sucks at it. He's too busy tinkering with his toys."

"Ben? I mean, the Mec?" I finish Lo's right foot and move on to her left.

"Yeah. That rat of a Mec." She leans forward and whispers, "Last run, he dropped a girl out the airlock." She winces. "Forget I said that. So anyway, greens are elite and live in the Family Room. We get Johnny's handpicked clients, and we don't have to handle money. You have to be a little exotic to be green."

I stare down at Kaya's tag. "So if green is the top shelf, what do the blue girls do?"

"Trade themselves to the passengers. They're a bit on their own, but they find regulars and rooms. I imagine it's not terrible to be a blue girl."

"And yellow?"

"They have to stay on the crew deck. Not a lot of money down there. Or food. Not a lot of anything." She stands up like she needs to run away from her words. "Wait here until it turns off." She leaves, and I put a second coat of color on Lo's toes. My skin tingles under the orange light, but it's not unpleasant.

"I feel a little nuts," Lo says. "You feel a little nuts?"

I nod, focusing on the job at hand and trying to project calm. "We're going to be all right. Between the two of us, we have the smarts to get through this."

"Yeah. Maybe." She touches my shoulder, and I lock my fingers with hers.

"I'm so glad you're here," I admit in a rush. "So glad."

She squeezes my hand. "Yep."

Something *dings*, and the orange light of the room fades. Kaya comes back, and I can't help but smile at Lo, who's admiring her newly pink toenails. We're still as naked as the hour we were born, which makes things awfully awkward when we step into the shower room and find Ben waiting.

I could try to cover up or turn away, but I'm too steamed. I wait for his eyes to fall down me as he turns to Kaya. I even plant my hands on my hips, almost wanting him to look, wanting to be able to kick him for looking.

"Johnny's already asking for Rain," he says. "Have her dressed and ready to go in five."

Kaya's tight mouth suggests that she's holding back a few choice curses. She must really believe that Ben killed that girl, but Ben had alluded to Johnny doing it before, hadn't he?

Ben checks his com. "I'll wait out there." He thrusts bracelets at us without letting his gaze drop to my skin and leaves. I turn the circlet of silver over in my hand.

"Mec silver," Kaya says. "All the way from the Edge." The bracelet shines like a mirror, and it's heavy and cold. It's the most expensive piece of jewelry I've ever seen, let alone held.

"You have to put it on to see your color," Kaya says. "And remember, once it's on, it doesn't come off unless Johnny takes it off himself. Otherwise you'll get zapped." I snap the piece of silver around my wrist, and it locks.

After a few trilling heartbeats, the silver glows scarlet.

"Ah, red," Kaya says. "Shoulda guessed."

"Is red bad?"

"Means you're his. No one else gets to touch you." She grabs a towel off a rack and throws it to me. "For now." She holds a second towel out to Lo, but she doesn't take it. Her hand is clamped over the silver bracelet.

"What's wrong, Lo?" I ask.

She holds out her wrist.

It's rimmed in yellow.

CHAPTER
17

Lo shivers while we choose clothes from an overstuffed closet. She'll need a drink soon or she'll start withdrawal.

"Kaya," I say carefully. "Do you know where Lo could get a drink? A strong drink?"

Kaya looks over Lo's shivers. "We have some wine in the kitchen, but Johnny doesn't like us drinking too much."

"Wine is good." I nod to Lo, and she follows Kaya to the kitchen area. My best friend looks back over her shoulder at me, and I smile, which hopefully looks less fake than it feels. At least Kaya has been easier on Lo since the reveal of her color, but as Lo's tiny frame stands out among the curves and grace of the other girls, I can't help thinking that Kaya wasn't just being cruel when she pointed out Lo's looks. Lo is on the bad end of a bad decade.

Despite all that, it sounds like Johnny approached her on purpose in the Blackstar. And what about our meeting on the pier? Was it accidental or was he really looking for a redhead?

If these pieces begin to fit together, I'm in more trouble than I thought.

I glance down at the slim-fitting outfit that Kaya chose for me.

It's comfortable, but I can't ignore the zipper that runs from one side of my collar to the middle of my thigh. *Easy access*, she said. I feel the tightness in my chest, but I force myself to breathe through it. I am going to sleep with Johnny. I am here. And this all has to happen if I have any hope of helping Walker.

I touch the tender spot on my cheek and find Ben by the door. "I need some answers."

"Not possible." He turns, leading me into the elevator. He plays with his com as we sink down a level, never looking at me.

"Still busy working your secret Mec magic with that bracelet? I'll really *try* not to mention it to Johnny."

He looks up hard and fast before pushing past me and through the doors. I jog to catch up, but he stops fast and turns. I run straight into his chest, my forehead hitting his jaw.

I swear, rubbing my head. "You have a ridiculously hard chin, you know that?"

"You won't tell Johnny I was messing with my com. I've sorted you out, and like I said earlier, you're not a bad person. You really want to see Johnny punish me?"

"It could slip," I say. "So you should probably do me a favor to keep my lips sealed."

I swear he looks at my lips for a moment before responding. "What do you want?"

"Make Lo a green tag."

He shakes his head. "Johnny sets the groupings."

"Well, how about a favor?" I look away. "When I need one."

"That's it?" He reaches for my cheek, and I almost smack him. He holds up the blue disc that he used to heal Walker. "Hell,

I was just going to fix your bruise. Okay?" He steps forward, and I let him heal me purely out of curiosity. His fingers are calloused but careful, and the device spreads strange warmth over my skin.

"So are you a doctor or are all Mecs like this?" I say to beat the awkwardness of being so close to him.

He snorts. "I'm eighteen. I'm as much of a career professional as you are. How old are you anyway? Seventeen?"

"You say that like it's a bad thing." I look over the steely rims of his eyes. "But you're a Mec genius. You could probably tell me what's . . . I don't know . . . 39,000 divided by 203.8."

He doesn't even pause. "191 and some change."

"Is that one of your fabulous jokes?"

He smirks. "Maybe."

"But that's the right answer, isn't it? It's a little sick that you just did that in your head."

"Yes, but you're missing a key flaw to Mec society. If everyone knows what 39,000 divided by 203.8 is, then no one is special. Being a genius is average, and being above average is scary."

"Is that why you're here? Why you left the Edge? To be different?"

"That's my business," he says quickly. He drops the disc into his pocket.

I touch my cheek; the soreness is gone. "Thanks, but that wasn't the favor."

"Ah, hell." He grins, and just like in the backseat of the cab, I'm not prepared for how cute it makes him look.

I spin and start down the hallway. "Don't smile like that." This time he jogs to catch up with me. "I'm not supposed to like you. Remember?"

"True," he says. "But can I ask you a question now? You're not terrified to face Johnny? Not even after you've found out what he does on this ship?"

"I need some answers, and he's the only one who has them, right?"

"He has plenty of answers, but that doesn't mean he'll give them to you." He stops at a glass door that looks in on a massive command deck. "Do whatever he says and you should be all right."

"What about my brother? Where is he? When can I see him?"

He looks away. "Those are questions for him, but I wouldn't ask them yet."

I touch the door handle, but I can't seem to open it. "Let me ask you something then. You don't seem *bad* either. What's your game in all of this?" I glance at his com. "Are you trying to get that thing off? Are you trying to escape?"

He tugs the door open. "If I was, would I really admit that to you?"

———————

The command deck is crowned by a wide window, giving me my first real view of the Void. Silver and white stars shine against a velvet black backdrop. Their magnitude and brilliance are so much more stunning than I ever imagined.

I can barely breathe.

Ben taps my shoulder, and I follow him around control panels and crew members. They don't look at us, their attention poised instead on Johnny at the center of it all.

And yet, the captain doesn't seem to be doing too much of anything. When he looks our way, he motions for Ben. I'm dying to step closer to that window and the teasing parade of stars, but I follow instead. I need some truth, and I need to find my brother. He better be somewhere safe.

He better be exactly the way we agreed.

Johnny waves everyone else away from him. He slides his shoulders out of his suit coat and tosses it to me without a glance. The fabric is surprisingly heavy and drenched with body heat, but still it may be the softest material I've ever touched.

"So that little hiccup?" he asks Ben.

"Taken care of."

"It better be. But I'm more interested in *how* it happened in the first place."

So Ben *was* the one who had to handle the tripped alarm just like Kaya said. What kind of secret things live in this ship anyway? I shift Johnny's jacket from one hand to the other, wanting to dump it on the floor.

"I don't know how it happened," Ben says after a long pause. Johnny's eyes have that flint to them that stirs up my arm hairs, but Ben is unmoving.

Johnny turns at me. "Tell me, Rain. What good is a Mec on staff if he can't sort out a simple security bug?"

"It branched," Ben says. "And you didn't give me all the pass codes."

Johnny sits on the edge of the control panel. He leans back until his leg is touching mine. "That, Rain, is a Mec trap. Do you really think he needs the pass codes?"

Both of them are looking at me, and I clear my throat. To side with Johnny or Ben?

Johnny, of course.

"He's probably just lazy," I say.

Johnny smirks at my assessment. He uses his thumb to unlock his communicator's clasp and hands it to Ben. "Here you go then. Make the system work." His tone has a playful edge that is too sharp. "Or else. Right, pal?" He knocks Ben in the shoulder, and I can't help but catch Ben's returning glare. A look that says, "Stand the fuck back and watch me."

But Johnny doesn't see it. He's too busy combing me with his eyes. "Let's take a walk, Rain." His hand creeps to my arm, then up my back until it's resting on the nape of my neck.

We head back toward the elevator, and I wait until we're out of view of the crew members before I shrug away from his grip. "I can walk. You don't have to leash me."

An amused grin plays on Johnny's lips, but he doesn't say a word—not until we've taken the elevator up to a floor where the only door is labeled *Captain's Quarters*.

⎯⎯⎯∿∿∿∿∿⎯⎯⎯

The room is the nicest I've ever seen. Deep carpet cushions each step and ornate silver light fixtures fill the room with a low glow. An overstuffed chair takes up one corner, backed by a bar loaded with dozens of bottles. Finally, my eyes are drawn to the large window at the foot of a huge slippery-looking bed.

Fear dawns like a brilliant sun. It was easy to say that I would sleep with Johnny, but the actuality of it is blinding.

He pours a drink, and I strangle the coat still weighing down my hands. "Come, Rain. You've never been shy before. Where's the 'say anything' quality?"

"You barely know me."

He collapses in the large chair, his knees spread a little too wide as he sips his drink with one hand and unbuttons his silky shirt with the other. "True, but let's not play strangers. That game is truly boring."

"Am I a game?" I toss the coat on the edge of his bed. "I'm starting to doubt our agreement. This ship is—"

"Is a Void ship that's taking you and your damaged brother to the Edge. I would treat her like a lady, Rain. Particularly if you want me to keep up my end of the bargain."

The truth is obvious: it doesn't matter if it is a game or not. I have to play. "So we still have our arrangement if I do . . . what I said I'd do?"

I watch his eyes wander up my tight outfit. This is nuts, and still, my heart beats in a rushing, warm sort of way.

"We have our agreement." He sips from his glass while his free hand touches his neck. His chest. "But I've been awake for three days to make sure we made it into the Void while you girls napped in storage, so check your bitterness."

I sit on the footstool, forcing a reserve that I don't feel. "I'm not bitter. So you didn't tell me that you're a pimp. I should have guessed as much, but it doesn't matter. You get my body either way." My words are meant to please him, but they also feel damned with reality.

"I don't like the word *pimp*. Clear it from your vocabulary." His eyes narrow for a moment. "But this attitude is refreshing. You don't seem to want to play the 'Oh, but don't you love me, Johnny?' game. Still, you must have questions. Tell you what, you give me something to take my mind off my exhaustion, and I'll answer a few of the concerns knotting up that pretty face."

My mind streams with images of red alarms and bracelet tags as well as Lo and Walker, but I know that I have to tease him. And I need to start at the beginning. "How old are you?"

"Twenty-two." He swirls the amber liquid in his glass.

"How'd you end up with a starship? You're so young."

He points to his knees, and it takes me a moment to remember that this is tit for tat. I massage the top of his legs, and he groans. "The short answer is that my father owns a fleet."

I venture a little further up his toned legs. One thing is for certain: Johnny may be lean, but he's no weakling. "So he just gave you *Imreas*?" This is the first time that I've used the ship's name, and I don't like the way it slips off my tongue.

"My father gave me nothing. He marooned me on Entra when I was fourteen, determined to make me 'Find my own way.'" He takes a drag from his drink. "I'd never been without my servants for so much as a day, and there I was in the middle of a fucking forest planet. Truth be told, I was starving, eating dead things that I found in the woods." I bring my massage back toward his knees, and he doesn't seem to notice. His eyes are glazed with a kind of crazy glow, which makes my breath go shallow. "But my girl came and found me. My Crysta. She stepped out of the clearing between two trees like a Void angel."

Johnny has withdrawn into a memory, but it feels dangerous. "She was my lifesaver."

"She helped you find your way out?"

"She gave me the way out through the casino. She has this *body*. I tell you what, finding men to pay for her was the easiest job I've ever done."

"You pimped her?"

Johnny sits up fast, knocking me back a little. His hand is on my neck in a second, tugging the zipper and opening my clothes all the way to my cleavage. "I warned you about that word."

"You did."

He touches my newly exposed chest. "Are you afraid of me?"

"Sometimes," I admit.

He leans back and finishes his drink. "You'll get over that. It's a virgin thing. To be honest, I detest virgins. Too high maintenance. By the way, what do you think of your color?"

I think that he means my bracelet, but he motions to my skin. I glance at my arm. It's got an olive tan to it like Johnny's. A healthy glow. "It's all right."

He puts my hand on his leg again, but when I start stroking him, he scoops me into his lap. "So where were we?"

"Crysta was making you money."

"Right, so I soon saved enough to collect the interest of other girls, and then my own ship. I used that ship to commandeer the best in my father's fleet. *Imreas* was his gem."

"Was he angry?"

"He was proud in his own way. You might say that I exceeded his expectations."

"How old were you then?"

"Seventeen." He sighs. "Now I run the Void with passengers. A self-made man at twenty-two. Are you impressed?" He fingers my jaw as I nod. And the truth is, I am impressed. I don't even have a set of clothes to my name, and yet when he was my age, he was in command of a starship. Pimp or no, that's no simple feat.

"But Kaya said you have even more lucrative business onboard." My curiosity gets the best of me. "Why do you keep trading girls?"

"Demand mostly. Plus I like giving beautiful girls a home and job. I take care of them like I'll take care of you. You'll come to respect me like they do. Or at least need me." He shifts forward, and I almost tumble off his lap. "*Who* says I have more lucrative business?" His arms have slipped around my waist so that I can't turn.

"One of the girls."

"You said 'Kaya.'"

"I did."

"Oh, Kaya." He sits back with a sigh, and I can't help but push him further, remembering his angry mumbling on the rooftop beside my greenhouse.

"So you don't work for your father?"

"Did Kaya say that I work for my father?"

"No," I say in a rush. "I was just curious. So you don't run errands for him?" I should have stopped sentences ago. His arm tightens me to him until I'm breathing his breath.

"I'm no *errand boy*." Johnny's eyes have blackened, sending a chill down my entire body. "But I'm glad you asked about my past as it might serve your future. I see through you right now. You're damming up your fears and growing as solid as stone, but"—he says while stroking my hair from my ear, and then whispers into it—"I don't want you like this. We'll wait until you want me. We'll wait until you've gone . . . soft. I have big plans for us."

He parts my lips with his thumb. "What do you think?"

I ache to bite his fingers. "I think you'll be waiting a long time. I'm not going to drool over you like these other girls."

Johnny smiles. "Yes, well, I loved Crysta. Before my exile, I couldn't have imagined trading her to other men, but then, it's amazing what you'll do when everything else has been taken from you. Nothing to lose. Everything to gain. It's the truest kind of freedom. You'll thank me for showing you."

"I already have nothing," I say through gritted teeth.

"Are you sure?" He smiles, but his lips are a tight line, and I can't help but think of Lo and her yellow bracelet. Walker in his frozen prison. "Just wait, Rain. Soon you'll be dying for me," he adds with the confidence of a stone-cold killer.

And with a rush, I realize that Johnny may very well be one.

CHAPTER
8

Lo is missing.

So is Kaya.

I stand by the small window at the back of the Family Room, hiding behind one of the many colored curtains. I'm sucked in by the outer space of my dreams—huge silver orbs gleam against the black stretch while in the distance, smaller stars streak like a hard rain.

And yet, it all weighs upon me like some great penalty. What have I gotten into?

The green-braceleted girls are silent or snoring, each one nestled on a bed mat in a different section of the veiled room. None of them would speak to me when I came back from meeting Johnny. Not one word about Lo or Kaya. Almost as though they had been warned.

Or maybe Lo had been right; I'm Johnny's red tag now. I'm the one to beat.

The lingering men left with their chosen girls when the lights dimmed for the night, and I find myself hoping that Ben might appear and leak his cryptic information. His body isn't so bad either.

"There's no reason to flirt with him," I whisper. "No good reason." And a whole host of bad ones. Not the least being, did he really get some girl thrown out the airlock?

But whether or not I want him to, Ben doesn't show, and all I have are the stars.

"Can't take those from me," I say, remembering Johnny's bizarre threat. "No matter whatever else you have in that twisted head of yours." I'm no longer foolish enough to believe that Johnny and I met by accident, and I've gathered that Lo is a pawn in this game he wants to play. He must have seen her on the docks and factored her into his plans. . . .

Lo's yellow tag must mean that she's somewhere on the crew deck, and yet her absence feels too sudden. Too permanent. She could be in trouble already. Knowing Lo, I don't doubt it for a second.

A guilty thought trips up my fears: if Johnny's going to use Lo, maybe he's not focused on Walker. I force myself to breathe, fogging up the window. Only a few weeks ago, Walker and I worked a double shift. He was so tired that I was practically carrying him home, and then I looked up, and that girl was falling from the sky, and everything changed.

I squeeze my eyes so hard that they ache. Samson put Walker somewhere on this ship, and I'm going to find him. "You haven't disappeared," I whisper.

But Lo has.

And Kaya is a green bracelet; she should be in this room, right? I remember Johnny's intense sigh as he said Kaya's name. Did I get her in trouble? Are they being punished?

I push the thoughts away. Lo, at least, is street tough. She knows about men and desperation. And if she were here, she could tell me how to *do things* with Johnny. How to kiss him. How to move against him . . .

SCHREECHEEENSCH! SCHREECHEEENSCH!

I fall to the floor, clutching my ears against the siren. A red light turns on and off, throwing an eerie pall over the room. Someone trips from behind a nearby veil, and Ben stumbles twice as he makes for the door. The siren stops, but the red light continues to flicker as he bolts out of the room.

So he *was* here! Right next to me the whole time! Was he watching? Did Johnny make him spy on me? My brain recovers from the searing volume of the alarm as I watch the door close in his wake.

It will lock, and I'll be a prisoner just like we were in the elevator. Shut in. Stuck.

I sprint, catching the handle a second before it clicks into the frame. I slip into the hallway, letting the door lock behind me. A far door slams behind Ben, and I follow slowly, stepping down a tower of steep stairs.

The air is grim on the low decks, and I breathe in a foul, steamy stench that is a little like livestock and more like a butcher's shop. I come out of the stairway before two huge storage units that stretch from floor to ceiling and duck behind a large support beam. High above, strips of fluorescent light attempt to dull the red glow of the lockdown lamps, but fail.

Ben paces before an enormous cargo door.

"The same one as earlier." Johnny appears as though he

materialized from the shadow. He throws someone at Ben's feet—a balding man in filthy clothes. His face is bowed to the floor.

"The same one," Johnny repeats. His voice is cutting, and my heart bangs with speed. I'm going to see Johnny, the Killer. I know it through to my bones. . . .

But Johnny tosses something else on the floor instead, and it clatters to a stop before Ben's boots. "Take care of it."

Ben doesn't move.

"Don't make me rethink our relationship, not after all we've done together." Johnny touches Ben's shoulder in a strangely friendly way. Too friendly. "You want me to trust you. You don't want this relationship to sour like it did with *her*."

Ben's face is red with the glow of the lights, and he slowly picks up the same knife that Johnny used to fix my shirt on the pier. "I know a more secure place where we could place him," he says in a raspy voice.

Johnny shakes his head. "Do it. I have a dinner to get to."

Ben's shoulders straighten, and a terrible sense of foreboding floods my veins. My fingers slip into my mouth, and I bite down as he pulls the man onto his knees by the back of his ragged clothes.

"Help *us*," he moans, but it's too late. Ben slams the knife into his chest and pulls it out in one slick movement. The man's head lolls forward, and Ben drops him facedown.

Johnny just smiles. "I do love watching you. As skilled as a surgeon."

"Shut up, Johnny." Ben shoves the knife into his hand and leaves, his heavy boots echoing like swears in his wake. Johnny wipes the blade on the dead man's clothes before dropping it in his pocket and disappearing into the shadows.

I taste blood. I've bitten into my knuckle, and my fingers are stiff.

The lockdown light vanishes, and the dank area fills with the yellowed overhead lighting. I stumble out of my hiding place and fall to my knees before the man. I want to check for signs of life, but my hands won't close on his greasy clothes. *Why* didn't I do something? I could have rushed out to stop them . . . right?

Wrong.

A circle of blood pools from beneath his body, and I scuttle back to escape it.

And still it grows and grows, filling the floor with crimson. The color slides after me like something insatiable—something drawn to me—until I have no choice but to run away.

———

People die on *Imreas*. The words chase through my mind as I toss on my mat back in the Family Room. People die when no one's looking. What could have been that man's crime?

Help us.

A shiver lights my spine. So there are more where he came from. If I was smart, I'd realize that I shouldn't be sticking my nose into the shadows of this starship, but I'm already desperate to find out what's happening. Where are these people? And why are they here? This is a passenger ship, but the passengers I've seen are rich traders and questionable personalities like Johnny.

The window throbs with whiteness, the view shifting from an

endless stretch of stars to a net of gossamer strings unlike anything I've ever imagined. They weave as they embrace the ship, and I catch my breath.

I have to warn Lo. And above all, I must find Walker.

I step silently around the bodies of the sleeping girls, but when I push through the shower room door I can't hold back a scream. My voice powers off the tiled walls as Ben faces me. His arms and hands are dipped in bloody water at the white sink. Blood stains his shirt.

He runs at me, and I bring my fists up, but he slams into the door, locking me in.

"Don't!" I shout.

"*Shut up!*" He returns to the sink and scours his hands like he's trying to take the skin off. "I'm not going to explain, so don't ask," he manages after a few moments, before adding, "Someone needed help."

"Yeah, right," I say as he yanks his bloody shirt over his head and tosses it down a garbage chute. His brown boots are stained as well, like he walked through a stream of red.

Wait.

He didn't have any blood on him when he left Johnny. Not a drop. That's how swift he was with that knife. How cold. Did he go back to clean up the body? Did he see me?

"So you were just *helping* someone?"

"That's what I said." He kicks his boots off and unbuttons his pants. I should be demanding answers or just looking away, but the quiver of his back stuns me—like he's trying not to cry. "You going to stand there and watch me change?"

I feel warm. "Maybe. You saw me naked."

"Not by choice." He slams his boots in the sink. "And I didn't look. I'm no pervert." His hair is askew across his forehead, his expression pained. He's a killer—I saw it, but then what am I seeing now?

"What did you . . ."

"Just get OUT!" Ben struggles with heavy breaths as he scrubs his boots over the rushing stream of steaming water. I switch the lock and go back into the dead quiet of the Family Room.

I sit under the starry window, curl my legs into my chest and squeeze my eyes against what I just saw. I can't afford to be naïve. No matter what I think I know about Ben, he is a murderer. Johnny may have been the one to order it, but Ben *did* it. I rock on my heels until something like sleep finds me, but it's pierced by a familiar nightmare of chasing my dad's bloody trail out of the apartment building, down the street, and this time, into a black sky.

Waking in a sweat, I press myself to the cool window. "I miss you," I admit to the universe, hoping that somehow, he can hear me. Just outside, purple and orange rings mark the spot where a supernova blew itself to pieces ages ago.

CHAPTER
9

I have to sleep with Johnny.

I unzip my clothes to the very border of indecency and wear a fixed smile as he takes me on a bragging tour of the passenger levels. I bury the image of the stabbed man as best as I can, needing to focus on Walker and Lo. Not to forget the overwhelming question of Johnny's endgame.

We pause in a meeting room with a wide window and strange pots filled with growing things. A few blue girls socialize with groups of sketchy passengers.

"Not exactly a family ship," I mutter. "You ever have kids onboard?" I ask Johnny.

"I don't do kids."

"What about things down in the cargo?" I ask, remembering Kaya's veiled words about animals in the lower levels that get loose and set off the alarms.

"*Why* would we have kids in cargo?" He's missed my meaning, but his tone is a razor. "No kids except that brother of yours, that is," he adds. I stiffen while he reclines into a plush couch. He enters something on his com. I guess Ben gave it back to him already.

"The Mec fixed the security?" I ask before I can stop myself.

"Probably. We'll see," Johnny says.

"Isn't it dangerous to trust him? Can't he do just about anything with technology?"

"Mecs do have limits, Rain. Just like everyone. Or, I should say, they have soft spots. You find one, and you put a finger in it." He leans forward and holds out his hands. "Skilled fingers are all it really takes to command a ship. I think you'll like them, too."

I blush from my knees to my ears, touching the leaves of one of the potted growing things. "I've never touched a plant before," I say, hoping to distract him.

"I always forget that you Earth Cityites don't know plants. Just wait until you get a glimpse of Entra."

The leaves are flimsy and soft like a dog's ear. I always thought they'd be tougher, more like the waxy brown vine that wove itself through the greenhouse. I wipe the gentle texture from my fingers and remember to smile.

He frowns back. "You're so eager to be friendly. What happened to me waiting forever for you to want me?"

"Maybe I'm seeing how you are on the ship. Your status as captain," I lie. I continue to smile, and he continues to frown. He fingers his belt in a *come hither* kind of way, but I lose my nerve and turn to the window.

Outside, the stars blaze. There's no sign of the strange ghostlike strings I saw before, just the pitch darkness with silver holes that gleam like Ben's strange eyes.

Below the window, I find an inscription: AS SEAN IMREAS NA UAIGNEAS.

"What does that mean?" I ask.

"That's my father's doing. He loves dead languages and other such ridiculous things." Johnny stands next to me, glaring down at the words. "It means: 'Strife is greater than order.'"

"*Imreas*," I read. "Is that the word for strife or order?"

His hand slips around my braid, tugging the waves loose until they're a scattered mess around my shoulders. "What do you think?"

Johnny's mood has soured. Whatever he might say, Johnny's father seems to have a hold on him that snakes right through to his soul.

"I need a drink." He squeezes the back of my neck and leads me to a place called the Rainbow Bar. Colored lights dangle from the ceiling, casting a collage of shades over the tables and drinkers. All ages of passengers bow out of his way, clearing a space at the bar for him to sit and a spot next to him for me.

The bartender places two glasses of violet liquid before Johnny and me. "Drink it. I've never met a girl who doesn't like it." I take a sip and my mouth fills with too-sweet syrup that tingles all the way to my belly. "It's drained from these strange birds on Entra."

I pause. "It's made from their blood?"

"Extraordinary, yes?"

I put the glass down but keep my fingers around it. "Sure," I choke out, knowing that I should be doing better. *Sexier.* I brush my hand along the edges of his leg.

Johnny scowls at it. "No forced affection, remember? Give me something real." He leans in like he wants a kiss. I close my eyes and press my lips to his.

They're as hot as though he just breathed fire.

I pull away and find his fist constricting my hair. His mouth touches my ear as he whispers, "Pathetic, Rain. I had such hope for you, but maybe this arrangement isn't going to work after all." He releases me. "Find your own way back."

Johnny parts the crowd, leaving me to the scrutinizing eyes of every passenger in the bar. I lick the still warm feel of where his lips had burned against mine. Lo and Walker need me. I have to thrill Johnny in order to find them. And yet, as I sit beneath the colored lights, touching the exotic drink, I begin to sink with doubt. Maybe I don't have what it takes to seduce him.

But I do.

I force a sip of that purple liquid. That blood. Johnny was right; it's delicious. Sinful. And even though he's a pimp—a handsome devil—he's *my* handsome devil. I check the scarlet gleam of my beautiful silver bracelet. He chose me.

And now I want to prove myself for a reason that isn't my brother's or my best friend's safety. I want to prove myself to him because I can. I want to play his game.

I want to win.

———————

I wander through the passenger levels of the ship for hours, looking for an elevator or stairs that might bring me to the crew deck to look for Lo. But *Imreas* is larger and more complicated than I imagined, and when I stop a crew member and ask about the crew deck, he takes a quick look at my bracelet and shakes his head.

"Only yellows down there." He escorts me back to the Family

Room, and by then, I'm so hungry that I push past the green girls and choose a piece of bread with some kind of sugary spread.

Then I sit on my mat until long after the lights have dimmed and the other girls have quieted down, going carefully over my next steps. Perhaps I had been going about this all wrong; I was trying to figure out how to make myself want Johnny.

What I need is for Johnny to want me.

I think Lo would be proud, and in the silence, I miss my best friend's chatter. I picture the way she leans in to tell me something crazy, her eyes huge. She would have tips for handling Johnny. Warmth blooms in my belly as I wonder what it will feel like to press myself against him.

Will I like it? What if it's too obvious that I don't know what I'm doing?

The thoughts are embarrassing even in the dark by myself, so I turn to the window. A single asteroid rotates through the Void, and my missing of Lo turns to Walker.

"Don't scream." Ben pulls back the veil which encloses my little area. I stand fast and make a fist, but he holds his palms out to stop me. "I just want to say that I swear what you saw in the shower room the other night . . . well, it wasn't what you really saw."

"I don't want to know," I lie. "If I know, I'm in more trouble, right?"

"Hell," he says. "You're right. It'd be a lot easier to let you be afraid of me."

"I'm still not afraid of you. Which is weird, I guess." I pause to think over my words; they're startlingly true. "I'm only afraid of what you do for *him*."

"What do you mean?" He takes a few steps closer, and I back into the window. "I'm sorry," he adds. "I wouldn't hurt you. Not by choice."

"I can try to believe that." Silence fills the weird space between us, and he crosses his arms over his chest, making his shirt constrict around his forearms. "You could prove it to me. Give me that favor you owe me. I need to see my brother. Like now."

"I can't take you until Johnny gives the clear. Not until you and he . . ." He grimaces. "He's given me strict orders. Not until after."

"That freaky bastard!"

"*Shhh!* Keep it down." He glances at his com. "Always assume there are security cameras everywhere."

"The security system that you fixed." My tone reveals my doubt.

Ben looks at me strangely. "I forgot you were there for that. Yeah, I fixed it."

"So . . ." I look around. "We're on camera now?"

He opens his mouth, but then closes it. "Always assume there are cameras," he repeats. "Unless I tell you otherwise. I shouldn't even be talking to you right now, but I turned them off. I wanted to explain about the other night."

"But you haven't explained. You've pretty much just told me that you can't explain." I pause. "Who's side are you on?"

"There are no sides. It's every man for himself in the Void. You do what you have to do to survive. You take what you want. Even Johnny lives by that rule." He pauses. "Especially Johnny."

I touch my hair, still so smooth and clean from my bath with Lo. "He found me on purpose because of my hair." I drop my hands to my sides. "But how? Did he just ask around until he heard that there was a ginger hanging around the pier?"

Ben nods. "He's made you into a weird challenge. I've never seen him do this before."

I pinch my leg. "And I've gone right along with it."

"Yeah, but he didn't know about your brother. About your insistence on bringing him along. Believe me, that was not in his plans."

"Will he hurt him?"

Ben rubs the back of his neck. "Rain, if you want to best Johnny, you can't play by his rules. They're already fixed against you."

"Ben, will he hurt my brother?"

He shrugs. "If he doesn't get what he wants, he can be pretty unpredictable."

I take a step closer. "What about Lo? And Kaya? Are they on the crew deck? Why haven't I been able to contact them?" He shakes his head, and I snip, "You don't know or you can't tell me?"

He shakes his head again and begins to back away. "Remember what I said about the cameras."

"Ben," I say, trying to bait him. "I think it's safe to assume that you're not on his side."

He shakes his head a third time. "It isn't safe to assume anything, Rain."

I will not react. I will act.

I will change the game.

I repeat this mantra through the next day, all determination and a little excitement. And after all, it isn't hard to slip into the captain's quarters. It isn't hard to strip off my clothes.

The hard part is waiting.

I twirl my scarlet-rimmed bracelet. It couldn't be a worse color, so carnal. So damning. And still, I need him to want me. To go crazy with wanting me. My hands feel numb, and I rub my fingers together. Is it cold or nerves? What will I have to do with my hands?

Will I bleed?

I can handle the pain, I think, but what if he expects me to know what I'm doing? To touch his body and give him . . . pleasure? Other than seeing Lo at her business from a distance, I don't know how I should lean or rock or moan. She made it look so easy, but what's easy about letting someone inside you?

I start to breathe too hard and slump into a naked heap of anxiety. He can't find me like this. He'll know in a second that I'm still forcing it.

My thighs shake as I get back to my feet. I bury every feeling except for the stars outside the window, watching a distant planet with orange highlights: a lava planet. I blow on the glass and draw a *W* in the fog.

The door opens, and I swipe the letter away with my forearm.

"Full of surprises." Even Johnny's voice smirks. Within heartbeats, he's standing behind me, his hands slipping over my shoulders, my arms, my chest. "This is not really what I had in mind. Are you forgoing the romance? The long talks and teasing caresses?"

I clear my throat. "I want to see if *you* can play."

"Oh, Rain." His tone makes things shrink inside me like they're being singed at the edges. "I'm game."

He unbuttons his shirt. Slides out of his pants. "To the bed?"

"No. Right here."

His chuckle is joyful, and I clench my teeth and squeeze my eyes against it. He wraps an arm around my waist and braces me against the window. His body is so firm—I wait for the warmth from within that I felt before, but it doesn't come.

Be soft!

"I don't know what to do." My heart *slams* in my paper-thin chest. "You have to show me." He doesn't say anything, and I grip the window ledge, my fingernails throbbing as they grind the metal. "You're going to have to help me."

Why won't he answer?

"Johnny."

"Shhh," he says. "First rule, you don't have sex with your head turned on. Actually, that's the only rule."

I believe him. Maybe I have to. I give in to his kissing and pressing. My legs relax so terribly slowly . . . like ice thawing against his heat.

I am here. And this is . . .

Pain streaks up from my insides, clawing all the way to my mind.

Happening.

CHAPTER
10

When Johnny lets go, I slip down the window. My hips tip like they've been realigned, and he laughs. "That's always a favorite part." He holds an arm out, and I brace myself on it to keep from falling to my knees. "You've got your Void legs now, Rain."

I watch him dress.

My own clothes are too far away.

"Your first time *and* standing. I knew you weren't going to disappoint me." He fastens his pants.

I have to swallow twice before my words will come. "Can I see my brother now?"

"Tomorrow. Ben will need to take you, and he's on his night duties." His brown eyes are too lively. "I'm hungry. You?"

"No." I may never eat again.

"Suit yourself." He leans in to kiss me, and after what we just did, I'm surprised to find his lips intimate. He presses his face against mine for a moment. "I can still be a gentleman," he says like he's trying to convince himself. He locks eyes with me. "Thank you. I enjoyed that."

I don't quite believe it when the door shuts, when I realize it's over, and he's gone.

"You're welcome."

I pull on my clothes and lean against the window. His body raged so hot against mine that it seemed to burn an impression of him into my back. I relish the cool of the pane, hoping the window can put the fire out.

Sparks and stars? How could I have been such a fool? The only spark between Johnny and me is the jolt of his needs. And what I need now is the strength of my family, or what's left of it. I need my brother.

Tomorrow, Johnny had said. Well, I can't wait.

My legs ache as I amble out the door, and the little bit of blood that left me makes my pants stick to my thighs. Still, I keep going.

The hallway light is dim, set low for night, and it draws spiky shadows down the walls. The Family Room's lights are off altogether, and I creep around the sleeping girls to the corner window where Ben resides. I pull back a curtain and find his boots at face level. His legs slide up and down on the wall for balance while his arms lift his body in a series of vertical push-ups.

"Wow," I say. "That's intense."

He kicks down, and I duck out of the way of his swinging legs. "On this ship, it's too easy to go soft," he says through pants. "You've got to . . . to try." He peels his sweaty shirt over his head and uses it to wipe his face. I look to the window to escape getting caught in the glisten of his damp chest by the light of the window.

The white web that was braided around the ship two nights

ago has returned. It makes me gasp. "What is that?"

He pulls a clean shirt over his head. "The edge of the worm-hole. The Void. You can't always see it, but it's always there." He draws a hand down the glass as though he wishes that he could touch what lies beyond. "It's brilliant, isn't it?" The strings fade into wisps and disappear with his words, dimming the curtained nook with the dark of space.

"So you did it," he says, still looking out the window.

"How do you know?"

"It's my business to know things on this ship." He sighs before adding, "You all right?"

I take at least a dozen breaths before I answer. "I'm still here."

"He's going to be out all night. He always parties after he breaks in a new girl." He turns around and sweeps a hand through his sweaty hair. "Hell. I didn't mean—"

"I'll take that favor now," I say. "Take me to my brother."

———~~~~~———

Ben leads me below the plush decks to the corridor where I watched him stab that man. He keys a code into his com to unlock a door, and we enter a musty cargo room similar to the one where I was strapped into that harness. And drugged. And stolen into this world.

A single light dangles from the center, throwing shadows alongside its rays. Large boxes and crates stand eerily against the glow, and Ben pulls a tarp away from one of them. I'm leaning over it in a heartbeat, staring into Walker's frozen face through the tiny pod window.

The tears come fast, and I scrub them, embarrassed that Ben is watching. Walker's small face is being overtaken with frost, and I itch to rub it away.

"Can we open this?" I tap the glass.

"Not without Johnny's thumbprint." He sits on a crate, his elbows propped on his knees. "Besides, he's safer in there than out here."

I wish I didn't agree. I lean away from the pod and swallow a moan. The cold stiffens the aches from what Johnny and I just did. "I thought I would feel better if I saw him, but now I feel . . ."

"Used? Assaulted?"

I scowl. "Lonely."

"The Void is about being alone. Get used to it." He shakes his head. "I don't mean to sound like an ass. Think of it this way: this ship is all smoke and secrets. Everyone's lonely."

"I saw you." The words slip out. I can no longer hold back my confusion. How can Ben be so careful and attuned, and then turn into Johnny's assassin? "I saw you stab that man."

"You what?" He stands.

"The other night." I touch the pod behind me for support. "I followed you."

Ben stops a few steps away. "Why—why didn't you say something?" He waves a hand in dismissal. "Scratch that, why did you follow me? Do you have any idea of what would have happened if Johnny saw you?"

"I imagine it would be something similar." I finger the flat area over my heart where Ben knifed that man. "You always kill on command?"

"I'm not a monster!" He takes another step, and I bring up my fists. Ben's shoulders sag as he watches me, and he crumples into a sitting position on the floor. "Rain, you have to understand. He's got me by the throat. He knows my weaknesses."

"What does he have on you?" Ben doesn't answer, but then, I don't really expect him to. "Ben, why do the other girls . . . well, they seem to hate you."

"They're afraid of me because of what happened to Bron. They're afraid of me just like you should be."

I force a laugh. "You're not so mean and scary, oh powerful Mec."

"Joke all you want, but most of the people on this ship won't acknowledge me. Mecs have become the weird alien race of the universe, regardless of the fact that we're the same damn species." He stands up. "Half the people on this ship are afraid that I'm going to eat their brains. The other half thinks I am going to read their minds."

"You can read minds?"

"Of course not. There are some Mecs, I'm talking top-tier intelligence, who seem like they can read minds, but that's only because they can assess a situation and predict outcomes with surprising accuracy. It's mathematical. Statistical. Not mystical."

My mouth might be hanging open. "That's quite possibly the coolest thing I've ever heard."

"See? This is what I mean. You're not afraid of the weird Mec stuff. That either means that you're too smart or too dumb to be afraid. I'm betting on the former. You can read, can't you? That's weird for an Earth Cityite." He grins kindly. "And when I think about how you just got right in my face on that old pier, it reminds me of . . . her."

"Bron?"

His smile disappears. "She was my . . . friend. Johnny got rid of her to punish me."

"That's the girl who went out the airlock? Why didn't you do something?"

He gets to his feet. "What could I have done? I didn't even know she was gone until it was too late. I just thought she was missing. I thought he hid her from me."

Missing. Like Lo.

I try to swallow but my mouth is too dry. "Ben, my friend is missing, and Johnny went off on this nutso speech about needing to take things from me to make me independent. You don't think . . ."

His gaze is on mine like an aimed weapon. "You mean the 'Nothing to lose, everything to gain' speech?"

My skin runs so much colder than Walker's pod. "You don't think he—*killed* her?" I wait for him to say, "No. She's fine. I know exactly where she is."

But he doesn't.

"There's a way." He gets to his feet and stands so close that I can't help but feel the differences between him and Johnny. Johnny is all heat and length like a blade under a flame, but Ben is broad and flexed—and yet yielding without seeming soft. My dad had that kind of strength.

"There's a way to find out," he says. "If you really want to know."

———wwwwww———

Ben leads me down a winding passage to a room full of greasy, churning machinery. Strange music plays over the clunk of grinding metal parts, and the combined sound spirals up and up without hitting a ceiling.

"This is the engine room. It runs the full height of the ship." Ben scans the upper parts and then crosses to a black box and shuts the music off. The riot of clanking machinery fills the endless space. Along one wall, stacks of books ascend out of my sight, and I gawk at what is easily the best collection I've ever seen. My dad's book must be among them. . . .

"What what?" a grumbling voice calls down.

"It's Ben," he yells.

Samson falls from the dim air, zipping down a rope that comes to a stop just before he smacks into the floor. He limps off a little metal seat, his black flight suit almost as faded with age as his hair. "Blasted bones." He rubs his hip. "Thought you were *Oh Captain, My Captain.*"

He looks me over through his large fogged goggles, his beard and hair even more grimy than when he was on Earth City. "Hey there, Rain Runner."

"Hey." I give him a short smile, hoping that he doesn't start in on that "rain must fall" business again. I don't think I can hear it right now.

He frowns at Ben. "Don't often see Johnny's girls in my engine room."

"I need to show her the population chart."

"You mean the Who's Missing Chart," Samson mumbles. He motions to the other side of the room, and Ben crosses, but before I can follow, Samson touches my arm. "You don't know any more of that poem you spouted before, do you? I've been trying to find it." He takes a tatty book out of his pocket—my book. The binding has been reglued and the pages are lined up neatly.

"Look it up on the network, Samson," Ben calls.

"That's cheating," he yells back. He looks to me. "So?"

"It's in there, but, well, it was something that my dad used to hum. That's how I know it." I clear my throat and begin to sing, *"I am the Poem of the Earth, said the voice of the rain, Eternal I rise . . . out of the land. . . .'"* Ben gives me a laughing look. "I didn't say I was a good singer."

"Then I won't call you a liar."

"Ass." I show him my middle finger and turn back to Samson. "I don't remember the rest, but the best part is the end. It's, *'Reck'd or unreck'd, duly with love returns.'* I don't really know what that means, but it kind of dances off my lips."

Samson whistles the melody. "'Duly with love,'" he repeats. He flips through the book, and I step over to where Ben taps a screen with hundreds of moving dots. He pauses, looking at me almost sideways.

"What?"

"Still just thinking how strange you are for an Earth Cityite." I give him a sort of grimace, but he smiles. "I didn't say it was a bad thing." He turns back to the screen, and text tags scroll across it too fast for my eyes to keep up. Ben sorts through it all at lightning speed until a cross section of *Imreas* appears. He taps the engine room and then a scarlet glowing dot with a single word attached to it: RAIN.

"You," he says. He selects the dot almost on top of mine labeled BEN RYAN. "And that's me."

Ben Ryan . . . he has a good name.

"Why isn't my last name on that screen?"

He shrugs. "Johnny must have put you in. You want me to add it? It's White, yes?" He clicks on the "Rain" tag again.

The red letters blink at me. He begins to tap letters, and I catch his hand, his fingers surprisingly warm. "I don't need to bring my family into this." I clear my throat and turn away from his strange look. "So this screen could find anyone on the ship?"

"Anyone with one of these." Ben clicks his com against my bracelet. "The passengers aren't tagged, so there's no way to keep track of them. Hence the alarm system. But the crew and girls are."

"Find Lo," I demand.

"Are you sure you want to know? If I can't find her, it means . . ."

"Find her."

His fingers move too fast, but in a few moments he breathes a sigh. "Here." He selects a dot and the script reads: Lo.

"So she's fine? Where is she?" I almost knock him off his feet as I lean over the screen. Lo's position is close to mine in the ship. She's only a level away. "How do I get there?"

"That's crew deck. Hell, I can't take you there."

"But she could be hurt or messed up." I face him, realizing how close we are in height. The scruff on his jaw is a little blonde and boyishly patchy. "You aren't the monster, I know it. Please. Take me."

He shakes his head.

I turn back to the screen and grit my teeth. "Show me Kaya then."

Ben taps the glass, but nothing happens. He tries again. "She's no longer with us."

"What do you mean? She's gone?"

His eyes lose their focus like he's slipping into a memory. "I thought for sure I'd find Bron. Just as soon as I came down here, I'd find where Johnny stashed her to punish me. But she was gone."

"Kaya's dead?"

Samson squeezes Ben's shoulder. "There are two ways to disappear off that screen, Rain. You either jump ship or you die." He places his other gnarled hand on my shoulder. "Of course if you go the way of the airlock, both happen at once."

"It's my fault." Ben's whole body sags. "I picked Kaya to take you upstairs. Clean you up. I should have done it myself."

"It's not your fault. It was me. I said her name to Johnny. I gave him something to use against me."

A small part of me waits for him to argue—to say that this isn't my fault—but he only murmurs, "So we both did it."

"Ben." I take him by the front of his shirt. His eyes have a tugging look, which catches me off guard. "I have to see Lo. I have to warn her about all this before something else happens. Something terrible!"

I shake him, but Samson answers for him in his stunned silence: "If Johnny finds out that he took you to the crew deck, something terrible will certainly happen."

CHAPTER
11

Johnny and his security be damned. If someone like Kaya, who had been with him for years, can up and disappear, I have to warn Lo. And I saw the cross section of this ship. The crew deck was on the second level, and Lo was all the way at the one end.

I'll find her.

The only problem is that Ben hasn't let me out of his sight in the Family Room, and from my seat on one of the center couches, I watch him move from one corner of the room to the other, weaving in and out of the veils. Always as aware of me as I am of him.

I feel his passage as though a string is tied between us. And maybe there is. After all, we are both at Johnny's command. We're both being forced into something, right? The question holds me: if Ben isn't so horrible—if he's been swept up in this dangerous game even though he's a good person—then why can't that be my fate as well?

My legs are sore and my hips have had an odd weight in them since I had sex. I shift on the couch, so lost in my thoughts that I almost miss the moment when Ben goes into the bathroom. A perfect moment to slip away . . .

I open the door but collide with the back of a sandy-haired girl.

"Don't tell Johnny," she pleads with a man, his shirt stained by something yellowish. "Everyone gets sick sometimes!" She's still standing against me, and she reaches behind her, taking my wrist for support. "If you tell Johnny, he'll bump me down. I'll be yellow tagged before the morning!"

He curses in a language I've never heard before leaving, and I touch her shaking shoulders.

"I threw up on him. I didn't mean to! I couldn't help it!" She watches him storm down the hall.

"Don't worry about Johnny. I'll talk to him," I try. "What's your name?"

She turns around and looks from my face to my scarlet bracelet, horrified. "Not you!" She backs further into the Family Room, and into the mass of girls who had collected during the commotion. Ben stands to the side.

They all glare at me.

"You got Kaya taken away." A girl with short brown hair stands at the front, wrapping her arms around the sandy-haired girl. "Do us a favor and don't pick any of us out for him."

"But I didn't . . ." I look to Ben, but he's glaring.

"Come on, Angel." He steps forward and takes hold of the sandy-haired girl's arm. She shirks from his touch but lets him pull her toward the door. "It will be better if you tell Johnny before your client does."

They leave, but not before Angel bursts into wails. And not before Ben whispers at me, "You stay here!"

I'm left in the quiet of the judging, green-braceleted girls.

"She's slept with him," the one who spoke before says.

"And she's still red tagged," another girl supplies. "He's not done with her. Yet."

"What's your game?" the first one asks. "What are you trying to do?"

I shake my head. "I don't know what I'm doing. What do I do when he's done with me? Please, I could use some advice." My pleas are met by their backs, each turned at me one by one.

The only girl remaining is the loudmouth with the short brunette hair. She squints at me. "You want some advice? Johnny comes first. Think about it, Red. And for all that's astral, keep away from the Mec." She leaves, and I'm alone in the center of the Family Room just like I was a few moments ago, but now every-thing feels blacker. Lonelier.

Johnny comes first. I dig into the words for more truth but come up empty. *Keep away from the Mec?* But Ben is the only one who talks to me. And why were they so shocked to find that I'm still red tagged after being with Johnny once? Does he go through girls that fast?

My heart pounds like ominous footsteps coming ever closer. When Johnny is done with me, he'll change my color. Green, blue . . . yellow? None of that matters because it all amounts to the same reality: I'll have to sleep with the other men. The ones who pay for me. Strangers. My breath is tight in my chest until I'm shaking, aching for Lo. She would know what to say—how to keep Johnny's attention. She *knows.*

I have to find her.

But I can't move from the couch, let alone slip through the belly of this claustrophobic ship. Someday soon, I'll have to sleep with strangers. The term *fucking* drips along my fears. And when Johnny appears in the doorway with his confident grin, I go to him like a shot. I tug him back to his room, and this time, I take him.

I kiss him, lean into him, slip against him, and all the while, my fears flare like fireworks through my body, aligning sizzles of pleasure that make me quiver.

When he's spent himself, he falls asleep, and I begin to hate him again. His lips twist into a demented dreaming smile, and I suddenly can't stand his heat. I escape his slippery bed, my body humming. I need to find Lo, but now I also need to rid myself of the lingering warmth of his touch—and to flee the whisper that I want more of it.

~~~~~~~~

I take the elevator to the second level, hoping that Lo hasn't moved too far since I saw her dot on that screen.

When the doors open, I'm blasted by loud chattering like a party—or a bar. I tug my sleeve over my bracelet and head toward the noise. Unlike the Rainbow Bar on the passenger deck, I enter a low-ceilinged room full of metal crates, which double as tables and chairs for a throng of drunken crew members.

A stenciled sign on the wall reads: YELLOW DOG BAR.

I breathe a sigh. If I'm going to find Lo, I'm going to find her in a bar.

A card game is the focus of the room, and almost no one looks my way when I slip through the crowd. Two crew-women stare each other down while everyone watches, and one slaps a card on the tabletop, making the others scream and cheer.

Someone grabs my wrist.

I'm yanked back and away from the cheering, pinned to the wall by a girl with a yellow-rimmed bracelet. Her straight, sandy hair is askew, and I recognize her too slowly. I saw her only hours ago, but this can hardly be the same girl. For one thing, she has a bruise on her throat in the shape of a hand.

"Angel?"

She pulls my sleeve back and glances at my tag. "What are you doing here?"

"I'm looking for—"

"I know who you're looking for. She was in here earlier talking about how her friend—Johnny's special girl—was going to find her."

I yank my arm free. "Where is Lo?"

"Oh no. I tell you and that Mec's likely to kill us all."

"I've made a deal with B—with the Mec," I lie. These girls really don't worry about Johnny. They're terrified of Ben. "He let me come down here to check on her. How else do you think I made it this far without tripping alarms?" I'm a little stunned by my own question. Where are the triggers? And how close have I already come to setting one off?

The card game takes another noisy, jeering turn, and Angel jerks around like she's expecting a blow. "Room 214," she says in a rush. "Jeb's got her in there. She was pretty out of her head when she left." Her eyes drop like the pity in them is getting too heavy. "But you didn't hear it from me. You didn't talk to me. You've never seen me before, got it?"

"Done," I agree, remembering Kaya.

She begins to say something but stops. "You did want to help me. You tried."

"Maybe I can still talk to Johnny for you—"

"No!" She shoves me, and I slip back through the crowd. Outside the Yellow Dog, I turn down a hallway dotted with narrow doors. Numbers are stenciled on each one, but many are worn away. It isn't until I come to 215 that I realize I've passed 214.

I press my ear to the door. Nothing. I open it without knocking. A bulging, hairy man sleeps on a small bunk. His head droops upside down over the side, issuing snores. I step in and almost trip on Lo's legs.

She's passed out on the floor, facedown in a puddle of watery vomit.

I pull her body against mine. "Lo," I whisper. "Lo!" I clean her mouth with my sleeve, checking her breath. It's shallow, but it's there. Her thin body flops like it's boneless when I try to shake her awake, and the bulge of a man grunts in his sleep.

I lift her up over my shoulder, my feet knocking against a pile of empty bottles and sending them into a cascade of clanking and rolling.

"Girl!" the man roars from his cot. "No noise!" He shifts on his filthy mattress, making it croak the annoyed sound of exhausted springs.

Please don't open your eyes, I pray as I take small steps to the door with Lo slung over my shoulder. *Please—*

"Get me a drink," he calls. I grab for the doorknob, knocking over several more bottles. "Girl—*WHAT'S THIS?*"

He's on me too fast and slams me into the door. Lo drops, rolling along the ground like she's just another one of those bottles. He presses my face to the back of the door with a giant hand. "Pretty one," he says. His breath is putrid. "Too pretty."

I struggle as his hands grope my hips and chest. He rips my arm up and slides back my sleeve—and jolts away.

"Re-red!" he stutters. "Get out! Get out now!" His wide, hairy face turns all over the ceiling like he's checking for a secret pair of eyes. I get my arms around a now groaning Lo and lift her by the waist. "GET OUT!" he roars again.

I trip into the hall only to hear yelling voices at the far end.

A mass of men coming our way.

I jog from their drunken calls, gripping Lo and ducking into a room labeled STORAGE. I drop her on a pile of rags and close us in, holding the door shut until I hear the crew members passing. I slide a crate against the frame.

Then I go to her.

Of all the times that I've found her passed out or beaten up, this is the worst. Her face is as colorless as the Earth City sky, and the greasy filth across her hair makes me gag. I fill a bucket of water from the utility faucet and kneel before her, scrubbing her skin. Her forehead is aflame with fever, and she moans.

"Rain," I think I hear her say.

"Right here." I tie her hair back with a rag; the dyed pink underneath has lost too much of its brightness. "You knew I'd come."

Her eyes tilt open, and I gasp. One of her irises is rimmed with blood. Like someone stabbed it. "Lo! Your eye!"

"Hit it," she tries. "Jeb hit it with bottle. Can't see out of it." She scoots a little higher on the pile of blankets, her eyelids suddenly flying wide. "Rain! It's you!"

"*Shhh.* I'm right here." I hold her shoulders to settle her back, but she fights me.

"Thank the stars! I've been trying everything to get up to you," she says. "I tried to sneak in the elevator, but Jeb . . ." Her voice falls away, making my stomach twist with guilt. Why hadn't I tried harder to see her before now? How could I be so blinded by needing to see Walker that I didn't realize that *this* was bound to happen?

Lo shakes me. "But I found them! I found them!"

"Lo, you have to calm down. You're a mess."

She pushes my hands away and takes a few rough breaths. "I was trying to get to you, and I found them in the cargo."

"Found *who*?"

Her bloody eye pierces my gaze. "The missing Touched."

"Shit, Lo. I don't have time for your paranoid stories." I prop up her shoulders. "Sleep, and we'll talk in a little while."

She springs forward faster than I would have believed possible and squeezes my face between her thin hands. "*Listen,* I found them. The Touched are here. On this ship. That asshole captain keeps them in cargo."

I pull her hands away. "Why would Johnny have the Touched in his cargo hold?"

"Because he sells them."

I laugh again, and Lo slaps me. Hard.

My mind spins as I refocus. "You hit me!"

"They're sold, Rain! Like slaves. Sweet freakin' mess, girl! They're locked in! They're starving!"

"You've had conspiracy ideas about the Touched since I met you," I say, "but I think this place has really screwed with your head." I glance around the dingy storage room. "Mine, too."

She kicks the crate away from the door. "If you won't believe me, I'll show you." Before I can stop her, she's streaked out into the hall, and I have to run to catch up.

⌁⌁⌁⌁⌁⌁

Lo throws up twice on the stairway. I try to hold her shoulders, but she keeps pushing forward. "Never seen you this bad. Let's stop for a minute."

"We don't have a minute. Jeb will be looking for me, and I'm assuming that the captain didn't just let you down here."

"I came to warn you, Lo. That Kaya girl—"

"She dead?" Lo glances at me from the side.

I nod.

"Figured. She got bumped down to yellow before you came back from meeting the captain, and then we were forced down here. I saw her once, and then, not again." Lo wipes her nose on the back of her arm. "This really takes the cake of all the freakin' messes I've been in, Rain."

"I know. Which is why we shouldn't be crawling deeper into the shadows. There are cameras everywhere." Lo has taken me to the level where Ben stabbed that man. To the very spot. "I've already seen what happens down here."

The huge cargo doors are closed, but an eerie sound slips

through them like the hum of penned animals.

"There's a window over here." She shimmies up a pile of metal crates and beckons to me. I climb, pulling onto my toes to look through a slit of a window.

"See now?" Lo spits.

I almost lose my grip.

Inside the huge cargo hold, hundreds of people stand in jumbled heaps and lie in sickening piles. Men. Women. Elderly. Even kids. Hundreds of them.

"Rain, there's another hold just this big and just as full!"

I open my mouth but my words are broken into sounds. I swallow and try again. "How is this real? I mean, these people . . . are those Earth City people?"

"Those are *Touched* people. The ones stolen by the cops." Lo crosses her arms. "Well? Say something. Who's paranoid now?"

I shake my head. Inside, I'm blank. I'm floating as though someone dropped *me* out the airlock.

"You told me that you didn't have time to care about the ones who disappear," Lo says. "You care now?"

The people are strewn all over one another, calling out and wailing.

Every one of them could be Walker.

"Mom and Jeremy." I scan the crowd as though I might find my mom or big brother's face among them.

Lo touches my cheek. "You're thinking about your family. I can't stop thinking about Mom. Who knows how long the cops have been shipping them off planet. I have a feeling, Rain . . . this is just the lip's tip of something huge."

"You said sold. You said slavery. How could they get away with that?"

"We're not on Earth City. We're in the middle of space freakin' nowhere. And there are no rules. No right and wrong." The width of her eyes shows off the bloodied one, and she taps her yellow bracelet against my red one. "There are no laws out here. Just deranged people with power. Like that Johnny."

"Who are they sold to? And for what purpose?"

"No one could tell me that," Lo says. "This is a huge secret. Most of the crew don't know anything, but Jeb talks when he's drinking. Still, he doesn't know much. But I bet I know someone who does." She jams her finger against the glass pane. "That Mec."

I follow where she's pointing.

Ben stands at the edge of the Touched crowd. He holds a tablet and scrolls down it, counting heads like he's running the whole. Damn. Thing.

CHAPTER 12

The rag slips from Lo's hair and *smacks* on the ground, and I remember the filthy, balding man that Ben stabbed. He was Touched! Helpless! Like my mom and Jeremy . . . and Ben—the guy who proclaimed to want to help the Touched—he killed him?

White-hot questions flare inside me as I watch a small girl claw at his pant leg. He pushes her back to slip through the door.

"I'll kill him," I say, already shimmying down the pile of crates.

"Whoa, whoa, Rain!" Lo charges after me, but she's not fast enough. Ben closes the cargo doors behind him, and I crash into him. He sprawls on the floor, his tablet skidding away.

I straddle his chest, pinning his shoulders with my knees, and punch him in his steel eye.

"Stop!" he yells, bringing up his forearms and grunting as my fists pummel his chest and shoulders. I connect with his mouth and blood spots my knuckles.

Ben gets his solid arms around me and rolls us so that he's on top. He squeezes my hips with his knees and pins my wrists.

"Rain?"

"Who else?" I grapple my legs up around his waist and pull so that I'm on top again, but he doesn't let go of my arms. One of his eyes swells with the onset of a bruise, and the other reflects the light of the ceiling strips. I twist out of his grip and slide off him.

He touches the blood at the edge of his mouth. "What in the hell was—"

"What is this? What is all this?!" I point to the cargo door. "There are *people* in there!"

He gets to his feet and offers his hand. "Get up fast. We have to move. The alarms will be back on in minutes."

"You can't explain this away!" I yell. "Are you that powerful and amazing, oh Mec?"

"Course not. But I have a few answers."

"You better have a lot of them." I ignore his offer of a hand and get to my feet. He's annoyingly calm after the way I just mauled him, and I rub my twisted wrists and call out for Lo.

She peers from around the corner.

Ben looks from her to me. "Hell, Rain. You really know how to complicate things."

———

Ben leads us to the docking bay where I first entered *Imreas*. We pass the hover cab in its airtight chamber along with several other heavy doors with small portholes. A rolling clank sounds from one, and I pause to look through the glass as the noise builds to a sharp *snap*. Doors tear open at the back, creating a roar of rushing air and revealing the Void beyond the ship—an airlock.

Ben has paused to watch, too. "Automatic air dump. It releases the pressure between the outer and inner hulls."

"Great." I grip myself, shaking away the idea of a person flying out of that room. At the far end of the catwalk a small space vessel hangs from the high ceiling by a chain net like a souvenir. The word MELEE is stenciled on its side.

"In here." He presses a door release and climbs into the side of the ship. I lead Lo through, and he shuts it behind us. "You're so damn lucky, Rain. The only reason you didn't set off a host of alarms is because I was down there. You realize how lucky that makes you?"

I ignore him. "What did I just see in that room?"

"Give me a second." He sits in a captain's chair before a control screen and his fingers fly across it.

"I want to know now!"

He pauses; his gaze is fierce despite the fact that one of his eyes is swollen shut. "Let me check the security logs before Johnny sees them and offs us all, will you?"

"He's asleep," I say. "I just left him." I swallow the sudden flash of Johnny leaning over me in his slick bed, his body working against mine. . . .

Ben pulls up an image of me in the elevator a few moments ago. His fingers fly over the controls until I disappear from the video.

"What are you doing?"

"I'm looping it. Deleting you from the record."

I step back and let Ben work. The vessel we're in is as small as a hover cab only more equipped. It reminds me of the small, rotting ship on the pier without the rust and age. Someone moans behind me, and I swing around.

A bald man lies on a bunk, his chest bandaged.

"Ben," I hear myself whisper. This is not just any man. It's the man I saw murdered—stabbed.

Ben finishes his work at the control screen and crosses to the bunk.

"Ben," I say again like it's the only word I know. "This is him."

"I know who it is, Rain." He sits beside the man and inserts a medical tube into the bend of his own elbow. Blood circles through it, surging straight into the man's arm.

"What's going on?" Lo asks from where she cowers by the door.

"I saw him kill this man. I saw him," I say.

"Yeah, well, you didn't see me save him afterward, did you?" Ben gives the man a shot of something that makes his moans stop.

"You're not a murderer." I hold back from adding, "I knew it," but I slip to the floor by Ben's feet. "Tell me what is going on here."

He checks the man's pulse while he speaks. "Johnny's business has nothing to do with passengers. Or girls. That's a front. He sells the Earth City Touched to a slaver known as Leland. The K-Force have been after both of them for years, but they do their trading in the Static Pass, and no one has been able to take them down so far."

"The who?" Lo asks at the same time that I say, "What's the Static Pass?"

He pauses. "The more you two know, the worse this is. You get that, don't you?"

I exchange looks with Lo. "We need to know," I say.

"Those are our people in that hold," she adds, tightening her arms around her chest.

"The Static Pass is a section of the Void near Edge space. Electromagnetic fields shut down there and ships kind of glide through—without power or any technology. Johnny does his trading in secret there without interference from the K-Force."

"The K-Force?"

"Mec space police. Or vigilantes, really. They have ties to the military on the Edge, but mostly theirs is a moral mission: rid the universe of filth."

"They sound delusional."

"They're the only ones doing something about the lawlessness of the Void."

"What does Johnny want the Touched for?" I ask.

"Mining on the asteroid formation beyond the Void. A place called the Ridges. It's dangerous work. Most of them die within a year or two. Some less."

"So they *are* slaves." My voice shrinks around the words. Mom and Jeremy . . . and even Walker, if they got their hands on him. For long moments, the vessel called *Melee* is silent apart from the ragged breath of the unconscious man. Lo holds herself, rocking back and forth until I rest her head on my lap. In no time, she falls into a dead sort of sleep.

Ben brings out his dose rod, giving the man something that makes his breath slow and quiet.

"He's Touched, isn't he?" Shivers break out across my arms as I remember the man's moan of *Help us.*

"He is, but he has these sane moments. He kept figuring out how to escape . . . that's what you saw when I . . . you know."

"But why bother curing him if Johnny's just going to sell him into slavery and a horrible death?"

Ben disconnects the tube from his arm and paces around the room. "Because he didn't deserve to die that way. Or maybe I just couldn't stomach being a murderer. I'm a human being, Rain. Give me a little credit." He takes the med disc from his pocket and hunkers down to my level, brushing Lo's hair from her face before running the blue light over the bruised lid of her blood-stained eye. She murmurs my name in her sleep but doesn't wake.

"How could I have let this happen to her?" I say in a hushed voice that doesn't reach Ben. He collapses in the captain's chair with a slight groan, the eye I punched turning purple. I have to do something to turn our fates around. Something good for once.

I slide Lo's head from my lap and cross the minor distance to him. "Give me that disc thingy. Let me fix your eye." I hold out my hand.

"Not the eye. But you can do my mouth." He wiggles his jaw and hands me the med disc. "Feeling guilty for attacking me?"

"Not especially." I raise his chin, looking down into his face. "You should have told me the truth upfront. Walker and I would never have gotten on this ship."

"Yes, you would. You couldn't hear me back there. You were blinded by your dreams about the Void and the need to help your brother." He's right. What could he have said to stop me? I hold the device like I've seen him do and pass it over his mouth. The blue light makes the bruise fade to yellow before it blends into the creamy color of his skin.

"You had some moves back there. When I jumped you." I

wipe a small crust of blood at the edge of his lip with my knuckle. "Like someone taught you how to fight."

"Someone did," he admits. "I've had training. You've got moves yourself." I can't get over how strong his stare is even with one eye—like it's another muscle he's honed.

"My training was living on the street." I press the disc into his hand. "And I have brothers."

"Brothers? You have another brother?"

"Had. Jeremy was—well, he probably ended up in a place just like that cargo hold. Maybe the same one." I look away. "I've got to go back to Johnny before he wakes and all hell breaks loose. Can Lo stay here?" I look around the small but cozy interior of the ship. It's different from *Imreas*. The metal walls are without rough bolt lines, and everything is neat, sparse, and, well, military.

He nods. "*Melee* is my ship—or at least it was before Johnny commandeered it. But he has no security tags or monitors here, and it isn't under the lock of his thumbprint. It's one of the only safe places on *Imreas*." He stands, and I'm too close to him.

"Give me a few minutes with Lo. I don't know when I'll see her again."

Ben leaves the vessel, and I wake her gently. "You have to listen," I say as she rubs her face. "Johnny is using you to get to me. To make me do what he wants."

She sits up tall. "He stole your virginity."

"He didn't rape me. I gave it to him. Like I agreed." I dig my fingernails into my arms, suddenly panicked. I've never under-stood that phrasing of "stolen virginity." How could he be the thief of what I was handing out? "It was easy, Lo. Like you said."

"Who do you think you're lying to? And if you've interpreted what I do as easy, then you've never been listening to me. Not one bit."

I look away, touching my stomach. "Lo, do you ever feel like . . . like it's not so bad?"

"You mean, do I ever like it?" Her tone is all business, and it makes it hard for me to nod. "Rain, there are two types of working girls. There's the ones who do it. And then there are the ones who *feel it.* He'll want you so much more if you put yourself into it, but that means you're giving away more than your skin. A lot more. And it's not worth it. Do you follow?"

"But I need to keep his interest, Lo. Otherwise I'll have to start sleeping with anyone who pays. I'd rather stay with him. I need to stay with him."

"Rain, in this business, *need* is just about the worst word there is. All you really *need* is to stay alive. To make it to the Edge with Walker. Everything else is up for grabs."

"He brought you on this ship"—I pause—"to use against me. And he could use Walker as well." The words fill me with the urge to break something.

"It's worse than all that." Her face is drawn so that I can trace the lines of her skull over her skin. Her sunken eye sockets. Her pointed chin. Tears veil her stare, but she blinks them back. "I shoulda told you sooner." She takes my hands in hers. They're shaking.

Just like Walker's.

"Lo," I almost yell, "you're—you're going—"

"Touched," she finishes. "I've had the shakes since before we left Earth City. I'm going away, Rain. My mind is hightailing it for better space. But you make sure they don't throw me in that hold," she says. "You make damn sure they don't make me a slave. You put me out of my misery when the time comes. Then he won't have me to use against you."

Her shaking hands fumble with her shirt, and she pulls out the picture of her mother. "I want you to take my mom. Keep her safe. If something happens to that, there's no proof she ever existed." Tears drop from her eyes. "She has to keep *existing*, Rain. Promise me."

I can't answer.

"Promise!"

"I promise." I take the picture but then press it back into her palm. "This isn't the last time I'm going to see you. You hold on to your mom, and I'll take her if the time comes." Lo wraps her twitching hands over the old photo like she's praying.

"Can't you fight it?"

She pulls me into a hug, and her back is all bones and paper-thin skin. "You already know the answer to that."

———✀———

I leave *Melee*, rethinking the two nightmarish reveals of the evening: Lo is going Touched, and *Imreas* is a slave ship.

"I'll walk you up so you don't get lost. It's almost morning," Ben says. "If Johnny caught you, well, we'd all be . . ." He draws a finger over his throat.

I barely hear him. I blindly touch the door release, closing Lo into the small ship.

"Hell, Rain. You look like you've seen a Void demon," he teases. I start down the catwalk, making him jog to catch up.

"Which don't exist, by the way. It was a lame joke."

I swallow. "Lo is going Touched. Got any jokes about that?"

"*What?*" He tries to grab my arm, but I walk even faster. I don't face Ben again until we're rising in the elevator. He clicks the halt button, and we slow to a pause. "How do you know?" he asks.

"Because I've watched it happen time and again," I say. His swollen eye stirs at my uneasiness. "She's stage two already."

"Out of how many stages?"

"Three," I say. "First they get headaches, and then shakes. The final stage is a sort of fog that they drift in and out of, until one day the fog becomes permanent."

"Hell," he says. "Are you afraid of it happening to you?"

"Why would you say that? Who asks a question like that?!" I smack his chest. "That's like finding a person chained to a cliff and asking them if they're afraid of heights!"

"I'm sorry." He rubs where I hit him. "I can't really imagine it. I mean, to watch that happen to everyone you love . . . your brother even."

I hold back the sudden image of my family, but now only Walker remains. "Yeah, well, we'll be at the Edge soon, and your people will have a treatment for him. And for Lo, too."

He presses the button, and the elevator begins to rise again. "If anyone can help, the Mecs can. Maybe. You should understand that it's a closed society. When scientists founded the colony, they were overly conscious of starting a new race. They were precise and clinical. For all its beauty and advancements, the Edge can be a very unfeeling place."

"Lo's going to get worse fast, and if Johnny finds her that way, he'll sell her with the others. She wants me to kill her before that happens, so I'll probably have to put her into a coma like Walker. You can do that with all your"—I say, motioning to his pockets—"gadgets, right?"

"Hell, Rain. Talk about rolling with the punches." He shakes his head. "You just found out that your best friend is losing her mind, and you've already moved on to saving her through elaborate and improbable schemes?"

"Not everyone likes to wallow and suffer." I watch him touch the edges of his swollen eyelid. "Why don't you use that disc thingy to heal your eye?"

"Can't," he says. "I've got hardware in there. You hit me in the one spot I'm vulnerable."

"Hardware?"

The elevator doors slide open. "Don't worry about it," he says flatly.

I step out before Johnny's quarters. "You shouldn't tell people where you're vulnerable, Ben."

He frowns. "Not everyone pretends to be invincible, Rain."

———~~~~~———

Lo's going to leave me now with or without Johnny. She's going to leave me to sort through the nightmare of this ship alone. I slide into the shadows of Johnny's room just to escape thinking about her. The room feels dimmer than I left it. I can only make out lumps and creases on the satiny bed. Johnny must be among them.

But I step through the darkness and into a black voice.

"Hello, Rain."

CHAPTER
13

"Lights," Johnny commands, and the room floods.

I squint against the sudden brightness.

"How was your walk?" he asks. "That's what you're going to say, yes? You were just out taking a *walk*?"

My blood has frozen in my veins. "I don't think I should say anything."

"Smart, but not smart enough." Johnny sits in the plush chair on the far side of the room. He wears his pants, but no shirt. "Come here."

I step to his knees, securing a fist behind my back. If he's going to beat me, I'm swinging back. But he just scoops me onto his lap, his arm chaining my waist.

He picks up a tablet from the side table, pressing his thumb into the security clearance that blinks a small red box. "Let's just see where you really were, shall we? Then I don't have to hear your lies."

My heart thunders into spiky questions. What if Ben didn't erase it all? What if Johnny sees me with Lo? Or Ben?

AIRLOCK.

He runs his fingers through the information on the screen,

his frown growing tighter, until he jerks, making me tumble to the floor. "So you were nowhere? You were a ghost through the night hours?"

My fear turns from his face to his leg. He's going to kick me. I've never been more certain of anything in my life. I curl my knees against my chest and shake my head.

"Still not going to spout lies?" He drops the tablet to the chair. Now he has both hands free. Now he could kick me and hit me—I eye his belt with new fear—his hips—and even lower.

I struggle to swallow. My terror won't do anything now, and it certainly won't distract Johnny from the events of my night. But I have to keep his attention on me and away from Lo or Ben or the fact that I now know about his true business.

"You wanted fiery." I glare into his glare. "A feisty redhead."

He laughs, and the sound spears my little reserve. He grabs me by the back of the shirt and hauls me to my feet. "Get out of my sight until I know what to do with you."

He throws me into the hallway, and I stumble into the Family Room just as the green girls are waking. They stare as I slip through the common area and back to my mat. I shut my eyes, but I don't expect to sleep.

This isn't over. This is the edge of Johnny's razor.

―――――∽∿∿∿∽――――――

I wake to a fat man leaning over me. He checks my hair as though he'd like to buy it.

"What do you think you're doing?" I pull from his reach, my back to the window.

"Inspecting an unusual specimen. He was right. I've never seen anything like it." He groans as he leans on a silver cane. His hair is missing in patches and streams of sweat work down each temple. "I'll have you."

"I'm Johnny's," I blurt. "I'm red tagged." I thrust out my arm and pull back my sleeve.

But my bracelet has turned green.

He chuckles. "Not anymore, it seems." He holds out his cane like an offer to help me up, but I get to my feet on my own.

"Johnny sent you to come get me? Did he tell you to punish me?"

He wipes his brow with a yellow handkerchief and shoves it in his pocket. "Am I punishment, little girl?"

My mouth opens and closes without an answer. I'm to please this man. I'm a green tag now . . . right? A *real* prostitute. Of all the horrific things that I imagined Johnny might do, it comes to this one: he means to whore me into submission. The walls of my mind melt, but I try to hide my panic. This is better than a threat to Lo and Walker . . . it only feels worse.

"Okay."

"Truly?" he smiles and a bead of sweat drops the length of his nose. "What a changeable creature you are."

I follow the man out of the Family Room, passing Ben at the door. His gaze tugs at strings in my chest, but I put the sudden emotion out of my mind. I touch my green bracelet; I have a job to do.

And I do it.

I turn my mind off just like Johnny taught me, my body slipping against the bare minimum. Afterward, the huge man is a pile of snoring pink flesh, and my brain clicks back on until I'm kneeling on the carpet, unsure of how I got there. I try to stand, but I can't, and my breath cuts at my throat. Half crawling, I make it to a small door—a closet—and hide inside. The narrow space wraps me up with darkness, and I weep.

⁓⁓⁓⁓⁓⁓

The fat man's name is Proffers, and I stay in his sauna of a room full of golden, ornamental things for days. He never asks my name but keeps me held up against his mound of a body until I fall away from myself, into an empty headspace. I am anonymous. Invisible.

This must be what it's like to be Touched.

Almost a week after Proffers came for me, I'm lying on a gold-cushioned window seat, watching the white strings of the worm-hole dance outside when Johnny leans over me.

He snaps his fingers in my face to stop me from saying something, and I scoot away from him, listening to Proffers hum a loony song in the shower.

"Follow," he commands, doing an about-face and leaving the room. I pull on my shoes while I tread after him. We weave through passengers in the hall who stare from Johnny to me. "Disgusting, wasn't he?" he says in the elevator. I had forgotten the way Johnny's eyes and hair can reflect the exact same shade of dark.

I level my shoulders. "I've had worse."

Johnny grinds his teeth. "That's a lovely thinly veiled insult, Rain."

"I'm cleverer than you give me credit for."

His thin smile matches his gaze. "You are. You really, truly are." The doors open, and we exit onto the floor for his quarters. "It took me this long to discover what you were up to all those nights ago. What a wild chase you've sent me on." My stomach drops in sudden fear for Lo. "For a few days there, I doubted that I would be able to uncover your secrets. But then, breakthrough." He holds his door open.

A man stands in the middle of Johnny's room. His flight suit is ripped open at the top revealing a patch of curly, grotesque chest hair. I remember his fingers smashing my face against the back of the door and hear his gravel shouting of *GET OUT!*

He twists his hands like a small boy before a disappointed father until his eyes fall on me. "That's the red, Captain. The very red. Stole my girl right out from my room, and I'd paid her up for the week and all."

"This is Jeb, Rain. But you've already met." Johnny's fingers slide along my lower back, gripping the material at my waist.

"Didn't touch her but for a second, Captain," Jeb adds. "Not the second I saw she was your girl."

"Would you like her now?" Johnny asks.

Jeb's head jerks around from Johnny to me and back again. "If you're done, of course, then I could—"

"How about it, Rain?" Johnny dares.

So he found Jeb, a man more vile than Proffers, to be my next punishment?

Well, it doesn't matter because I won't let Johnny have the best of me. I braid my hair back to shift out from under both of their looks. "Okay, Johnny. Whatever you want." I step toward

Jeb, but Johnny's grip on my waist yanks me back into his chest.

"Changed my mind. Go," he commands. Jeb stands there for an ugly moment, his eyes like loose marbles while he looks from me to Johnny. "I said, go!"

Jeb hustles out, and Johnny swings me around, gripping my shoulders like he's about to break me. His perfect skin is blotched with anger, but instead of crushing me, he lifts me by one arm and marches me to the command deck. The handful of crew members on duty exchange glances before disappearing altogether.

Johnny shoves me away and collapses into his captain's chair. I take a few steps toward the large window, looking out on the rush of a cluster of passing stars. Johnny is smiling again by the time I turn, showing off his teeth. "I'm so *very* frustrated, Rain. I didn't want this, you know."

"You did," I say, gripping my elbows. "You asked for complication. For ruse. You dared me into this."

His smile twists into a frown for the briefest flash. "Maybe I did. But you have no one to blame but yourself." He presses a few buttons on the control panel beside him. "Take a look." He waves his hand at the window, and I turn to find it altered into a view screen. And the view is a dingy cargo room with one dangling bulb.

Walker's pod beneath it.

A choked sound leaks out of me before I can stop it.

"Apologies," Johnny says. "Wrong screen." His fingers tap the panel, and the view switches to a bare metal room with a pair of massive sliding doors.

An airlock.

And in the middle of it, Lo's tiny frame. On her knees and sobbing.

"Johnny, don't take this out on—"

"She's a distraction, Rain. That's what your little midnight stunt proved to me. If you can't have her on this ship without sneaking out then we can't have her on this ship. Haven't I already told you the lesson of having nothing to lose?"

My mouth opens, but nothing comes. He really means to launch her out the airlock.

"This is just a trick," I blurt. "You brought her onboard to hold over me. You were never interested in trading her or—"

"You're right. She was here to help you learn to separate from everything else."

Was?

"Before my father marooned me on Entra, he gave me my own ship to captain for three weeks. Later on, he admitted that he wanted me to have it all before I had nothing." Johnny's brow creases into a knot. "A genius maneuver. If I hadn't known that I wanted to be captain, I wouldn't have tried to regain it. Build from the bottom. Nothing to lose. Everything to gain."

"I get it, Johnny. Your dad was . . . right. I'll forget I even know her. I promise!" I look to where Lo is ripping at her hair.

"I tried the same tactics with my father. 'Let me stay onboard. I'll work up from the lowest crew position. . . . '" His voice drops, and he stands. "Eleven minutes to the next automatic dump. You'll have enough time to say good-bye. Probably. As long as you stop wasting it blathering on, trying to make me change my mind."

I sprint so fast that my vision fragments—images blurred by the wetness in my eyes. The silver-walled halls. Black flight suits. The docking bay and the smashing clatter of my footsteps on the grated walkway.

Lo is in the last airlock.

I break against the porthole, pounding on the thick glass pane. "LO! LO!"

She stops tearing at her hair. Her filthy cheeks are whipped with tear tracks, and she comes to the window slowly.

"Rain." She presses her hand to the glass. A few ripped-free strands of her pink hair hang from her fingernails. I throw myself against the wheel lock on the door without budging it a fraction.

"Rain." Her voice is muffled to a whisper, and I press my forehead against the porthole to hear it.

But the rolling clank sounds first.

She looks back at the doors. "Don't trust the Mec. He's not telling you the truth."

"Lo! Don't . . ." But I have nothing but her name. "Lo."

Clank. Clank. Clankclankclank . . .

"Those are our people, Rain." She takes out her mother's picture from her shirt and smashes the scrap against the window. But there's no hope. Lo's mother is going with her now no matter what. They'll lose their existence as one.

The *snap* sounds, fracturing the seal on the door.

"Sweet freakin' mess," she mouths as the doors break apart.

And Lo flies backward . . .

. . . falling head over heels into the Void.

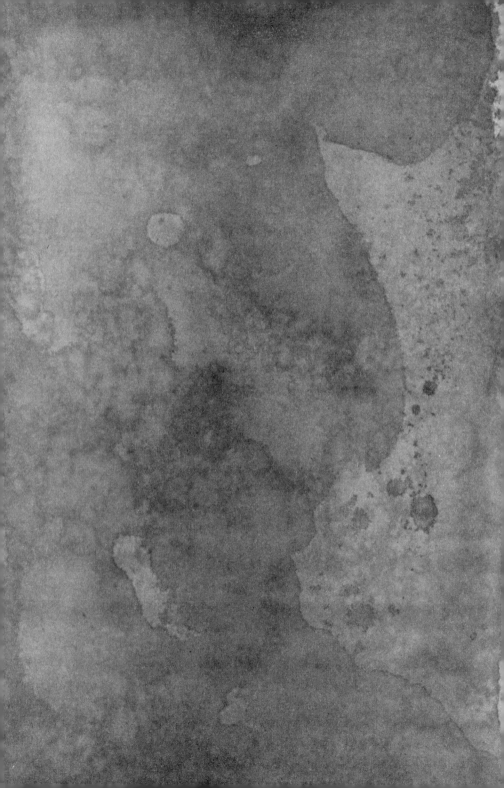

PART II

BLUE

CHAPTER
14

My body swings to a lewd rhythm. If I rock forward, I can see silver-white stars through the tiny passenger room window. If I rock back, I face a dingy ceiling and a spidery water stain.

And he likes it best when I rock back.

So I do. Over and over in ugly syncopation until his grunts climax with a wrenching squeeze of my hips.

"Rain," he moans.

"Don't use my name." I slip out of my voided state and slide off him. My feet touch the ground in the exact spot where I shed my clothes to begin with, and I'm redressed in a move so refined that Lo would be proud. Now I know what she meant about doing it without feeling it. Sex can be nothing.

It can be *it*.

I button my shirt to my collar and hold on to the edge of the bunk. Remembering Lo no longer makes me sob, but I get dizzy . . . spun up like some fist is twisting all my insides, and though I'm the best at deluding myself, there are still moments when I cannot turn my brain off. When I'm too aware of all that I've lost.

"I said, *here*." Tobern thrusts a fistful of coins. I drop them in my pocket while he fingers the ends of my ratty hair. "You're looking like shit."

I tug my matted curls and force them into a rubber band. "Same night next week?"

"Just take a shower before then." He sags back on his pillow and folds his hands behind his head. He stretches and groans, and though the room is small and he's not a big man, he seems like an acre of flesh.

I'm about to duck out the door, but I pause. On a small shelf, a bit of white glass is shaped like a heart.

"Go ahead," Tobern says. "I've been seeing you eye that every time you're in here."

I pick up the beautiful, light trinket. "What is it?"

"It's a bit of that Mec glass that their whole city is built out of."

"This is from the Edge? You've been there?" I love the touch of the glass so much that I sit back on the lip of his mattress just to hold it for a few more minutes.

"This stuff is amazing. You tell it what to do. What to be." He takes the glass from me. "Spoon," he commands. The glass slides out of its shape and into the shape of a spoon.

"Wow." I take it back from him. "What's the Edge like?"

"Hard to say. I've only seen the spacedocks. They don't much like Earth Cityites just walking around."

I try to avoid looking my clients in the eye, but I look at Tobern now. He's probably thirty, and he has a decent chin. That's the best that I can think of him. "You're from Earth City? So am I." I look back to the glass. "Coin," I say, and the glass slips into the new shape. "Is the Void what you thought it'd be?"

"This is my third run from one side to the other," he says. "And every time, I'm blown away by how crazy things can get out here, but you get used to the crazy. Then the crazy is normal. Boring, even."

I hand the bit of glass back to him, wanting desperately to keep it.

A piece of the Edge. What I wouldn't give to show it to Walker.

"Stay the night if you need. I've got room on the floor," he says kindly.

"Thanks, but no. See you next week." I tuck out the door and into the muted light of the late evening. No one is in the passenger halls at this hour, not even the other blue girls, and that's the way I like it. They work so hard to have clients who keep them on for weeks or months, but I'd rather drift from bed to bed.

I have to keep moving to escape the reality that my body is no longer mine.

I tug my sleeve over the sapphire light coming from my wrist. The color no longer reminds me of the spacedocks above the old pier—of starships or Walker or my dreams of the Void. Instead, it speaks Lo's name and the blue engines that backlit her freefall until her body was lost to the blackness beyond.

The color also echoes the screams that ripped me in pieces while I collapsed beneath that porthole, my wrist blinking from green to blue.

I knew then that I had to move or it would become yellow. I had to move or I would soon be watching Walker's pod fall into the stretch between the stars. Johnny's game was just getting

started, and I was already behind. So I came straight from the airlock to the passenger levels and became a real working girl.

And it only took me these few weeks to get the rhythm.

I head across the deserted common room and deposit all but
two of my coins in an ornate box. The other girls wait for Johnny
to hand in their money, but I get slivers of joy in denying him the
chance to see me in my new situation. I'll keep it up until we reach
the Edge, if I can.

My body begins to fold inwardly as I think about needing to
keep this up, but then I remember the cameras. Cameras everywhere. And I push myself onward.

Johnny doesn't get to see me fall apart. I wait until no one is in
the backroom at the Rainbow Bar for that. I slip in and shake so
hard that my bones rattle. There's no way he can see me then . . .
I think.

My shoes slosh with the sound of coins, and I curl my toes
over them. I've been amassing a secret hoard from my nightly col-
lections, and I'll use it to bribe a crew member to get my brother
off this ship. Johnny may have a good lock on me because of this
damn bracelet, but Walker could still be freed.

Everything may have changed since I trudged through the
streets of Earth City, but I still need a faithful plan. Hope remains
my sharpest tool.

I head to the Rainbow Bar where Lionel, the bartender, sleeps
with his head dropped on the countertop like he went down in the
middle of serving: a rag in one hand, a glass in the other. I pull his
shoulders up until he looks around with sagging lids.

"Come on, scrawny lion. To bed."

"Righty, Dara," he mutters. I take him to the storage room and drop him on his bunk, tucking the holey blanket up to his neck. Lionel and I have a decent relationship. He calls me his barmaid, and I help out, using the place to find clients and then coming back here to sleep.

He's never tried to sleep with me, and I love him for it. Although he does call me Dara when he's topped-off drunk. I've gathered enough to know that she was his daughter from a now distant life before the Void, and I let him think so. In fact, being his Dara stand-in is one of the only warm things left in my very cold life.

I clear away the rest of the glasses, shut the door, and turn off the colored strings of lights. Now the only glow comes from the far window, and I drag the most comfortable couch underneath it and tuck myself in for the night, staring at the ghostly strings of the Void. I haven't seen the edges of the wormhole in a while, and they remind me of Ben.

His eyes have that kind of sheen—at least that's the way I remember them. I haven't seen him since that day I was sent off with Proffers. Johnny might've found out about our connection and killed him along with Lo. Or he's avoiding me.

I now know what Ben meant when he spoke of the Void's inherent loneliness. I feel it. The Void is a hollow place that breeds hollow existences. To be fair to the other working girls, the other blues, they've tried to be friendly. But I refuse to learn a name or take a favor. If Lo's and Kaya's deaths taught me nothing else, they proved that I cannot afford friends on this ship. Or they can't afford me.

I settle into the beaten cushions, ignoring the stench of spilt liquor and an aching in my joints, but I can't avoid my yearning for Walker. I press my hands between the folds in my knees and watch the dancing weave of the Void until I hear something.

The bump of a chair against a table.

I catch my breath just as a shadowy man leans over me. His hand closes over my mouth, and I jerk out of my seat, biting and kicking until my attacker stumbles. I crawl to an empty bottle and swing it against his head.

He goes limp.

I hold the spot in my chest where my heart is trying to riot free and poke at the outline on the floor. I step over the toppled chairs, gripping the bottle high and ready to conk the bastard again. But there's something familiar in his sturdy legs and toned body.

Not to mention the boots and cargo pants.

"Ben?" I drop my weapon and slide the table away. I shake his shoulders, but he's out cold. I grab a glass of water from behind the bar and dump it on his face.

He jolts awake, fists up. "For hell's sake, Rain." He spits water and lowers his hands. "You didn't have to attack me." He touches the knot now swelling above his temple. "I covered your mouth so you wouldn't cause a riot."

I fetch a rag full of ice for his head from behind the bar and hand him the bundle. "At least I didn't pop your eye again."

His eye has healed over our weeks apart, and his hair sticks forward as though it was actually combed before our tussle. I can't help taking in each piece of him by the window light, and he seems to be doing just the same with me.

"You look pretty rough, Rain." He presses the ice to his head.

"What'd you expect?" I finger-comb my hair. "I've been on my own for weeks."

"I couldn't come earlier. Johnny's been watching your every movement through the cameras. He's been waiting . . . wanting to see you break down."

So he couldn't see me in my hiding place. "I'm surviving." I get up and pace the floor. "What do you want anyway?"

He rights the toppled table. "I thought we could go see your brother. I've looped the security feed for the next few hours, and Johnny's down a couple bottles."

I'm at the door before his voice has stopped. "Well? Let's go." I feel a smile that, for the first time in weeks, is genuine, and it flips onto Ben's face like a mirrored image.

———————

I press myself to the frozen pod. The small window is covered in frost, and I have to chip away at it with my thumbnail before I can get a glimpse of my little brother.

Walker is so much smaller than I remember.

"He's only twelve. And I know you haven't met him—not the real him, but he's a damn firecracker. The best kind of pushy loud-mouth."

"Must run in the family," Ben says from his seat on a dusty crate. He heals the lump on his head with his med disc and then probes the spot with his fingers.

"He's smart, but he gets distracted." I look for the orange scruff, but the pod's growing frost has masked my brother's cheeks. And there's nothing I can do about it. Walker's never seemed so distant—not even through the longest of his fogs. It's like he's already left me.

I tug the tarp back over the pod.

"That's it?" Ben asks. "I thought you'd want to stay for hours."

I smooth the rough fabric. "Johnny showed me this room before the airlock . . . before Lo. He wanted me to know that she wasn't the only person that he could dispose of."

"Hell. I'm really sorry about Lo. I tried to help her, Rain, but he"—Ben pauses before adding—"Remember that Johnny thinks this is all for his entertainment. His game. But I'm smarter than him. So are you, I think, which is kind of awesome."

I push past Ben's somewhat backward compliment and yank the door open. "But he worked it out last time. I'm not taking the risk again."

"That's because some crew member saw you. If you told me that, I could have taken care of him." The way he says *taken care* makes me think of the Touched man Ben stabbed. Blood like floodwater spreading across the floor.

"Don't do me any favors, Ben." I start out the door, and he follows. I was an idiot for leaving my level and crossing *Imreas* with him. "It's like you said all those weeks ago, I'm not your friend or your ally. We're nothing to each other."

"Whoa, whoa." He grabs my elbow. "I thought we were friends. Or at least friendly about each other's secrets. Isn't that what you wanted?"

"Didn't you get the last girl you were friendly with thrown out the airlock? What was her name again? Bron?"

He lets go of me. "Don't be cruel."

I press the elevator call button. "Right before Lo died, she said 'Don't trust the Mec. He's not telling the truth.'" I brace myself on the wall. "If we're friends, explain that."

"Lo heard a transmission while she was in *Melee*. Do you want to know what it was?" The doors open, and I step inside. Yes, I do want to know. But should I? Damn my curiosity. I slide to the floor. Ben steps in before the doors shut and presses the halt button.

He hunkers before me. "Are you all right?"

"Of course not." I press my head into my hands, trying to hold myself together while I shake like a Touched person. Ben tries to put an arm around my shoulders—and I feel like breaking it. "Don't!"

"You're having a panic attack. I can help you." He pulls a silver gadget out of his pocket, and I knock it away.

"Don't. Touch. Me."

Ben sits back against the doors. I hold myself even tighter and work to get the air out of my lungs. One breath. Then another. One more. I try not to look at him, but he's too enticing. He even smiles kindly, which is so weird that I almost laugh.

I scrub my face, surprised that it feels good to have him on the other side of my panic. "What am I doing?" I shake my head. "I promised myself that I'd play it safe from here on out, but I think that's against my nature."

His smile grows. "Me, too. That's why I'm K-Force."

"You're what?"

"I'm a spy."

blink at him. "K-Force? The Mec vigilantes?" I laugh. "You're dreaming. You're just a teenager. When did you have time to join the space cops?"

He shifts into a cross-legged position. "I was fourteen when I volunteered. Bron and I presented ourselves to Johnny as defectors in *Melee*. The K-Force knew that he wouldn't turn down the chance to have two young Mecs for servants, but they didn't know about what he would make us do." Ben sighs. "We were supposed to subvert that first run so that the K-Force could intercept *Imreas* and rescue the Touched in his cargo. We failed.

"We weren't able to get in contact to regroup as easily as I hoped," he continues. "And I didn't even figure it out until the last run." He holds up his wrist. "I'm routing the signal through this." I remember the squealing sound that came from Ben's com back on Earth City when we were above the smog in the hover cab.

I get to my feet, and Ben follows, still waiting for me to say something. "So you're a spy, and everything you do here . . . organizing the girl trade and killing for Johnny . . . that's all just a front so you can bring him down? Which you can't really do?"

He leans in so close that I flatten against the wall. "If you haven't noticed, Johnny's pretty good at punishing people who don't follow the very letter of his commands. Hell, Rain! He *murdered* my girlfriend! Shot her out the airlock like a hunk of trash metal!"

A speck of his spit hits my chin, but I don't wipe it away. I'm hearing the clanks. I'm seeing Lo fly backward into the tomb of black space.

Ben blinks and his eyes have lost their fight. "You know how that feels." He wipes my jaw with the back of his hand. "He was jealous. . . . I tried to deny my feelings for her, but he killed her anyway. Said I needed to learn a lesson in loyalty."

"Nothing to lose," I say.

"Everything to gain," he finishes. "Except it's everything to lose with him, isn't it?" He clears his throat. "I'm close now, but . . . I need your help, Rain."

I barely hear him. I hit the button for the first passenger level over and over. The elevator begins to rise too slowly.

"What are you doing?" he asks.

"Getting away from you as fast as I can." My pulse tumbles. "This plan is fatal. Why would you even share it with me? Are you trying to get me killed or my brother?"

"I need your help." He touches my arm, and I cock my fist back like I'm going to nail him.

"You need to stay away from me, that's what you need."

He steps back. "What about the hundreds of Touched in the hold? You don't want to help them? That's why I'm here, Rain! We—you and me—are going to stop Johnny's slave trading. I have a solid plan."

I hit the floor button again and again, urging it to rise faster. "I'm busy enough trying to save one of them. I don't have time to care about the rest."

Ben overrides the elevator with his com. We halt jerkily and begin to drop.

I fling around. "What'd you do? Let me go back!"

"Not until you see something," he says.

~~~~~~~~~~~~

Ben opens the lock on the cargo hold and then rolls the doors open just enough for us to slide in. The stench knocks into me like a toppling skyscraper. I'm beneath it. I can't breathe. It's in my eyes and mouth and I swear I can *hear* it—human waste and filth trickling everywhere.

I grip Ben's shoulder and look down at the grated floor. Feet below, the sloshing surface of an open sewer glistens with vile fumes.

Ben's arm circles my waist, holding me up. I cover my mouth and nose, and he tugs me further into the mass of Touched people. They linger this way and that, bumping into each other. Mouths ajar and gazes unfocused.

"I get the point," I say, and the filth feels like it's crawled across my tongue.

"I want to show you something." He leads me through the mess of bodies to where two young, blonde girls hold each other. "I found them a few weeks ago," he says. "They must have known each other before they lost it. Look how they won't leave each other."

Their hair is so much the same color that they might very well be sisters, and their eyes are slack, yet they hug with a fervent need to be close. Just like Walker always clung to me, even in his deepest fog.

"I don't understand this disease." Ben shakes his head. "But I think that if they can still recognize loved ones, they can't be altogether lost. I mean, these aren't my people, but—"

"They're my people."

Ben slips a hunk of bread from one of his pockets and holds it out to the girls. They reach for it together, each girl holding one end while they pass it back and forth to bite. "They have hunger. If I didn't know anything else about them, I'd still know that they don't deserve to be worked to death in the asteroid mines."

The girls have green eyes like Walker's, and I can't look anymore. Ben leads me back the way we came, back through snagging fingers and moans and filth. He locks the door behind us, and I throw up. I begin to fall forward, and he catches my hips, holding me up against him.

"I did the same the first time I went in there. If you—"

Footsteps clamor around the corner, and Ben tugs me into the stairwell by the waist. I try to say something and he whispers, "*Shhh.* Come with me." He draws my arm over his shoulder and leads me down the steps. His closeness is friendly. The closest I've had to Lo or Walker in so long that I keep tightly to him and let him take me anywhere.

We pass the clanking whirl of the airlocks, and into *Melee*.

"So this really is your ship," I say, sitting on the bunk where the Touched man recuperated the last time I was here. "Where is that guy?"

"I put him with the others, but Johnny shouldn't remember him, so he's relatively safe."

"Relatively."

"Yeah." He sits in the captain's chair, leaning his head back. "This ship is . . . I don't even know."

"From everything I hear about the Edge, it doesn't sound like a place you should leave. How'd you get here?"

"I ask myself that question all the time." The steel behind his eyes is more silvery than usual, highlighting the blue. "I wanted to be a doctor, to help people, but somehow I got on the military path. It was probably because of my dad. He was K-Force. A slaver ship like this one rammed his into the Static Pass, and without thrusters or a way to call for help, they spun off course," he says. "They drifted for months until they all died of starvation."

"Was it this ship, Ben?"

"It was too many years ago to be *Imreas*. It was whoever Johnny works for . . . the head of the slave trade." His hands tuck into tight fists.

"So if you disable the trade—"

"I punish my dad's murderer. But that's only why I volunteered. I stay in it now because someone has got to help those people." His fingers uncurl, and he grips his knees. "My uncle Keven is a high-ranking official in the K-Force, and he was the one who okayed me to take this mission with Bron even though we were so young. Bet he's sorry he did it now." He takes a deep breath. "Bet my mother's all but killed him for letting me go."

"You had a mother?" The thought is weird for some reason.

"Of course, I have a mother. Just like you."

"But I don't." I run my hands over the bunk until I find the metal edge. "She went Touched when I was seven." I remember her smooth face and emerald eyes for the first time in years. "She was a real beauty. The kind of redhead that Johnny would have gone nuts for."

"Like you."

I flinch. "Yeah, well, the cops took her, and my dad had his hands full with my brothers and me, I guess. He didn't try to stop them. He didn't even fight back."

"He was taking care of your family. Don't doubt him."

I cover my face, but my memories come with anger instead of the usual drowning pain. "When they came again, he did fight. Jeremy was helping our neighbor hide from the cops. Someone told on him, and they came for both of them. My dad went nuts. He tried but . . . they beat his skull inside out on the stairwell and dragged him into the street."

Ben moves beside me. "He did what he thought he had to. Just like you do for Walker."

"What *I thought* I had to . . ." I pull at my shirt, feeling ghostly fingers. How many men have I given myself to? I've given up counting.

The smell of the Touched cargo hold refills my senses until I have to cover my mouth. Of course Johnny should be stopped, but if I help Ben, I'm gambling with not only my life but also my brother's. And Walker needs me now more than ever. But Lo needed me, too.

Our people.

I clench my knees. "What is it that you need me to do?"

CHAPTER 16

Johnny is the lord of the common room. He sits on a navy couch amid blue-tagged girls, taking questions from a line of passengers about our upcoming arrival at Entra.

I swallow my excitement for seeing a whole new world and sidestep the crowd, waiting for the moment when he sees me. Waiting to see if there's a speck of humanity within him.

Maybe just a glimmer of his regret at having killed my best friend.

My coin hoard is now hidden beneath the dustiest can in Lionel's storage room, and my feet feel loose in my shoes. What I'm about to do may drastically upgrade my position on this ship, but I'm not foolish enough to cut off other avenues. I may still need to pay someone to help Walker. Maybe Samson would do it. . . .

Ben's so-called "solid plan" has more holes than the worn-through sleeves of my shirt, but what he needs me to do is simple: distract Johnny. And that means giving him what he wants: the proof that killing Lo made me more independent—just like his father's order of banishment "freed" him.

I have to admit that more than a little piece of me revels in the idea of taking on Johnny again. Making him pay.

Johnny's black clothes stain the navy couch like the harshest center of a bruise. "No, I won't be joining you on the gaming floor," he says to the first passenger in line, a chubby middle-aged man. "You'll have to repay what you owe in credits instead of slippery offers." He looks up from his tablet, wearing a thin smile. "Hello, Rain. I was wondering when you were going to grace me with your unique coloring."

"Am I still just a color to you?"

He turns to his screen. I forgot how tall he is. Even sitting down, he's just a head below eye level, and his thighs splay out like a dare. "Do you have something *more* for me?"

I push past the chubby man and stand between Johnny's legs. A blue girl reclines across the couch with her hand resting on his knee, and I knock it away. I lean over the tablet in his hands, making him look into my face.

He still steals my breath.

Beyond the sex, the slaves in his cargo, and the darkness in his too-deeply brown eyes, he has the allure of something unknowable. Unfathomable. And with a start, I realize what he's always reminded me of.

The stretching black behind the stars.

I lower my mouth to his lips. His initial response is lax, so I take his collar in both hands and bring him against me. I am the hungry one now. My tongue finds the edge of his, and my hatred twists my attraction until I could almost suffocate him with this kiss.

When his hands mount my hips, I push him back against the

cushions. "I'm done with this level. Give me a new challenge."

Johnny's neck is tinted with a rare blush. "Such revamped interest." His tongue flicks across his lips, and I can tell that he's pleased. "Does this mean you've forgiven me?"

I hold back the urge to kick him in the balls, and then maybe kiss him again until he turns as blue as my bracelet. "I've"—my voice threatens to break as I remember Lo's horror-stricken face— "adjusted."

"Let's test that resolve." Johnny's fingers tap his tablet, and my wrist switches from sapphire to scarlet. "But clean yourself up first. You're a little disgusting at the moment."

Johnny motions for the chubby passenger, and I take a few steps back. "I've changed my mind. Maybe I will join you at the casino. What passes for high roller tokens these days?"

I take this as dismissal but don't move fast enough to miss the man's response. "Girls, credits, or stones," he supplies. "But girls take the cake."

With each step, my bracelet seems to grow heavier and heavier until I have to hold it up with my other hand. This is what had to happen, right? Johnny is distracted, and we'll arrive at Entra soon. Now I just have to pray that he doesn't lose me in a card game.

I take the elevator to the Family Room and walk past the ugly stares of the green girls and into the shower area. It's mercifully deserted, and I strip, looking over the deep tub where I bathed with Lo—where Kaya tortured us with the mysterious burning powder.

Frightened and unaware but together—I wish I knew then that

that moment in the water with Lo was going to be one of our last. I should have tried to calm her. She was already scared for her life.

And poor Kaya . . .

I blink some raw wetness from my eyes and get into one of the wide, tiled showers. I turn the water on as hot as it runs and step into the scalding stream. I wash my hair dozens of times, letting the water melt my muscles and sore hips into a less horrible form. The rush and flow steals the lingering filth from all the other men, and I bask in a rare carefree feeling.

"Rain!"

I poke my head around the curtain and find Ben frowning. "Hey, I'm showering here."

"You're red-tagged again! First off, how the hell did you manage it? And secondly, *why?*"

"You wanted me to help."

He waves his hand to shut me up and leans against the divider between my shower and the next. "I didn't mean for you to throw yourself back under him," he whispers, something like jealousy darting between his words. I find that I like it on an entirely unhealthy level and let the curtain close in his face.

"I don't do anything half-assed. Besides, I can't just wink at him and make him do what I want, you know."

"I realize that," he says. "This just complicates things. He's going to keep you near him now, especially when we land on Entra. That means you're going to be in the danger zone when I . . ." His words stop at the sound of someone entering the shower room. "Someone's coming!"

"Didn't you lock the door?"

"I forgot."

I reach through the curtain and grab him by the front of his shirt, pulling him into the shower with me. He spins so that he isn't facing my nakedness, which means he's staring down the stream of the water.

I do a poor job of trying to cover myself even though he isn't looking, and then, while girls' voices resonate in the shower room, I begin to enjoy the fact that he's getting soaked, fully dressed. And the thrill that I'm *embarrassed*, my nakedness seeming like a crazy powerful thing.

Which is something I haven't felt in far too long.

In a few minutes, the girls leave, and the door wallops closed behind them. Ben steps out of the shower without turning back to look at me. "That was close," I say. "What's the point in keeping a stern eye on the security feed if you forget to lock the door?"

"Even geniuses can be forgetful," he says, and I think I hear a smile. "Especially geniuses. But a locked door might have been *more* suspicious, so maybe I was just being inadvertently smart."

I stick my face around the curtain. He's leaning so close that I bump foreheads with him. "You wanted my help, so I'm actually going to help. And your plan, by the way, completely sucks. I have a better one, but you have to do something for me first."

Ben's face is an inch from mine, his gaze so keen that it'd make me feel naked even if I wasn't already. He looks as though he's about to complain, but his rather full lips—which I can't believe I haven't noticed before—curl into that boyish smile instead. "I'll hear you out, but not here where the other girls might catch us." He pauses. "It's going to be hard to get you away from him."

"Give me one of your gadgets. Let me dope him."

He cocks an eyebrow. "So much for playing it safe." He fishes into one of his pockets and hands me a small tin. "Drop one of these in his drink. It'll knock him out and cloud his memory of the whole evening. Then I'll come get you, and we'll talk."

"This is a gamble."

"Yeah, well, we're both in deep now." His smile is uneven, smirky, and I have the craziest urge to kiss it.

So I do.

I peck his lips so fast that he stumbles back and falls straight into the deep tub with a wild splash. I laugh, ducking back into the shower as two green girls enter. Over the rush and flow of the stream, I hear Ben's sloppy, boot-stomping exit from the tub.

"You should take your clothes off first, Mec," one of them dares to say.

"Very funny," he says. The girls' feet patter on the tile as they hustle by my shower, and I peek out to watch Ben struggle out of his wet shirt. He shakes the water from his dripping hair and glances back at me.

I drop the curtain. This is nuts. I'm giddy and running warm inside like the insanity of our plan has given me new life. It's probably just the promise of being proactive, but it feels like I'm really running the Void for once.

~~~~~~~~~~

I turn the tin of drug strips over and over in my pocket. Johnny's room is just as I remembered it—satiny sheets and the daring window that he first took me against. Not to mention the dim lighting that draws shadows down the walls like reaching hands.

I keep to the window and observe a passing lava star so huge and fiery that I'm caught in the sweeping, licking flame-covered surface.

"I hoped to find you naked. Isn't that your special move?"

Johnny enters, pulls his collar free, and undoes the string of buttons down his front. His chest seems thin next to Ben's, but it's still toned with the right curves and dips.

"I don't do anything twice," I say.

"You look much better." He untucks his shirt. "I didn't enjoy watching you get all filthy on the passenger floors."

I laugh. "You call that filth? I grew up on Earth City, remember?"

"True." He's shirtless now and already undoing his pants. My mouth has run dry, and I finger the tin in my pocket.

"Do you want a drink?"

He smiles. "Always."

I move to the bar and pour from the first bottle I see. I slide a tab out of the tin, but before I can drop it in the glass, he corners me from behind. His desire and impatience press into my back as he combs my hair away from my neck.

"My fiery girl," he whispers. "I watched you every second you were away. You didn't enjoy those other men, did you?"

Heat rolls up my body. How would he know a damn thing about what I enjoy? But even as I think these words, Johnny's closeness—his caresses and warm breath—make me feel a very forgotten thrill. I had thought that I could go to him like the others, all numb and robotic, but he does things to me without my permission just like before. He makes my skin tingle and my belly warm.

My heart bangs with both the anticipation of it all and the anxiety of enjoying it.

I can't. I have to keep a straight head. . . . I have to . . .

He turns my shoulders, and I slip the tab between my lips. It dissolves in a hurry, and I spin and kiss him so fast that even he fumbles to get a hold on me. I reach into his mouth with my tongue, the whole experience running much sloppier than any other kiss, but it doesn't matter because he's passed out on the floor before I can gag.

I feel a little woozy myself and grip the edge of the bar. I wipe the spit from my lips and chuckle at my success . . . only to fall, landing on top of Johnny.

Lights out.

"You weren't . . . supposed to . . ." The voice is a blurry mess. My eyesight is a blurry mess. My neck stings as something is zapped into my skin, making me jolt up into Ben's arms.

"I said, you weren't supposed to take one as well." Ben fixes the needle back into the silver dose rod.

"What'd you give me? Not that limp dick drug." I rub my neck as my eyes adjust. I'm on Johnny's black satin bed. Johnny is beside me with his mouth open and tongue lolling out like a butchered animal. I lean away from him.

"I gave you adrenaline." He turns the rod over before me, showing the different colors of the injection settings. "Red is adrenaline. See, I can switch out the meds for whatever purpose, and right now I've got it loaded for emergencies." He flips it to the next setting. "Yellow is Limpicilin." He cracks a smile and hands the heavy silver instrument to me.

I flip through the settings. "Can any of these kill a person?"

He tugs it out of my grip. "Don't even think about it, Rain."

"This could be it." I look over at Johnny's limp, shirtless body. "We could kill him."

"If Johnny were to die, the crew would be loyal to his father. They would dump the passengers and girls and hightail it for the asteroid belt beyond the Void. Believe me, we don't want that. The Touched would go straight to the mines, and we'd be in enemy space.

"Besides, Rain"—Ben says, nudging my chin with his knuckle until I look his way—"you don't want to be a murderer. Trust me."

I try to imagine Johnny dead, and a quiver slips from my lower back to my scalp. Of course, I don't want to be his killer.

What I am is bad enough.

Ben offers a small smile. "You ready to tell me your brilliant plan, oh fearless Earth Cityite?"

"Don't mock me," I say, hiding my own little smile. I try to stand on my own, but I stumble too far to the side and have to grip his arm. "Stupid drug," I curse. "Can you give me another shot?"

"Not unless you want your heart to explode."

I squeeze my eyes and try to shake away the grogginess. "All right, well, we have to go down to where he keeps Walker. We have to move him."

"That's your plan?"

"That's my price for helping you. We have to hide him in case Johnny figures out what I'm doing and decides to take something from me." I close my eyes against the memory of Lo flipping through the black. "He won't be able to get his hands on Walker. At least not as easily as before."

By the time we make it to the room with the solitary swinging light, my head and body have recovered from the knockout drug. Ben wastes no time in maneuvering Walker's pod out the door, and I find a similar-sized crate to replace it, covering it with the tarp as a decoy.

Of course it won't fool Johnny if he comes down here to check, but I have to trust that he's too reliant on the technologies at his fingers to do any actual legwork.

I twist the scarlet bracelet on my wrist.

"Don't do that," Ben says. "It could shock you."

I leave it alone but itch to tug it off my arm. "I thought it was beautiful when I first saw it."

Ben pauses, leaning against the pod. "Bet you thought Johnny wasn't so bad either."

He's right, but I won't tell him. I push my brother's frozen prison to keep from revealing my lingering problems along that front. Despite everything, Johnny still knows my pleasure zones like he mapped them, and yet he killed Lo.

What's wrong with me?

When we finally make it to the suspended mass of *Melee* in its chain net, Ben works his magic on the ship's control panel until the lower side of it opens like a secret door. We push Walker inside and close it off.

Ben steps into the small ship and I follow. "Johnny will have a hell of a time finding him in there." He rotates this way and that in the captain's chair while I flop back on the bunk. I hadn't realized how nervous I was about moving Walker until now. My heart spins like an engine and my breath is uneven.

"Of course, we'll be in trouble if he checks in person. . . ."

"We'll jump that bridge when it crumbles under us." I don't want to think about Johnny's wrath. Or Johnny, period. "So my plan"—I say and then sit up, folding my legs underneath me on the bunk—"is to free the Touched on Entra."

Ben stops circling in his chair. "No way."

"Well, you wanted to sneak them off the ship and store them somewhere until the K-Force could pick them up. That's stupid. If Johnny figures out that they're gone, and they're all in one place, it's only a matter of time before he finds them. Right?" Ben opens his mouth to object. "*But* if we release them on this forest planet, they'll be much harder to find. They'll certainly scatter, and then how easy will it be for Johnny to round them up? Not at all, right?"

"Rain . . ."

"Plus, they'll be free. Who knows? Maybe not being locked up and starved will set something loose in their minds. You said it yourself: they still have hunger. Humanity. They deserve freedom."

"My plan might have been crap," he admits. "But that plan is crap as well."

I bring my hair back and braid it. "It's not genius, but even you said that Entra's our last chance to save this group. After that stop we'll be in the dead zone. What's it called?"

"The Static Pass."

"Right. And you said that the K-Force are on the wrong side of it, which allows Johnny to just go about his business. We can't let him deliver all those people into the hands of that slaver. And this way the Touched aren't waiting on the help of some phantom space cops who may or may not ride in to save them."

Ben gets out of his chair and paces around the cabin. "Have you thought this through, Rain? I mean, have you thought through the aftermath? If you're too close to him, if you're still red-tagged, he could take his anger out on you—even if he has no idea that you're in on this." He stops moving. "He could punish you just to make himself feel better."

I look away. "Or you."

"I am one of his favorite punching bags." He sits beside me so hard that the whole bunk bounces. "He could do anything if he realizes that they're missing. I mean, he'll most likely keep up appearances as a passenger ship and head to the Edge, but if things go crazy, your already slim chances of getting out of here with Walker decrease significantly."

"I *have* thought about that." I pick at a small hole on the knee of my pants. "You still have to get off this ship. You said yourself that the K-Force are out there. Maybe when you rejoin them, I'll come with you. You can get me and Walker to the Edge."

His hand moves over mine, but at the last second, his fingers curl into a fist that doesn't touch me. "Hell."

He stands and palms the release to open *Melee*'s door. "I'll try, but I can't promise anything. Recovering me or anyone else is not one of the K-Force's priorities. Especially after all my years of failure . . . regardless of who my uncle is."

On the walk back to Johnny's quarters, Ben is too quiet, and then, the whole ship blares.

SCHREECHEEENSCH! SCHREECHEEEENSCH!

I fall to my knees on the swinging catwalk, clutching my ears against the siren. The red light flicks on and off, eerily matching the glowing scarlet on my wrist. Ben is swinging around in a circle, confused.

"What do we do now?" I yell without being able to hear myself. "Did we set that off?"

He screams something back, but I can't hear. He's panicked; the color is draining out of his face. Through the breaks in the siren, we hear footsteps. Running footsteps and many of them.

"We need to hide!" I shout, but he just gives me a confused look. I get right in his face "HIDE!"

He blinks awake, pulling me by the arm from the walkway. We haul down a corridor, and he beats his fist on a wall until a panel pops free, and then he shoves me into a very narrow space. He slips in behind me, snapping the piece of wall back in place.

The flashing alarm light is now just an outline to the panel.

And we are in the dark.

The siren stops after a minute, and the space is so small that I can't get my arms free to rub the tingling sensation from my ears. I work my jaw while Ben twists so that he's leaning into me, almost on top of me.

"Did we just set that off? I thought you shut the alarms down!"

"*Shhh*," he says. "There are going to be crew members all over this hall. And don't blame me, I did my best with the feed, but I'm not perfect. And Johnny's been updating the system behind my back."

"Will the alarm wake Johnny?"

"Nothing's waking Johnny before that drug wears off."

I breathe a sigh that must knock right into Ben's face. He's so close that I can feel the heat of his body, but I can't see a damn thing. The edging glow of the lockdown light doesn't reach into the wall space, and my bracelet does nothing outside of coloring my arm with a bloody tinge.

"Are we—"

Ben presses into me as a warning just as voices sound outside. A number of crew members bark commands back and forth. The loudest being, "Check every room."

"Hell." Ben's lips are against my ear. "They're looking for us."

~~~~~~~~~~~~

What may be hours later, I try to shift toward the wall but only succeed in knocking into something that jolts my back. I jerk forward, smashing full-bodied into Ben.

"Stop moving!"

"Something stung me."

"A bared electrical pulse. There are dozens in here. Just try to stand still."

"Easy for you to say. You're the one leaning on me." I twist until my hips are off-center to his. "If you wanted to be in the dark with me, you could have just asked."

Crew members return through the hall. Ben and I fall into a dead silence, and my idiotic words linger as being entirely too slutty or flirty. Or both. *If you wanted to be in the dark with me?* Good lord.

The voices move further down the corridor.

"What are you complaining about?" he whispers. "You're the one who kissed me."

"I was joking. Just kidding!"

"If you were kidding, why are you blushing?"

"You can see me?" I back up into the pulse and receive another electrifying jolt in the shoulder. "You can see in the dark?"

"I can see a scale of temperature signatures when there's low light." There's a smile in his voice. I clear my throat and try to think about something other than how very close we are and the fact that he can freakin' *see* my body heat.

"You Mecs really are evolved."

He breathes an annoyed sigh and leans back, causing me to tilt into him in the narrow space. "You've really got to stop thinking that I'm super human. If I was . . . well, we wouldn't be in here, would we?"

I prop my arms on the wall beside his waist and lock my elbows for maximum distance. "I don't get why you're so embarrassed about being Mec. You could have been born on Earth City, losing your friends and family one after another like a string of old lights."

My throat gets tight, but I can't seem to stop. It's been too long of a night—too long of a run through the Void. "You could have been walking across the square one day only to look up into the eyes of someone committing suicide. Someone falling over you like human rain."

Ben doesn't say anything, and I stare into a corner of the wall space that I can't even see. "Just ignore me," I manage. "Being shut in here is making me say stupid things."

He's quiet for a moment. "I won't ignore you. You're not the kind of person that anyone could ignore. No wonder Johnny is in love with you."

"He isn't—"

"He is, Rain. It may only be Johnny's brand of lusting love, but seriously, he's hooked."

My cheeks blaze with embarrassment as I remember how I mauled Johnny's lips before that line of passengers. "Yeah, well, I'd rather not talk about him."

"All right." He's quiet for another long stretch of minutes. "I've been doing some more research on the whole Touched phenomenon. I think it's genetic, and that's a sort of specialty with Mecs. It may just be a weakness in the DNA of Earth Cityites."

I've never heard it put so simply. "So maybe your people do know a cure."

"They should know more on the Edge, but don't delude yourself, Rain. Mecs aren't perfect." His chest heaves and bumps into mine. "For example, I was born blind."

"What?"

"Every Mec is born blind. Our scientists messed with genetics to boost intelligence, and somehow they wiped the code for eyesight. They haven't figured out how to fix it without losing the enhanced intellect, but they figured we're wicked smart now, so who needs natural eyesight." He takes a long breath. "I'm not evolved, Rain. I've been engineered this way."

"So how do you see?" I touch his face, finding his hair and twisting it behind his ear.

"Optical cameras were implanted in my brain after birth," he says as though the words taste foul.

"So *that's* the silver? You've got machinery in your head? Is that what you meant when you said you had 'hardware'?"

"How's that for enforcing the Mec stereotype? We've got technology on the brain. Literally." He forces a laugh. "So don't go so hard on the Earth City. Mecs are just another brand of freaks."

"You seem pretty human to me. Particularly all your flaws. And you'll be a doctor one day. Once we get out of here. I know it."

"Right. When we get out of here." He swallows a laugh, and I think that he's going to make fun of my rather naïve scratching around for hope. But he doesn't. He clears his throat. "So, what will you be once we're out of here?"

The immediate answer is *anything else than what I am*, but I manage to keep that to myself. "I don't know. I guess, more than anything, I'd like time to think about it. On Earth City, I was always scraping to stay alive. To protect Walker. I used to dream about running the Void, but beyond that . . . maybe I just wish I had time to try a bunch of things. I'd like to use the smarts my dad gave me." The idea fills me with a real warmth. "Does that sound crazy?"

"Not at all. There are universities on the Edge that could help you do just that."

"University," I repeat, loving even the sound of the word. My elbows are stiff from supporting myself, and I bend them, nudging into him.

"You can lean on me," he says in a husky voice. "We could be in here for another few hours. I don't know how long they'll look for the cause of the alarm." I loosen my elbows until I'm resting against his chest. His heart thumps beneath my ear—a little too loud and fast.

Of all the men that I've let inside me since I boarded this claustrophobic metal, his closeness feels the most risky. Of course Johnny would lose his head if he knew how much I think about Ben—how often we've had . . . moments.

"Ben, you really think the K-Force won't save us? We're doing *their* job, aren't we?"

"It's difficult to say. I just don't want to make promises to you that I can't keep. They have greater priorities than rescue.

Large-scale missions. Their brand of justice is really eye for an eye. They'll blow *Imreas* to hell if they get a chance, and it won't matter who's onboard." His arm tucks around my waist, and his voice lowers. "And they certainly didn't do anything when I let them know about Bron. 'A necessary casualty,' my uncle called her through the transmission. *A necessary casualty.*"

"She was your girlfriend?" He'd called her that before and the word lodged someplace deep. To think that they were together, *really* together despite Johnny and the girl trade . . . I can't help but feel an itch of jealousy.

His fingers tug at my belt, and I relax against him a little more. "Not exactly. I wanted her to be, but nothing is simple on this ship. And Johnny had his hooks in her almost as deeply as he has them in . . ."

Me.

I know that's what he wants to say, but he continues in another direction. "He was enraged by the idea that she could like anyone other than him. I bet he beat her before . . ."

His hand turns into a knot—an unyielding fist pressed against my hip. "Hell, Rain. I'm going to get you killed."

"Not if I get you killed first," I point out.

He hiccups a surprised laugh. "True." The muscles of his shoulder are the best balance of firm, both warm and inviting. I rub my cheek against his shirt just as the red lines around the edge of the panel stop flashing and are replaced by the yellowed brightness of the overheads.

The lockdown is over. Ben shimmies around my body and pops the panel free, spilling unnecessary light into our secret space.

CHAPTER 18

Ghostly bodies fall through the Void.

They scream my name.

And Walker's pod is among them, flipping and spinning until it's gone beyond the blue engine lights of the ship. I try to jump after him, but I'm held back by gripping, stroking, stealing fingers. I'm prodded and stripped. I'm taken apart by faceless men—skin from muscle, muscle from bones.

Soul from body.

Someone touches me, and I snatch the hand, bending back the thumb that I've caught. I open my eyes and look straight into Johnny's hair-ruffled halo.

"Let go."

I drop his thumb. "You startled me."

He shakes out his thumb joint but wears a smile. "You were nightmaring." I try to push up on my elbows on the satiny bed, but he moves closer. He's naked, but then so am I. I stripped both of us when I returned from being with Ben. And I destroyed the room. The plush chair is on its side, clothes are strewn about, and a bottle has been emptied on the bar.

"We did all that?" I fake.

"Apparently. Must have been a wild night. Wish I could remember some of it." He squeezes his temples for a moment. The drug I slipped him last night has left him groggy but not dead. The sheet glides between us like a film of lotion as he presses his length against my side and draws circles on the lowest part of my belly.

"Tell me what you dreamt about." A smile is fitted to Johnny's face, but for once it isn't cold or malicious. If anything, I would call it searching. "I don't remember my dreams," he adds.

"I saw my brother," I say, leaving out the rest.

Johnny groans. "Boring. And here I was hoping you dreamt of me. Crysta used to have nightmares where she'd call out for me." His eyes reveal their deepest brown as his gaze falls out of focus. "I loved watching her twist and cry. Watching her ache and sniffle. Sometimes I would wait for her to hit that breaking point—right before she might wake herself—and then I'd kiss her."

His lips seal mine, reeking of the alcohol that I smeared over his unconscious mouth, and his body arches as he moves his kiss from my mouth to my neck to my chest. I begin to slip into it—to run my hands through his hair and massage his back.

But Johnny sags, and he presses his forehead into my neck. Strange emotions seem to freeze him where he lies, and for just a moment he is nothing like the cold commander of this ship. His whole weight sinks against me as he sighs, and if I didn't know better, I might call him heartsick. Ben said that Johnny has a sort of love for me, but it feels more like he has an overwhelming need for another's love. A craving.

A deficiency.

His com buzzes next to my ear, and he grumbles out of his

trance and slides off. He presses something on the wristband, and the door opens.

Ben enters.

Johnny has taken the sheet with him, and I grapple to cover my nakedness, tipping off the bed and landing with an unlady-like *oof* on the floor. Johnny chuckles. "That Mec stare is a bit much, Ben. Do try to blink once in a while. Then maybe my girls wouldn't be so terrified of you."

"Your girls are scared of me because you make me punish them," Ben says while I tug myself into the first bit of clothing I can find, Johnny's black dress shirt, and get to my feet.

"True," Johnny admits. "But what order would we have if I was always the one knocking them around?"

Ben doesn't respond, and my fingers struggle with the shirt buttons. I can't help but remember last night—that small space between the walls—and the way Ben and I leaned, breathing each other in.

"We'll be arriving at Entra tomorrow," Ben says to Johnny.

"And all is in place?" Johnny gets out of the bed, naked and apparently not the least bit shy about it. He picks up the bottle on the bar and drinks from it before tugging on his pants. "No surprises like last time?"

Ben shakes his head. "No sign of her—"

Johnny's look kills Ben's words. Then he beckons me with a come-hither finger, and I step over and into the curl of his arm. "There was an alarm tripped last night. What happened?"

Ben's good. His face is blank and sound. "We didn't find anything. It could have been nothing."

"Nothing." Johnny's arm gets a little tighter around me. "Why don't I believe you? Oh, that's right, it's because you still think you're smarter than me, but I know that Mecs are only as capable as their toys. Empty your pockets."

Ben pulls all sorts of interesting things out of the deep pockets in his cargo pants, dumping them on the edge of the bed. In the meantime, Johnny slides his shirt off my shoulder and kisses the nape of my neck. A sort of moaning sigh slips out of me that's entirely too loud, and Johnny chuckles, nuzzling my neck some more.

I glance at Ben, feeling the rush of my embarrassment. But his eyes are held up on the place where Johnny kisses me. He chucks the blue medical disc onto the bed last.

"That's everything," Ben says, and when Johnny doesn't look up from caressing me, he cuts in, "Johnny. That's it."

Johnny doesn't look up. "Rain," he says. "Pat him down for me."

A torn feeling swells in my chest as I step between them. I manage to kneel before Ben, feeling his pockets—and the tensed muscles of his legs beneath. All the while, my heart slams around in my chest. I should not be between them. This is more than a little dangerous. This is what happened to that Bron girl.

I find a bit of metal in the pocket at Ben's calf and freeze.

"Well?" Johnny asks.

Ben must want whatever it is, but what if Johnny figures out that I lied? What if he starts to think that Ben and I are together? I pull out a tiny screwdriver from the pocket. "Just this." I hand it to Johnny, and he turns it over in his hand before tossing into the pile on the bed.

"Thank you, Rain. You can go." I turn to leave, but he grabs my arm. "You're coming on planet with me tomorrow, so make sure you're presentable." I nod and make it to the door before I'm stopped by the unmistakable sound of fist against face.

Ben holds his mouth. He's bleeding. Johnny shakes his fingers loose.

"Well, I feel better," Johnny says rather jovially. He glances at me. "Get out, Rain."

I wrap Johnny's dress shirt tighter and go to the Family Room. The green girls hush when I enter in a way that prickles up my bare legs, but I'm too hungry to care. I change into a plain top and pair of pants from the community closet, trying not to think about what happened to the clothes' former owners.

I'm also trying not to think about Johnny and Ben in that bedroom. Will Ben fight back? Probably not. Would he even win? For all Ben's strength, Johnny has always felt more dangerous—more capable of violence. Maybe for the simple reason that he enjoys it.

A short-haired brunette glowers while I select a weird ball of purple fruit and some grainy bread in the kitchen. I return to my mat with my food. It's been weeks since I slept here on my own, and yet somehow the spot is comforting. For one thing, Ben's area is only a stone's throw away at the far end of the window, and for another, there's the window itself.

Bright strings weave and dance beyond the glass.

We'll be on Entra tomorrow . . . and tomorrow is when Ben and I try our risky plan. I keep trying to bite into the colorful fruit, but I can't help but think of the Touched down in the cargo hold. Most of them are starving. Ben says they rarely get food, and when they do, they fight like animals over it. I set the waxy purple ball down and tear into the bread, making myself take a huge bite.

WHAM!

Something slams into the back of my head, and I sprawl on my mat. In seconds, half a dozen girls pin each of my limbs to the floor while the short-haired brunette crashes down on my chest like she means to flatten me.

I try to cough up the bread, but she presses a pillow over my face. Kicking and struggling, I fail to get a hand free or a leg. *Are they trying to kill me?* The brunette finally lifts the pillow, and I launch my half-chewed wad at her face . . . and am rewarded by another stretch of minutes under the cotton.

"What do you want?" I gasp when I'm released.

"Where're Sare and Lula and Dom? What'd you do with them?"

"Me? I don't even know who those people are!"

"What about Kaya?" the girl holding my left arm barks. "You knew Kaya."

I can't get enough air beneath the brunette's crushing weight. "Kaya?" I manage through puffs. "Kaya is dead."

One of the girls holding my legs cries out, and the girl on my chest hisses at her to shut up. "You had her killed. Admit it!" She tugs at my hair until I have to bite down to keep from giving her the scream she wants. "My mother always said that red was the color of the devil!"

"Don't leave a mark, Amanda," another girl warns.

The brunette's grip on my hair slackens. "Wouldn't want to hurt Johnny's pet."

"What makes you think that I made your friends disappear?"

"You show up and green girls go missing," the short-haired girl—Amanda, I guess—says. "What do you whisper in his ear that makes him get rid of us?" Before I can answer, she shoves the pillow over my face again. This time it doesn't come up when I start kicking; my body thrashes from the lack of oxygen.

It doesn't come up until I stop moving altogether, ready to pass out.

And I don't even breathe when the pillow is removed; it's like I forgot how. Amanda smacks my chin, jolting me into a gasp. Then she presses her face down on mine like she's going to bite my nose off. "You go off with him, and we disappear. Explain it!"

"Maybe it's Johnny's fault. You ever think of that?"

Several of the girls cry out and let go of my arms and one of my legs.

"Don't question Johnny." Amanda slides off my chest.

"What's wrong with you?" I get up on my elbows. "*Why* would you stand up for him after all he does?"

"Don't bite the hand that feeds you," Amanda says.

"I'm just trying to get to the Edge in one piece. I don't have anything to do with your missing girls."

"The Mec!" a girl standing lookout calls. The rest of them disappear in various directions, but Amanda gets to her feet and looks down on me.

"You won't get out of this untouched." She slips away through the curtains, and I'm left in a mess of fruit, picking at my smashed bread. They were careful. I won't have one bruise from their attack, but still, every part of me aches. I don't even remember the names she listed, but three girls are missing, and they all think that it is somehow my fault.

I believe them.

※※※※※

I stand before the window, unable to sleep. The stars are like a web of lights, two of them growing brighter and brighter: the two suns of Entra. When Kaya spoke of them, her eyes glazed with longing. Is there someone waiting for her to come back to the planet? Friends who won't see her again? A family she left behind?

At least Lo didn't have anyone else. Just Walker and me.

"Are you ready for Entra?" Ben says through my thoughts. "We'll be there in a few hours." He steps around the veil to enter my small area. I press my fingers to the cool glass and am reminded of Walker's pod. I should find a minute to visit him. If things go bad on Entra, I may never see him again.

"Hello?" Ben steps closer. "We can talk now. I've bumped the feed offline so we can go over the plan."

"The other girls could hear, Ben."

"Most are out with clients," he says. "But we'll be quick. I— I wanted to check in with you after this morning." I take in Ben's face for the first time and find his bottom lip swollen, split down the middle with a puffy, scabbed line.

"Oh." I reach for him without thinking. He catches my hand before I can touch him and pulls it down. Still, he holds my fingers for a few moments before letting go. "He won't let you heal that?"

"He took my *toys*, remember? Besides, I think he likes seeing me hurt more than actually hurting me. But then, he does enjoy a good streak of violence." Ben's tone is joking, but his words are heavily serious.

"I'm sorry about your . . . screwdriver." I almost joke, too.

"That was for you, so you could prove your loyalty to him."

I should have guessed that he had thought all that through. "You really are smart."

"I just knew that he'd make you check me. He'd like to think that you're afraid of me like the other girls. He really thought that he was *having fun* with you as well as punishing me." Ben frowns, and I remember what he said about Johnny making him hurt the girls.

"What does he make you do to them?"

"The usual is lock them up. The unusual is worse." He's staring at me with a bared sort of intimacy, and I can't quite keep his gaze. "So," he clears his throat, "the plan."

I'm ready for this part at least. I've been going over and over our scheme for the past two days. "I drug him when we're at the casino, and then we boost the hover cab and steal the Touched from *Imreas*. Then we free them on the far side of the planet."

"I'll take care of the mechanics and security. Thankfully we don't have to move the Touched from the cargo holds. Those bins work like huge drawers; they come right out from the side of the ship. We can empty them and replace them without anyone noticing . . . hopefully."

"So that's how Johnny has people loaded up without anyone

suspecting. They were sealed into those holds before they even left Earth City."

Ben nods. "500 per hold."

"A thousand souls. I didn't realize there were that many." So many people to damn if we fail . . . not to mention what will happen to me and Ben. And Walker.

Ben nods. "Of course this all rests on your ability to knock Johnny out."

"Easy." I rub my stiff neck, failing to hide a groan.

"What's wrong?"

"I got blitzed," I say. "The other girls think I'm some sort of evil omen that caused three of them to disappear."

"Ah." Ben writes three names in the fog I left on the glass: Dom, Sare, and Lula. "Johnny marked them for liquidation."

"What the hell does *that* mean?"

"Means he's going to trade them on Entra. He'll use them as gambling tokens, most likely. Gaming is huge on that planet and *very* corrupt." He wipes the names from the glass with his arm. "We'll never see them again."

I tug at my sore neck, remembering Johnny's conversation with the chubby passenger. So it is my fault. Johnny wasn't planning on gaming until I showed up and got his blood moving.

"Did they hurt you?" His hand slips from my elbow to my wrist.

"Not as much as they wanted to." And now I don't blame them. "But Ben, what was up with Johnny this morning? What's he afraid of on Entra?"

"Crysta."

"His old girlfriend?"

"His old love," Ben corrects. "We shouldn't run into her, though . . . not this time. I've reserved his room on the farthest side of the casino, and there's no record of her name in the outpost's current manifesto." He hooks his thumbs under his arms, making his biceps round up. "You don't want to see Johnny when she's around."

"I thought she helped him start his girl trade and all that. What happened?"

"What happened is that Johnny could turn her into a prostitute, but he couldn't reverse his success. You should see her now—drop-dead gorgeous but as lethal as arsenic. He really messed her up. Too many men. After awhile, all these girls get . . ." His voice falls off level, and he drops his arms. "Hell, Rain. I'm not trying to make you feel—"

"Save it. I'm fine." I face the window. "I'm nothing like Johnny's old love." I cradle my aching body, but something feels off. "What—"

I feel his shadow inexplicably.

His height. His leanness.

I swing around. "Johnny."

"Hello, Rain. Ben." He is a black pillar among the dim veils. "What's keeping you two up? *Bonding*, are we?"

CHAPTER
19

For a long moment, Ben and I stand speechless. How much did he hear? My heart slams, and I search for words, but Ben beats me to an excuse.

"She's filing a complaint. Rain was attacked by the other girls."

I glance hastily at Ben. "I can handle it, Johnny. I—I didn't want to tell you."

"Which girls?" Johnny steps forward and takes my chin. He examines every angle of my face.

"I don't know their names." I can feel his rage growing through the glints in his eyes. "I didn't see them. They put a pillow over my face," I add in a hurry. "I couldn't breathe for a few minutes. It was just some hazing."

"And I suppose this was another one of those times when the security feed was down, Ben? Another *hiccup*?"

"I didn't catch it on the feed," he says. "They were careful. Besides, I told you we could have the system checked over once we reach the Edge. I know someone who—"

"Lights!" Johnny commands across the Family Room, cutting Ben off. The light level rises to full brightness, and I have to shield my eyes until they adjust. Johnny flings back the curtains as he charges to the center of the room.

"Follow him," Ben whispers.

"What have you done?" I murmur. "He'll kill those girls."

"We have no choice. Our plans are too important."

"Wake!" Johnny yells from the front of the room. "Get up here!" From every secret nook, sleepy-eyed girls stumble forward, creating a group of startled and frightened faces. I stand at the back, trying to breathe air that has become useless in my lungs.

"Some of you attacked my Rain. My *red tag*. The leader will step forward."

No one moves. My eyes dart to Amanda's short hair. She wears nothing but a light green dressing gown.

"Step forward or you'll all be yellow tagged before dawn," he commands. Amanda shuffles through the shaking mass of girls. Her bare feet and calves remind me of a small girl, and it no longer matters that she half suffocated me. She was acting for her missing friends; she did no less than what I would have done.

Johnny's hand closes around the back of her neck, and he leads her toward the door without even glancing at her face. "The rest of you get back to sleep," he barks. "Lights out!"

The room falls dark so fast that I swear I'm falling with it. I feel the scatter of the frightened girls and hear a few whimpers in the aftermath of the slamming door.

Ben's hand closes on my shoulder. "We didn't have a choice," he says into my ear.

"Don't touch me." I shove him away and curl up on my mat. Johnny will kill her. I'm certain. Maybe the airlock. Maybe he'll choke her in the hall. Or a knife.

I remember the great crimson puddle spreading out beneath the Touched man and then the spray and smears of Walker's blood all over the empty pool. I shake hard, gripping my shoulders and letting my fingernails sink into my cold skin.

A river of red runs from one end of the cosmos to the other, and it's darker than the Void, and carnal, and all over me. I pull at my bracelet until I've bruised my wrist, not caring if it shocks me. And when it won't budge, I yank on my hair.

Maybe Amanda was right about me. I am red—the color of the devil.

The signature of blood.

⁓⁓⁓

During the last hours of the night, I wander down to Samson's engine room to check the population chart—that screen full of people dots—for Amanda's tag. I can't seem to think about anything else.

The last person I want to see is Ben, but he's there, climbing a rope that ascends far out of sight in the ceilingless place. His pants sway with the loose bottom of the rope as his arms work to carry him higher.

"Try not to fall!" I yell. "Would suck if you got yourself killed instead of someone else!"

Ben glances down, and I can't stand the oblivious look on his face. I turn to leave, but he leaps down, hitting the metal floor with a loud clop from his boots. "Wait." He blocks the door. "I have to talk to you."

"I'm still in, if that's what you're worried about." I try to shoulder past him, but he holds his arms out. "I just don't want to look at you right now."

"Hear me out."

"You sold out Amanda. *You* got her killed."

"Samson!" he yells into the ceiling guts of the engine room. "Get down here and tell her what I told you!"

Samson rappels on his little seat to a level just above our heads. His eyes are covered with his fogged goggles, and his beard is flecked with something ashy.

"'Reck'd or unreck'd, duly with love returns,'" he sings at the sight of me with a wide-mouthed smile. The words bang up through the room with echoes that reach into me. "Hello there, Rain Runner. A pleasure to see your face this late, although I don't know if I agree with your decision to wander these unlucky halls."

"Don't waste your breath, Sam. I've already given her that lecture." Ben crosses so that he's right under the greasy old man. "Tell her what I just told you. She's not likely to believe me."

"She can read it herself." Samson pulls a piece of paper from the breast pocket of his flight suit. He lets it flutter down to the floor, and I stoop to grab it.

"Samson has agreed to send that transmission in the event that we—" Ben clears his throat. "Disappear."

I unfold the note:

TO TITAN SHIP HOLMES. ATTN: K. RYAN.
MELEE LAUNCHED PASSENGERLESS WITH
BEACON. LIVING CARGO TO THE EDGE.
BEN RYAN DEAD.

I read the message several times. The last three words thunder through me in a way that makes me need to sit down. *Ben Ryan dead?* It's too reminiscent of the awkward line from the warning posters on Earth City. "Do not sorrow," I whisper and lean against the edge of Samson's table. "What in hell is this, Ben?"

I take in the mess of his hair, struggling with the sudden sensation that the words in my hand are a terrible prediction. A given—Ben will die.

"I've rigged *Melee* to launch itself through *Imreas*'s side when we reach the other end of the Static Pass. My ship's made of a harder metal and should cause a good deal of damage to *Imreas*, although we'll be too dead to know. It might even slow Johnny down enough for him to be caught.

"Samson will send that transmission," he continues, "and my uncle, Keven, will recover *Melee*. Maybe not right away, but your brother will be rescued. They'll see him to the Edge and someone will help him." He looks up into the deep shadows of the engine rigging. "Keven will have to go back to tell my mother what happened to me."

I hold the note out by two fingers. "This is . . ." Depressing? Horrible?

The opposite of the hope I need to get through all this?

He takes the piece of paper. "It's a little insurance. I owe you that much for helping me. Not like this plan will necessarily work, but it's something."

"It's something," I repeat. Ben passes the note up to Samson.

The old man takes the paper and presses it inside his pocket. "So you two really mean to go through with it? Thought I'd seen it all in the Void, but you pair are brand new." He pulls his goggles off his forehead revealing a circle of pink skin around brown eyes. *Silvery* brown.

"You're Mec!" I exclaim. "Why didn't you say so before?"

"Because then people either quiver with fear or expect too damn much. And you two are just a couple of teens. Don't forget that while you're off saving civilization and upholding the moral code or whatever." He yanks his goggles back over his eyes. "Don't forget to enjoy yourselves where you can."

I manage a small laugh. "Sure thing, Dad."

The title was meant to be a joke, but saying *Dad* sends a terrible shock through me. What would my father think of all this? What would he say to his daughter who is now little more than a prostitute? A prostitute who's in the habit of getting her peers killed?

Samson presses a button that recalls his seat up into the engine rigging. "*Reck'd or unreck'd . . . ,*" he sings as he goes.

"You'd think he'd help us," I say.

"He does in his own way. He's a decent soul, but he's been in the Void too long." I can feel his stare, but I won't look at it. "Samson may not agree with Johnny's ways, but he isn't about to interfere with them."

"You think all Runners are like that?"

"All the ones I've encountered," he says.

"What about these K-Force? You said they'd hardly prioritize a rescue mission for you. What makes you think that they'll pick up Walker in *Melee*?"

"Because *Melee* is a Void-capable vessel. She's valuable."

"Everything is ranked by a depraved value system in this universe, isn't it? Human life should mean more."

Ben shrugs. "Depends on the human. I can tell you that Johnny gets forty credits a head for the Touched."

"Forty!" The number is both sickeningly low and much higher than I expected. "And what about Amanda? How much was she worth?" Ben looks away, and I turn out of the engine room. He stomps in pursuit. "Did you even bother to check the population chart to see if she's still alive?"

"I did." His steps slow until I know that he's given up on trying to catch me.

I swing around. "And?"

"And she's gone." His forehead creases with a frown. "Don't try to shame me, Rain. Remember how long I've been on this ship. Remember that I've lost friends as well." He gets in my face, and I can't help but look at the split in his bottom lip where Johnny punched him. "Our plan is too important for this!"

"I know that!" I press my face right under his, but his words beat mine.

"So if I have to choose between one person and the lives of hundreds of sick people, I'm going to make the easy decision. And if I have to choose between one of Johnny's sickly obedient girls and you, I'm going to pick you every time." He wavers after his outburst, and I feel a little blown by such a passionate admission. He squeezes his eyes like he regrets his words but doesn't lean out of our standoff.

My hands slip up his arms, and I clutch his shirt like I need to find some way to hold on to him. *Ben Ryan dead.*

"This is too important," he says without opening his eyes. "Right?"

I squeeze the soft fabric. I could almost press myself to him. Let him feel and see and know the real me beneath all my terrible deeds.

Almost.

CHAPTER
20

Entra is a wonder.

The planet's forest surface swirls with emerald and jade colors even from the upper atmosphere where *Imreas* is parked. I press myself to the hover cab window as we leave the docking bay, only to be half blinded by the brilliance of two orange suns.

Johnny touches a button, causing a shade screen to drop over the windows and mute the new world to a tolerable, but less vivid, hue. Ben sits across from me, his eyes shielded behind his hair, and Samson's ratty head is haloed by light in the driver's seat. Despite their silence, I can't help feeling surrounded by secret friends. Samson might not go out of his way to help us, but he's on our side. I can tell.

Johnny's fingers slide from my knee to my thigh, under the hem of the crimson dress he presented to me just this morning.

Here I am, obedient. And the color of blood from head to knee.

I refuse to look at Ben, not wanting to know if he's watching. Glaring. In the days since our tryst in the secret wall space, I've taken to rethinking the hell out of that moment. Of course it doesn't mean anything; it can't. But that doesn't mean I can't go over it in my head and just pull the pieces of those hours apart, savoring them. I feel myself run warm as I remember the low husk to Ben's voice when he said, *You can lean on me.*

Johnny pushes my hair behind my ear. "You look perfect. We'll go straight to the hotel," he commands.

I begin to respond, but my voice is rough. "All right," I say, unable to keep myself from glancing in Ben's direction, but he's looking out the window, only the hint of a clenched muscle along his jaw.

Johnny's touch turns from caress to grip, and I can't help but feel the sway of his nerves. Entra has put him on edge, or perhaps it's the thought of running into his old love. Whatever it is, it's making him unpredictable, which spells danger for our plans. I turn to the window, watching the mass of green sharpen into an endless forest.

"I've never seen nature before. That's the word, right? *Nature*," I try. "Not outside of a document screen anyway." No one responds, and I continue to watch the swift magnification of the planet through the window, remembering the brown vine that grew around the glass ceiling of the greenhouse. Would it grow in this environment? Or does it need hardship and constraint?

Could anything from Earth City flourish here?

Maybe the Touched won't survive in the wild, but at least no one will be hunting or enslaving them. Who knows what they're capable of when they're finally free. I twist the bracelet around my wrist.

Johnny knocks my hand away. "Don't play with that."

The hover cab turns toward a massive white structure, which sits atop the tree line on thick pillars. Samson sets us down on a parking lot of other hover cabs on the building's rooftop.

We exit, and though it stings my eyes, I watch the crowns of the two suns settle out of sight until the whole horizon bleeds a citrus rainbow. The hover cab lifts off from behind us with a gust that throws the hem of my dress up to my hips. I tug it down and take a deep breath to ask where Samson's going, but instead my lungs burn so hard that I have to lean over and hack to breathe.

"Breathe shallowly," Johnny orders.

I try to ask why but only succeed in coughing harder.

"The atmosphere is packed with oxygen because of the trees and a few other gases that don't exist on Earth," Ben says. "Your body will adjust to it, but it'll take awhile. Best to sip at the air until then."

I take a very shallow breath and the burning abates. "Where is Samson going?"

Johnny smooths his hair and grips my elbow.

"He will run disembarking passengers down from *Imreas*," Ben says.

"Shut up," Johnny barks. "Since when do we answer the girls' questions?"

"A slip." Ben's footsteps fall behind as Johnny marches me around a variety of hover vehicles. When we reach a silver platform, he steps on a lighted square in the center, and the whole platform drops below the parking lot level. We come to a stop seconds later on an inner floor.

"Welcome to the Entra Suns Casino, Rain," Johnny says over the bustle of hundreds of people.

We're in the center of a corridor overflowing with bodies and chattering voices. Restaurants, bars, and storefront doorways spot the white hall as far as the eye can see, but most striking is that the floor is not a floor at all, but a wide expanse of seamless glass that shows off the forest running beneath the whole structure.

I almost trip as it feels very much like standing on air.

Johnny's grasp on my elbow flexes as we push through the crowd. People jostle by, bumping into him in a way that notches his already aggravated demeanor until even I want to scream, "Out of the way!"

He stops in the flow after awhile. "Take the lead, Mec. Turn your blinders up and stare them down."

Ben frowns. "No."

Johnny's eyebrows twitch, and Ben shakes his head, submitting, but making a point about not wanting to. He tucks his hair behind his ears and closes his eyes. When he opens them, every drop of blue has been replaced by shining silver—like he's turned into a ghost. I can't suppress a shiver as he turns his gaze through the crowd.

And they part. They whisper and point.

Some people look away while others gawk. Either way, they clear from his path like he's some kind of lord. It's the damndest thing I ever saw.

"What the . . ."

"In a universe full of unveiled wonders"–Johnny says, not bothering to hide his annoyance–"everyone still freaks at the sight of a Mec. You should have seen them when I had a Mec girl. Like I'd stolen an angel from the heavens."

Ben looks back at Johnny with burning hatred, and even I feel the heat of it. Johnny means Bron—Ben's Bron. So she was *that* valuable and he still killed her? Ben and I are crazy. Johnny is both the armed weapon and the itchy trigger finger. And we want to drug him and steal his valuable shipment of human cargo?

"Stop fidgeting," he commands and swipes my hand from my hair.

Ben leads us toward an entrance engraved with the words SILVING SUNS HOTEL, and we follow the wide berth his presence commands, passing through the hotel's posh lobby to an ornate hall. I linger behind Johnny as he lists orders for Ben.

"I want those girls brought down immediately. I'll be out for the evening," he says.

Girls? He means the three green girls who Amanda died for. I stare through the glass floor as I walk, longing to touch the leaves and branches only a few feet away. What I wouldn't give to escape. To walk among growing things . . .

I knock right into Johnny's back.

He's frozen in the middle of the hallway by the sight of an incredibly tall woman. Her blonde hair pours down her shoulders like a cascade of gold water. She, too, has gone still except for a creeping smile.

"Hello, Johnny."

He clears his throat. "Crysta." Another shiver lights my spine, much worse than the one when I saw Ben's eyes. Johnny yanks me forward until I'm at his side, but she doesn't even look at me. She's too busy staring into Johnny . . . ungluing him.

"Welcome to my hotel," she says.

"Your hotel?"

Her smile slips into something so cold that even I am stung by it. She snaps her fingers at one of the two huge men flanking her, whom I didn't even notice until that moment, and holds her hand out for a tablet. She runs through information on the screen. "I see that you're booked in the Helena Room. That won't do for your . . . tastes." Her glossy nails click against the tablet's glass screen. "I've switched you to the Fina Suite. One of our best. The last door on the left."

"Wonderful." Johnny's tone is full of barbed pleasantness.

She doesn't look up from the tablet. "I have business to attend to. Enjoy your stay." Her curvy form sweeps around Johnny, followed by her two servants, and my pulse beats warnings as his face folds. He hauls me to the end of the corridor where the door on the left opens as though it saw us coming.

The suite is built into the corner of the massive casino. Two of the walls are made of seamless glass, which, along with the floor, makes the whole place feel like it's floating. A stream of water pours down the corner of the two glass walls, emptying through slits in the floor and into the forest below. Our own water-fall . . .

Johnny slams the door, stripping his coat away. "What is she doing here?"

Ben shrugs.

Johnny muscles him into the pristine glass wall so hard that Ben's breath busts out of his chest. I swallow a yell. I can't believe that he didn't go smashing through the pane and plunging into Entra's surface.

"Her hotel?" Johnny yells. *"Hers?"*

"She probably won it in a gamble, Johnny." Ben's face is tinting into a red hue as Johnny squeezes his chest. "Ch-check yourself. She's probably watching you now."

Johnny's eyes flick up at the ceiling, and he drops Ben to the floor. "You're right." He straightens his shirt and pulls his jacket back on. "I'm going out." He bends down to where Ben kneels, catching his breath. "You bring me those girls *now*."

"And you," he swings at me. "Move from this room for any reason, and I'll—" He holds the back of his hand up. His fingers twitch, no doubt dying to slam into my face. All the smoothness of his youth has vanished under his expression, almost as though Crysta made him age a few decades in a few seconds.

He leaves, and the sound of the falling water fills the sudden quiet. Ben looks up from his crouched position on the floor and glances at the ceiling. *We're being watched*, his silver gaze warns. I help him to his feet.

"Mind turning your eyes off," I say. "They're freaking me out."

Ben blinks hard, and when he opens his eyes again, they're blue and natural and lovely. "I'm sorry you had to see that. Pretty alien, isn't it?"

"Not at all," I lie. I glance around the room. "What do I do now?"

He points to the shoulder of my dress. "That's all twisted," he says in a weird tone that I've never heard before. He moves behind me, brings my hair out of the way and fusses with my straps. "You need to lay low," he whispers. "Crysta is bad news, Rain. He *was* dangerous; now he's damn *explosive*." His fingers brush my neck, sending sparks all the way to the backs of my legs.

"Please," his voice drops to its lowest yet, "don't give him a reason to hurt you."

I pace the glass floor all day, very aware that somewhere in this bizarre casino, Johnny's gambling with the lives of three girls. He's drinking himself into oblivion. But most importantly, unless he returns, he's ruined our plans to save the Touched.

Outside the glass room, the suns set into a citrus rush, and the sky turns to violet velvet.

If he doesn't come back, I can't drug him, and if I can't drug him, Ben and I can't sneak away. I squeeze the tin of drug strips in my pocket. If Ben could do it all without me, we'd be set, but he needs two people—one to fly the hover cab and one to release the Touched from the cargo crates.

Damn!

I sit on the silky white sheets of the enormous bed only to stand up again and pace to the other side of the room. Does Ben even know that Johnny hasn't returned? I finger the silver lamp on the bedside table, and it springs on at my touch, glowing with an eerie green light.

I return to the bed and sit down just as the door opens.

Johnny enters with a lurch and stumbles. I rush to his side and catch him before he falls. He tugs at his collar like it's choking him and screams at two bouncers in the hall. "Fuck off now! I'm outta your precious way!"

Crysta stands a little further back in the hall, and her eyes lock with mine in a way that threatens and smiles all at once. Johnny tries to swing around in my arms to face the door, but one of the men slams it in his face.

He tumbles back into me, pressing me against the glass wall and groping blindly. His lips fall over mine until I can't breathe. I manage to turn my face away, and he moans, "Crys. Baby doll."

I lead Johnny to a lounge couch and press him into the seat. I pour a drink from the bar and slip one of the drug strips into it, watching it dissolve before I take it to him. "Here."

Ben could be here any minute. What if Johnny realizes that he didn't call for him? Is he too drunk to suspect something?

"You don't want it?" I shake the glass in his face.

His eyebrows bend over his gaze like black clouds, but he doesn't answer. I set the glass down beside the lamp and sit on the footrest before him. I pull his shoes off, letting them *thunk* to the floor. Then I rub his calves. A kiss worked last time; maybe it'll work again. I move to his thighs. Nothing. I finger his belt, but still he doesn't engage. I tug my dress over my head and start to unbutton his shirt.

One of his hands closes over both of my wrists. "She owns half the damned casino. Rigged it," he says. "Took every last credit from me."

I try to twist out of his hand, but his fingers constrict, and his expression strips me. I should be careful, but I feel damn careless. "Maybe she wants revenge for the life you pushed her into."

"She wants to play with me like I played with her." His head tilts back so that he's staring up into the hidden security cameras. "I offered a way outta that life, but she wouldn't take it. Damaged goods!" he yells upward.

When his face turns back to me, his eyes have blackened. "Why aren't you as pretty as her?" He yanks me closer and pulls at my hair. "You are . . . exotic . . . but not a goddess. She's a goddess, especially now. Did you see her?"

"I did," I say through clenched teeth. He's squeezing my wrists so hard that my fingers are growing stiff.

"She was different before. Less confident. Liable to cry. I used to make her weep." His tongue lingers on the point of his eyetooth. "Would you cry for me?"

I can't answer. My hands are numb except for a pain that shoots up my arms every time he twists his grip.

"You wouldn't, would you?" He yanks me onto his lap, wrestling my chest under his arm. I want to fight back. I could take him in this state—probably—but Ben's words sound through my head.

Don't give him a reason.

He reaches into his pocket with his free hand and pulls out a small silver lighter, the same kind of lighter that the Earth City factory workers receive after twenty years. He pops the lid, igniting a flame as long as a finger, and holds it a foot under my wrist.

"Sure you won't give me a cry?" he says into the side of my hair. "You sure?" He brings the flame closer and closer until its warmth turns into a biting pinch. I grind my teeth, concentrating on the glass wall, on the forest beyond. On the trees . . .

The burning switches to a screeching pain, and hot tears fill my eyes, but I won't make a sound.

"Better than nothing," he says, snapping the lighter shut. He fingers the wetness on my cheek. "You may not best her in looks, but maybe you're a better brand of girl for me." He tosses me onto the footrest. My arm sears with pain, and my wrist is bubbled. Swollen and *melted* in places. It swells until my fingers curl and stiffen.

Johnny has disfigured me.

"You bastard!"

He stands, glaring down with a chuckle. He's picked up the glass—finally—and holds it only inches from his lips. "Rain, Rain. Why do I have the feeling that we'll never get rid of each other?"

I want to kill him.

"To you and your unflagging stubbornness." He presses the glass to his lips, but a knock interrupts him. He sets the drink down and crosses to the door to face a very stunned Ben. "What is it? I didn't call for you."

Panic and anger rear up in my body. I grab the silver lamp with my good hand and charge, smashing it against the back of his head.

Johnny crumples to the floor.

"Rain!" Ben gasps. He hurries to shut the door behind him, but I've already fallen to the floor, holding out my burnt wrist. The pain is all over me, hot and tingly like I showered in it.

Ben kneels. "*Hell*," he breathes, taking my claw-like hand and turning it over so that he can see the full extent of the burn.

He pats his pockets but comes up empty; Johnny still has all of his gadgets.

"Hold tight," he says, darting around the room. He rips part of the bed sheet and doses it with liquor from the bar. Then he wraps it around my wrist, and I shake as the alcohol soothes and stings as it begins to numb the burn. Ben pulls me into a hug, holding me tightly while my breath levels. "What happened? What did you do to provoke him?"

"*Do?* Are you kidding? I was simply here. Then I was not as beautiful as Crysta or as weak as her. I didn't *do* anything!" My irritation gives me a degree of stability that hugging Ben couldn't match. I get to my feet, checking the ceiling. "What about the cameras?"

He laughs and stands. "You think of that now? After you've ruined hotel property and knocked out your pimp?" He nudges the dented lamp with his foot. "Don't worry. It was a pathetically simple system to hack. The only thing they're going to see on this room's feed is that it's empty."

I cast a look at Johnny's crumpled body and wipe away residual tears. "All right. Let's go. Let's do this." He doesn't move, and I have the sudden urge to hit *him* with the lamp. "Well?" I step toward the door. "You ready?"

"I think we're going to attract enough attention between your hair and my race, but . . ."

"But what?"

"Walking through the casino half-naked might cross the line."

I glance down at my underwear. "Shit!" I dart after my clothes, and Ben stifles a laugh as he hauls Johnny over to the bed and tosses his body onto the mattress. I yank my dress over my head and tie my hair back into a braid.

"Now you look ready," he says.

I feel the hint of a smile that I won't give him. "Not a word about that ever again. All right?" I touch my bandaged wrist, wincing a little.

"All right." His own grin fades. "Rain, if you want to change your mind, I understand. This is damn near suicidal. I've rigged the cargo holds' security, but if he actually checks them in person . . . or if he has other ways that we don't know about . . ."

"A thousand souls, Ben." I pause. "A *thousand*."

CHAPTER
21

The sky has turned from velvet to coal outside the transparent walls of the casino. We push through the stream of people, getting separated more than once. I was used to directional crowds during the factory shift processions on Earth City, but this swirling hoard is much different. Here, people change directions after only a few steps. They pause unexpectedly, causing me to run into them and other people to run into me. I'm frustrated before we're even beyond sight of the Silving Suns Hotel.

When a large group of men comes straight at us, Ben reaches back for my hand at the same moment that I reach forward for his. Our fingers weave and lock together, and I swear my heart thuds doubly because of it.

We take stairs to the rooftop parking instead of the fancy rising pedestal that brought us into the casino. I welcome the familiarity of handrails and concrete steps, but I must be gripping Ben a little too firmly because he pauses at the door to the roof and looks at our entwined hands.

"It's a weird place, isn't it?" he says as though he feels as awkward on this strange planet as I do. "Many of the spaceports along the Void are crowded and crazy like this. Everyone is for hire here for one thing or another."

"Is this what the Edge is like?"

He smiles. "The Edge is very different. Probably unlike anything you've ever imagined." We release each other's hands slowly. "There are some places there that I would love to take you. Like the rockfalls out beyond the blue lakes. Or the underground steel market. Or the crystal caves on the far side of the moon."

"Moon caves?" Now I'm smiling. "Sounds unbelievable."

"It'll blow your mind," he says. I have to look away from the very affectionate tone of his voice and the sudden desire to leave everything and go with Ben to the Edge. Just the two of us. No Walker or Touched. No Johnny.

Could we do it alone? I bet we could.

The back of the exit door is hammered out of a crude metal, and the small window frame bears a familiar stamp: MADE ON EARTH.

"Samson was right." I point it out to Ben. "He said I'd be impressed to find Earth City stuff at the other end of the universe. I didn't believe him, but"—I say while running my fingers over the letters,—"it's pretty great, isn't it?"

"Sure, it is." His tone is still too low and intimate, and then the stairwell becomes too quiet. "Are you ready?" he asks.

"I'm always ready," I say and lead us out. Tiny stars penetrate the black sky alongside dual silvery moons. We make our way through the maze of vehicles on the rooftop parking lot until we find ours.

I slide into the driver's seat beside Ben, and he grips the

steering post. "You do know how to pilot this thing, right?"

"Of course." He clears his throat. "I could have done it when I was a kid, but . . ."

"But?"

"I'm having doubts."

"No doubting this, Ben. All those people need us."

"Yes, but . . ."

I wait for him to continue, but he doesn't, and I'm annoyed that he could think about going back when we've come this far. "Don't freeze up on me now. Not after what I had to do. You just had to play with the network; I went back to *his bed* for this chance. Think about that for a second!" I settle down. "Actually don't think about it. I don't know why I said that."

"I like you, Rain," he deadpans. I bark a laugh, and he darts a look at me. "I mean it. I thought that maybe if I say it, I can think about something else. I should be terrified about what we're going to do. I should have my mind on the plan, but I can't stop imagining what he'll do to you if he catches us."

"You're not thinking about me. You're thinking about Bron," I say. "It's just remorse. Believe me, I'm guilt incarnate. You don't want to feel guilty about causing my death like you do about hers."

"Nevermind." He circles the engines to life, and the vibrations hum up my legs. "I shouldn't have brought it up," he adds under his breath and pulls the hover cab into a steep ascending spiral that flattens me against the seatback.

I grasp the straps. "Damn, Ben. Samson doesn't drive like this."

"Samson isn't under a time crunch. We've only got until sunrise before what we're doing becomes obvious to any sky traffic." He shuts off the headlights as we zoom higher over the planet.

"Whoa. I can't see a thing!"

"And that's why you're not driving." The blue engine lights make their way up through the cracks of the cab, lighting Ben's stern face.

"So you like me?"

"You want to talk about this now?"

"You brought it up." I twist in my seat to face him. "I like you, too. At least, I don't dislike you the way I used to."

He cracks a grin. "That's progress."

"Plus you don't really make me feel like a girl, so that's good."

"Great," he says, giving the word an extra syllable. I had said *girl* instead of *prostitute*. He should follow that, right? I watch him, teetering on the edge of giving away too much. Ben says he likes me, but as a friend or as something more? His words dangle either way . . . and I am Johnny's girl. Is there a chance that he thinks and rethinks our moments like I do?

Suddenly, I can't think of anything other than the fact that he can see my body temperature flare through the darkness.

"It's not fair," I say, and he looks back at the controls. "No one should be able to see in the dark. That's where people need to be able to keep their secrets. Maybe that explains why people don't trust Mecs."

"I could watch you all night without figuring you out. Believe me, your secrets are well hidden." He adjusts his grip on the steering column and clears his throat. "We're coming up on *Imreas*." I peer into the night, making out a black spot in the sky that's blocking all the stars. It looms larger and larger until the dark mass becomes a wall of silver metal.

Ben inserts a few commands on the control board. "I've got the catch out. I just need to hit the sweet spot." He brings the hover cab up to the side of the massive starship where I can see the handles of the two cargo crates fitted like drawers into the outer hull.

"That's how he gets them onboard without anyone realizing it, isn't it?" I say. "The cops put them in those crates. And Johnny takes the crates away. No witnesses except a handful of trusted crew members."

"They were designed for food shipments. You pull them out, fill them on planet, and then hoist them back into the side of the ship. Easy. Except, of course, that Johnny's never used them for supplies." The hover cab shifts as the catch clicks into a large loop on the side of the first crate. "But then that works to our benefit; so few people know what Johnny really does with those crates that no one will ask why we're unloading them. They'll just think it's a supply run."

Ben steers us clear of *Imreas*, and a banging sound shakes through the vehicle. "That's just the chain letting out," he says. Something *clangs* like a great lock, and Ben brings the hover cab further away. I squint, seeing one huge crate separate from *Imreas's* side, swinging free in the limited gravity but connected to us by a thick cable.

Ben breathes a huge sigh and pilots us back toward Entra's surface. "Now it's your turn. There's a harness and a drop line by the back door."

I shimmy over the driver's seat and into the passenger section of the hover cab. "A harness?" I pick up a unit of straps.

"Yeah, get it on over your waist. I can't set this cab down on the surface through the trees, so you'll have to rappel down, get the door open, and lead them out."

I find leg holes in the harness and secure the clasp over my hips, then I follow the connecting line to where it hooks to the ceiling. By the time I look out the window again, Ben has us over the forest on the far side of the planet.

Here the moons are large and looming.

A crash sounds as the crate lands on the ground below, and the hover cab comes to a jerky halt just over the tree line. I fling open the door and look down. I'm a hundred feet from the ground, nothing below but the huge crate resting between the trees on the forest floor.

"You've got to be kidding!" I scream at Ben.

"This is as close as I can get!" he yells back. "Go now!"

I get my hand around the release and move to the edge. My heart slams in my throat. The hover cab sways in the wind, and I look down at the longest drop I've ever faced, let alone considered jumping from.

"Go!" Ben calls.

I step out.

And that's all it really takes to fall.

I swing to a stop in the harness only feet from the top of the crate. From there I have to let the line out by hand, zipping down to the ground a few feet at a time. As soon as my feet touch the soil, I circle around to the crate's doors, turn the wheel lock and pull the gates open.

Hundreds of faces peer through the crate. Their eyes blink glassily, and the stench of their captivity fills the cool night air.

"You're free." My mouth is dry, and my voice cracks. I point toward the woods. "Go!"

But none of them move.

I grab the nearest man and tug him out of the crate. He turns in a full circle but won't keep walking. I grab another and another, but they linger, bumping into each other.

"Go! Go!" I scream, pulling at arms and shoulders to get more of them out, but they stiffen in clustered groups, blocking the exit. A few hold on to each other the way Walker always held on to me. They're afraid. How can people say the Touched are brain dead when they clearly feel fear and pain? When they cry when they're hungry or flee when there's danger—

That's it!

There were words that I used to help Walker through his fogs. *Food* was one. No matter how lost he became in the quicksand of his mind, if I said "food" he would open his mouth.

And the other one was instinctual as well, the word I used to trigger his flight response.

"RUN!"

I'm beaten back by the stampede, gripping the hover cab line to keep them from knocking me over as they flee and scatter on old bones and starved limbs. They must know. Somewhere beneath all those blanked surfaces, they can smell the clean air and the soil underfoot.

When the last one has disappeared through the shadowy

trees, I close the crate doors, seal the lock, and press the button that returns me to the hover cab. The wind kicks my hair from my face while I soar toward the blue glow, and I feel my dad. My missing family. I feel their pride through me like a blaze of fiery light.

Once inside, I shut the door.

"Well," Ben says. "Are they gone?"

"They're free."

I collapse across the backseat as we surge up in a spiral toward the night sky and the black shadow of *Imreas* for the second crate. This time, I'm brimming with joy when I leap from the hover cab and fling open the doors. I imagine my mom and Jeremy sprinting into the woods, and am filled with the hope that saving these people is like helping them.

The cops on Earth City tried to make the Touched disappear, but all they did was sever our society into pieces too small to function. Too small to thrive.

Toward the end of the second group, the two small blonde girls, still holding hands, streak into the dark like links in a chain that can't be broken.

———⁓⁓⁓⁓⁓———

Ben and I return the empty crate to its spot on *Imreas*'s side and head back to Entra. I slip the harness off and climb over the front seat to join him. "Johnny won't even know that they're gone until it's too late to come back for them."

"That's the hope." He takes a deep breath. "Now we just have to go back and pretend like nothing's changed so he doesn't suspect anything. We were fast," he adds. "Still two hours until dawn."

"Do we have to go back?" I ask.

"You know we do."

"My brother," I say, answering my own question.

"Not to mention the fact that if we don't return and act normal, Johnny will suspect something. Our entire plan rests on the idea that he doesn't bother to check those crates in person."

"Yeah, yeah. I get it." I glance out the window at the shadowy rush of the tree line.

He clicks his com against my red bracelet. "Plus, running away is a death wish. All he has to do is press a button and we're zapped. Remember?"

"Yeah, yeah," I say again. I had almost forgotten that Johnny could electrocute us through our tags. "But it's not dawn yet. And he's still out. We don't have to rush back."

"You're right. We don't." He steers the cab out over the forest, bringing us down with a jarring thump on the only spot wide enough for the vehicle to land—a cliff face overlooking a wide, glistening lake.

We get out in silence. The light is different here. Brighter. Ben's silhouette is lit against a navy sky, and the white moons shine within an aura of clouds.

"What can you see?" I ask.

"It's deep water," he says. "A submerged canyon."

"This planet is so empty of people and yet full of life."

Ben rubs his arms and nods. "It would make an amazing relocation place for Earth Cityites. There used to be talks about it on the Edge, but that was before they started to become entangled with Mec culture. Apart from the K-Force, my people don't care much for the rest of humanity, Rain. It's embarrassing. Heartbreaking, really."

"But you said that they never really leave the Edge. So maybe they don't know about Earth City. About the Touched or the slaving in the Void."

"They know enough to ignore it," he says sadly.

I step to the edge of the canyon, peering over the side. The water is black, but the reflecting moons highlight a slight ripple on the surface. I sit on the ledge, my feet dangling over the drop.

Ben shuffles down next to me. "I can't really believe that we did it. You?"

"I believe it." Out over the water, small bats swoop, diving toward the surface only to swing up like a dance. "When Walker was little, he would run through alleys with his arms out, singing high notes that echoed off the bricks. Dad called him the Night Bird like it was his superhero name."

"You make me wish that I wasn't an only child." Ben scoots over until our legs touch. I turn to face him, finding him so very close. "What do you want to do now?"

"Enjoy what time we have left." I sigh. "At some point, he'll figure out that we're the ones who stole his cargo." And then he'll kill us. Walker, too.

"We'll find a way to get away from him before then."

"Let's hope." I throw a stone. It drops for long, long seconds before echoing a minute splash. Jumping from the hover cab was terrifying, and yet it filled me with a sense of crazy freedom that

I've never felt before. I throw another rock and touch the bracelet on my wrist. Even at this distance from Johnny, the scarlet glow is strong.

The second rock splashes, and suddenly I would give anything to be that stone, dropping through an unknown freefall. No harness this time and nothing but the air to comfort me. No memory of gripping fingers and stripping men. No Johnny.

Maybe that falling girl wasn't so far off after all. I touch the bandage on my burnt wrist.

"Does it hurt?"

"No. Is that strange?"

"Nerve damage," he says. "It's not a good sign. I wish there was something I could do." I run my fingers over the linen, wondering if being Touched feels like a kind of whole body numb like this burn. Or like slipping into that voided mental place I frequent when I touch the other men. When I let them touch me.

"Johnny will be awake in a few hours. We'll have to come up with an excuse for why he has a concussion. We could tell him that he passed out."

I get to my feet, my toes over the edge.

"Rain, what are you doing?"

"I don't want to talk about Johnny." Or remember the heat of his skin and lips and constant taking. I pull my dress over my head, toss it away, and leap out over the cliff face.

The air whirls as I drop through the night, crashing into the silver-lined black surface. My skin stings from my heels to my hips, but my body is mine in the weightless plunge. I sink into the cool of deep water, only clawing upward when my lungs begin to spasm.

I emerge to the biggest breath of my life. A newborn breath. It stretches to the soles of my feet, and I splay every finger and toe. I shake the water out of my ears and hear the echo of Ben's shout.

RAIN!

Rain

rain

"I'm here," I call back. A dark body hurtles over the cliff's edge, and Ben comes falling after me, dropping past the shine of the moons until he explodes against the surface.

I laugh and swim to where he thrashes.

"You scared the hell out of me!" he yells, spitting water. I crawl closer and closer to him, unable to stop. I wrap my arms around his neck and kiss his wet lips.

He goes still for a heartbeat.

But then his arms seal around my waist, and his mouth is alive against mine. Waves of warmth roll through me like when I kiss Johnny, but there's more—an added jolt of surprising joy. My tongue finds the edge of his, and his breath rushes into mine. And all the while, our feet churn the water to keep us above the surface.

To keep the moment.

We kiss until we're both gasping. I press my face to his cheek, his hair dripping on my nose, and though I don't feel at all like crying, my eyes leak.

"Unbelievable," he murmurs, and I can't help but agree.

22

We kick to a sandy shore beneath the sheer rock face. I swim through a mass of old leaves before my feet touch down, stepping out covered in bits of foliage. As I pick the leaves away, I'm more aware of my knees, hips, and breasts than I've ever been in my life.

Ben yanks his wet shirt over his head, and the moons' light shades his chest with a gray color as pale as death. The same color as Walker in his cold prison.

I have to look away. The rush of the water and the kissing was one thing, but this is land now. Land means Johnny and the girl trade and my frozen little brother.

He wrings his shirt and swings it over his shoulder. "You've got leaves in your hair." He reaches for me, and I back into the rock face. His hand drops. "What's wrong?"

I breathe in—and then out too fast. His naked chest and half-open mouth sting even as I close my eyes against them. He's my Ben, not some sleazy passenger with grubby fingers and a hairy smell. But when I open my eyes, my heart is throbbing . . . and no longer in that good way.

He steps closer, and I back up again, scraping my shoulder on the rock.

"I need a little distance," I say.

He laughs. "After all that?" He points at the water. "After what we just did? You're shy now?"

I move away from him, feeling the lightning in my nerves. My panic rising. "Just listen to me, okay?"

The moons slip behind a cloud, and Ben is shadow. "Okay. I'm listening."

I rub at the shivers on my bare stomach and arms. I want to tell him about the other men. About the nights and the deals and the horrible things that I've done. But I can't.

"We shouldn't get caught up in this."

"You mean us?" he says in a tone that makes my shivers worse.

"Remember Bron?" I can't see him wince, but I bet he does. "The closer we are to each other, the harder it will be to hide it from Johnny."

"Hell, Rain! You really should have thought of that before you jumped me." He wrings his shirt over and over until he's in danger of ripping it to pieces. "I wasn't being guilt stricken earlier. I really do like you, and I think about you all the time. Are you trying to torture me?"

Heat flares up through my cheeks, and I don't care if he can see it. He shouldn't be this thick. He should know what I am and what I've been through.

"Sorry, Ben"—I say, resisting the urge to knock him back into the water—"but I'm not going to sleep with you just because I kissed you."

He drops his shirt to the sand. "Are you serious?"

I look out across the lake. The moons have dipped low, and in the distance, the navy sky melts to a lighter blue.

"You think that I want to . . . that I'm trying to . . ." His words sputter out. "I have real feelings for you. But if you can't tell the difference between me and Johnny, you are damaged."

His words dump icy water all over me.

We're quiet for a moment, and I watch the whirl of red that's starting to streak out of the blue dawn. "We have to go."

"Rain." He reaches for me, and I push past his fingers.

I scale the pockmarked surface of the rock face. At the top, I wring my hair out and find my dress. Ben follows right behind me, and I don't care if he's watching me dress. He's seen it before. So many have, and they're all the same.

He stands at the hover cab, his damp shirt clinging to his chest. "I didn't mean that," he says. "I don't think you're . . . damaged. You're different from the other girls. Better."

"What's so different, Ben? Men give me money and I take my clothes off. Just like the other girls. Unless it's Johnny, in which case I'm apparently free."

"Hell, Rain."

"Doesn't matter," I manage, getting into the vehicle. When the door shuts us in together, I feel like screaming, but I swallow my voice.

"You liar. How can you pretend this doesn't matter?" he asks. "If anything matters, it's this. At the very least, we should be able to be honest with each other."

"Yes, but don't forget." I stare out the window. "I belong to someone else."

We return to the Entra Suns Casino in an ugly silence. Tonight we saved the lives of almost a thousand people, and yet we can't look at each other. We take the dropping platform back into the corridor of the large glass-floored building, and I'm thankful for the stream of people moving through to the restaurants and bars, and the wash of colored, gaudy lights.

We weave and bob through the crowd, getting pushed apart from each other. This time we don't reach out. This time, my hands are buried in my crossed arms and his are in his pockets.

"I can find my own way to the hotel from here," I say.

"We stick to the plan," he responds coldly.

The Silving Suns Hotel is much more deserted, but I walk faster and faster, feeling the tug of Ben's presence at my shoulder.

"Remember, he'll be disoriented. Just say that he fell while drunk, and you took care of him. I've fixed the feed on *Imreas*, so if he checks the control board, he won't realize they're gone. We have to lull him into a sense that nothing has changed so that he doesn't check the cargo in person." I keep walking, and he catches my arm a stone's throw from the end of the hallway.

I tug my arm free. "I can do this."

His expression pulls on me. The anger that had boiled up in him by the water has evaporated. "I'm sorry."

"So am I." I almost choke on the words. "But that can't change this."

He nods a terrible nod and leaves. I wish I knew why I love being near him one moment, and then the next I can't stomach the pressure between us. I wish I could tell him that my mind and body are at war . . . that he is 100 percent correct. I am damaged.

I push forward, and when I get to the end of the hall, the door opens.

But I freeze in the frame.

Johnny is propped up on pillows against the headboard. His head is tilted back, eyes closed. A woman with hair like a golden waterfall sits beside him, running fingers over his chest.

Crysta's smile is menacing. "Johnny, your red girl is back."

He lifts his head, his stare groggy and yet somehow full of fire.

—— ·····/\/\/\/\/\····· ——

I'm not breathing.

I have to breathe.

Dawn breaks over the forest line and pours orange-red light into the glass-walled suite. I squint from the brightness as Johnny tries to stand on unsure legs.

"Sit, my love. You're still out of it." Crysta touches the spot at the back of Johnny's head where I blasted him with the lamp, and he winces. The door shuts behind me, pushing me further into the room.

"Where were you?" Johnny asks, leaning back against the bed. "Fucking someone?"

"I was taking a walk. I wanted to see the casino."

Crysta stands, her hair falling over her shoulders in silky waves. "She's a bad liar." She picks up a tablet from the couch. Her nails click on the glass screen until she's found what she wants. "There was a hiccup in our security, but we have a backup system."

"A *hiccup*?" Johnny sits up too fast and has to grip the edge of the mattress.

"No doubt installed by your Mec in pursuit of your girl." She touches the tablet, turning the view screen in her hands into a life-sized holographic image before me.

And the image stings.

Ben is kneeling on the floor beside Johnny's body, pressing my wrist between his palms. Then he holds me—an almost naked me—stroking my hair so tenderly that something flares in my chest at the sight of it.

"This is moments after she knocked you out," Crysta says. It's only a few seconds, but the clip loops over and over, and even the angle is incriminating. The camera must have been outside the hotel, recording through the window like a secret stalker.

Crysta smirks. "If you were smart, little girl, you'd realize that a glass-walled room is no place to throw stones or a lamp. Or choose a lover."

Now Johnny really gets to his feet. His neck is stained with a brilliant red as he watches the repeating embrace. He fingers his com, and I know that he's calling Ben.

"Don't bother summoning him," Crysta interrupts. "My men already have him." She clicks something on the tablet, and within heartbeats, the door bursts open. The two bouncers who threw Johnny earlier now muscle Ben into the room.

He gets the better of one of the men, stringing the man's arm up behind his back, but the other bouncer pulls a blade and holds it to Ben's cheek until he releases. The men get a secure grip on Ben as his gaze turns to the holographic image of our embrace.

He stops struggling.

"Shall I have him beaten? To think that your own servant

would bed your girl. You might be losing your touch, John."

Johnny snarls loud enough to shut her up. "I don't need help with my servants." He crosses the room to Ben. "You were so much easier to deal with when you were a skinny nothing, no more than the weight of one of my legs."

Ben? Skinny? I examine the way they stare each other down in a new light, full of familiar dislike and competition. Jealousy. Not unlike the hatred between two warring brothers.

"All those push-ups," Johnny sneers and touches something on his com.

The bouncers drop Ben—throw him. But no, that's not right. I choke on a scream. They jump away because Ben's rioting from the shock now surging from the silver band on his wrist. His body beats the floor, vibrating so hard that his teeth clack.

Johnny lets up on his com, and Ben's gasping fills the room. He leans over him and kicks at his forearms. "All those push-ups for nothing." Johnny looks to Crysta. "He may be a Mec, but he doesn't have the balls to go after one of my girls. Not again. This is *her* doing."

"No." Ben gasps. "I wanted her. I went after her."

Johnny looks my way, but I have nothing. Why in the world would Ben egg Johnny on about this? He'll go crazy with jealousy! He'll—wait.

He'll be blind to our other plans, and the Touched will have a chance.

"Johnny," I start, but he swings at me, backhanding my face so that I lose my balance and wind up on all fours, my palms and knees spiked with pain.

Johnny hunkers beside Ben. "And to think, I wasted a perfectly good girl Mec trying to teach you a lesson." He leans even closer. "You know I had to kick Bron's teeth out before she'd admit to being involved with you. You must not have left a good impression. But I suppose it was worth it. You should have seen her gummy expression when I hit the airlock release."

Ben surges to attack him, and Johnny sends another shockwave through him. Ben's back arches and he yells, clawing at the glass floor.

Somehow I'm both screaming my heart out and not making a sound.

"Pipe down," Johnny says almost playfully when the torture has ceased. He digs into his pocket and pulls out the dose rod he took from Ben. He flips the setting to adrenaline red and gives himself a shot.

"Didn't he make you into a prostitute?" I hiss at Crysta standing over me. "How could you help him now? Didn't he hurt you?"

She leans down, her golden hair falling past my face. "Girl, what part of this *isn't* hurting him?"

Johnny gives himself a second shot, and he yells as it courses through him. His shoulders straighten, and he grows stronger and crazier before my eyes.

"Look at this, Johnny." Crysta plucks a leaf from my hair. "They must have been down in the forest. Remember when you used to take me to the woods and lay with me in the leaves?"

Johnny's face is briefly frozen. He looks at Crysta without the aggressive possession that I'm so used to—like he's lost in her presence. And just for a second, I catch something like regret and sorrow in Crysta's perfect face. They might both be stuck on the same memory.

But Crysta breaks first.

"Enjoy your little mutiny, John. I have business." She presses the leaf into Johnny's palm. "I'll see you next time your daddy sends you back through." Her golden hair twirls as she pivots and leaves, the bouncers slamming the door in her wake.

Johnny stares at the leaf before he crumples it in his fist. Rage returns to his bared teeth, and he surges toward me so fast that I fall backward long before he kicks me.

And still, he kicks me.

My stomach. My ribs. My chest. I curl into a ball that does nothing to stem the thundering pain of being stomped. Johnny's foot comes to a stop on the side of my head, pressing my cheek into the glass floor. Ben's eyes meet mine across the distance where he sobs to breathe. He mouths something that I can't understand.

"Know that this is only our warm-up," Johnny growls, pressing even harder on my head.

And even harder . . .

Pressure sears from my eye to my neck in the second before my jaw *snaps*.

CHAPTER
23

I'm wrapped in a blanket of stiffness and suffocating pain. I pant through my nose, unable to open my mouth. And still, I try, but only manage to wail through my teeth.

"Stay asleep." Ben's voice hovers over my ear. "You don't want to wake up to this."

He shouldn't be this close. I open my eyes. My head rests on Ben's lap. He combs my hair from my face over and over as though he's afraid to stop. "You never listen."

I try to sit up, but the lead blanket that I thought I was wrapped in is really my body. I'm dead weight. And I can't open my mouth to talk.

"He won't let me heal you," Ben says. "And he locked us in here together as punishment. He wants me to watch you suffer. How creative of him." His voice breaks. "He broke three of your ribs. And your jaw. Your only luck was that your lungs weren't punctured."

Lovely.

His fingers stroke my hair a little faster. I manage to push his hand away and lift my shoulders and then my head. I look around at crates and boxes. *Where are we?*

"We're back on *Imreas*," he answers as though he can hear my thoughts. "We're in the cargo den where I first brought you." I slowly recognize the high ceiling—as well as the line of harnesses on the wall. "I don't know if he realizes what we did," he whispers. Ben slips his arms around me and lifts me against his chest. I cry out my pain through my clenched teeth, huffing horrible, animalistic breaths.

I feel his face in my hair and something like a nuzzle. Groaning a warning, I point up at the ceiling. *Remember that we're being watched, Ben?*

But his lips press on my neck until I feel the air of each of his words. "He thinks we're lovers. We could act like strangers now, and he wouldn't buy it."

What is happening?

"We're back in the Void already," he says, apparently still reading my thoughts. "You're lucky you were out through takeoff. I had a hell of a time keeping your bones from popping through your skin."

I groan something that sounds a little like *Thanks.*

He opens his hand palm up on my knee. "Look, I don't know how much longer we have, but you have to know that I'm not after you like the other men. I'm not trying to possess you. Or buy you. You should know that."

I know.

I lift my hand with enormous effort and squeeze his. He tries to interlock our fingers, but I seal mine into a fist and knock his palm a few times.

"You trying to tell me 'thanks but no thanks' again?" he asks.

I pound his hand a little harder, but even I don't know if I mean yes or no.

"I know this is complicated." He sighs and holds me a little tighter. "I wouldn't push you, you know. Just don't forget that you kissed me first. Twice now."

Hours pass in silence. A few times, I break into tears and moan because the pain in my jaw spikes or something in my chest sears with pressure. Each time, Ben's hold grows tighter like he's determined to keep my shattered body together with his own.

If only he knew the real feelings that swing around in my mind. The way I dream about his twisted hair and steel blue eyes before the demon fingers find me . . . the way I don't mind the nightmares so much when they come with pieces of him.

But then, how can it matter? None of that will help us now.

We don't know if it's night or day as the lights never change in the cargo den, but at least a day after I first woke, Ben stands and positions me against a crate. He paces the open floor, pressing his com, which seems to have been turned off.

"It's been too long," he says. "I don't know what in hell is going on, but something is amiss. He should have killed one or both of us by now. He should be torturing us. He's planning something."

I make a grunting noise to shut him up. He may not care if we're under surveillance, but I know Johnny, and he's somewhere watching us with a magnifying glass. I guarantee it. But Ben is right; Johnny is planning something.

He comes for us within the hour.

"Get her up," he says from the doorway. His shirt is half-unbuttoned. "Rain and I need to have a little chat."

Ben helps me to my feet, and I feel at least two ribs try to bust through my side. "Let me carry her," he says. "She can't walk."

Johnny holds a hand up to stop Ben. "She'll walk. Do you know nothing of the girl who plays with you? She could walk from here to Earth City if she set her mind on it." Johnny beams at me with a strange pride, and I push Ben's arms away, standing on my own. After all, he's right about me; I manage a step and another. I keep my arms woven around my chest, which helps with my torso, but does nothing for the spearing ache in my jaw.

As I make it through the door, Johnny slaps an arm around my shoulder so hard that I scream through clenched teeth. He ignores it, hustling me away and slamming the door behind us. The great lock clangs behind me, sealing Ben in.

~~~~~~~~~~

On the command deck, Johnny sits me in his captain's chair. He kneels, and I breathe through my locked teeth while his eyes search my face.

He flips open his knife and slices the shoulders of my dress, tugging the material down to reveal his handiwork—a patchwork of purple bruises across my chest that highlight my broken bones like halos.

He takes Ben's med disc out of his pocket and holds the warm blue light over one of my sides. He's going to heal me? Why? So he can hurt me all over again?

I feel my bones heating and maybe melting back together. A pop sounds when the rib has stolen back into its place, and he heals the others while he talks.

239

"You haven't disappointed me, Rain. I've spent days trying to be angry enough to deal with you, but it just keeps slipping through my fingers. The truth is that this little chase you've sent me on has been more exciting than anything I've encountered in many runs. So, it would be foolish of me to kill you when you might just be giving me exactly what I need."

Pop.

"I wanted to start out with a compliment since you have put so much work into duping me and that Mec. Poor Ben. He has no idea that you used him, does he?"

Used him for what?

"To think that you let him hope that you liked him . . . that's cold. But I want you to know that I'm not going to kill him over this. Mecs are too hard to replace." He smirks. I don't believe him. Johnny's ruffled hair and lighter eyes can't quite make up for the snap that seems to be arching in his words. He could still kill Ben and me. He's waiting for something.

Pop.

"You know you made me hurt you. I didn't want to, but you were so persistent, you and that damn Mec." He chuckles. "But even there, wasn't it a bit fun? The way he flopped around when the shock went through him! I've always wanted to try that."

I take a few deep breaths through my set teeth as he holds the med disc up to my jaw.

"I'm tempted not to heal your face. You're so much more manageable without all that lip." His look is aching. "Still, I'm dying to hear how you did it."

He runs the warm light over my jaw until it jolts back into

place with a painful click. I let out a yell, startled at how loud it is now that my mouth swings open on its usual hinge. He moves away, and I fall from the chair.

"How I did what?"

Johnny hunkers down to my level, his eyes glinting with the next bit of malice that he can't wait to release. "Stole from me."

My pulse whips through my body. "Stole what?"

He waves his hand and slouches in the captain's chair. "I'm not there yet. I want to show you something first." He presses his com, and within a minute, a young crew member enters. His hair is ratty, and his scraggly moustache makes him look even younger.

"Captain?" he asks. I can tell how hard he's trying not to look at where I sit on the floor by Johnny's feet, still working my jaw to remove the stiffness and only wearing half a dress.

"Take out your tracker," Johnny says.

"Out, sir?" His face has paled.

"Out." Johnny holds out his knife.

The crew member looks from me to the knife to Johnny before he takes it. He folds back the sleeve of his flight suit and presses the blade over the back of his wrist. He takes a few ragged breaths before digging the knife into his flesh.

I look to the floor, which proves to be a mistake when drops of his blood splash down only inches from my knee.

Johnny holds out his hand, and the now ash-faced crew member drops a tiny piece of metal in it. Johnny leans toward me. "These trackers are much cheaper than the bracelets we use for the girls' safety. For example, they don't give off a lethal shock if forcibly removed like yours would or Ben's. But they are highly effective at keeping the bulk of my crew in line. Still, some might call me paranoid for using them wide-scale. A thousand of these, for example, is a serious investment."

A thousand. Sweat slips icily down the back of my neck.

"But how handy these little babies are when things go missing." Johnny drops the tiny piece of metal back into the crew member's hand. "Go to medical and have it replaced."

The young man leaves in a hurry, a trickle of blood in his wake.

I get to my feet. "Johnny, what—"

"Quiet. I'm almost finished." His fingers dance over the control panel next to his chair, and I turn to face the huge command window. The screen is split between the two cargo holds, both jam-packed with the Touched.

I can't take in the squalid mass of them without feeling an urge to throw up. My body heaves, but having been without food and water for days, nothing but sour bile lines my mouth.

"Such a headache to round them all up down there, but I want you to know," he stands behind me and places his hands on my shoulders, "not a single one escaped."

All our work and gamble . . . all for nothing.

He chuckles as I begin to shake harder. "You know, some of them had even set up rudimentary shelters and collected food from the forest like they were actually going to have a life there."

"They did?" I breathe, turning to face him.

"*Wrong, Rain!* 'Who cares' is the right answer!" he yells. "They're wastes of space, and the only reason I deal in them is because my father wants them so damn bad. Now, I've taken great pains to have this ship locked down and most of the crew in the dark about this business, so before I find out how you found out about your pathetic brethren and how you managed to free them, we're going to play a little game."

He turns me around to face the screen. Half of it now shows an airlock. An airlock with dozens of Touched inside.

"Would you choose the lives of say, a hundred crazies, over the life of one?"

I grind my teeth. "If you mean to kill me, Johnny, just get it over with. Of course I won't let you kill a hundred people in my place."

His arm snakes around my chest, anchoring me in front of him, and his face lowers to my ear. "Oh, I wouldn't trade you for a hundred thousand of these. You're *much* too valuable. I meant that ice cube you call your brother."

The other half of the screen switches to show a second airlock. It's empty except for Walker's pod in the center . . . maybe in the very spot where Lo knelt in her last minutes. I can even see a hint of his small face through the narrow window.

"Johnny!" I try to spin around, but he keeps me where he wants me.

"Time to choose."

I can't breathe, and shudders wave through me from my neck to my ankles. Walker's airlock is as silent and still as death. The other hums with life. The Touched knock into each other, their moans soundless through the window of the command deck.

"Of course if you don't choose, I eject them both," Johnny adds. "You have one minute."

Hardly able to breathe, I squeeze my eyes and lower my head. I can't trade my brother for the lives of a hundred people! I can't. But if Walker doesn't make it, I'll be alone in this universe—and I'll have ruined myself for nothing. Every traded kiss. Every grope.

Every fuck.

I close my eyes. "This is evil, Johnny. You're trying to make me inhuman. Just like your father did to you. It's not fair what he did, but it doesn't have to be permanent. You could let them all go."

"Wrong." He grinds his teeth too close to my ear. "I'm not making you evil. I'm trying to make you invincible. You make the right choice here, and you will get what you want, Rain. I promise. That's what my father did to me. He taught me how to get what I want regardless of anyone or anything else. He taught me how to win the game."

I open my eyes. The right choice?

Of course! This *is* a game, and Johnny's rigged it. Only one choice will make him keep me around. The other must mean death, not just for me, but probably for those Touched and Walker as well. Maybe even Ben.

I'd bet he'd love to dump us all into the Void together.

So I just have to sort out what he wants me to choose. By Johnny's rule of *Nothing to lose, everything to gain*, I should guess that the right choice is to save the Touched, letting go of my brother would prove that I've moved on. But suddenly it doesn't seem so simple. After all, Johnny isn't simple. He's been hollowed by his choices. He's incredibly capable, yet haunted. And lonely.

After all, he came looking for me that day on the pier.

And what he really wants is for me to end up like him. That's what this whole game was about: finding someone who would run the Void and not bat an eyelash at his true nature and business.

Finding someone to love him as he is.

His ragged feelings for Crysta only prove that he's been aching for too long. I risk a glance at his smooth cheeks and lips. His eyes reveal their inner brown as his look searches me. Maybe this is simple. He's waiting for me to make the choice that he would make, the self-interest choice. *What I want.* Well, that's Walker. Johnny's known from day one that this has been about saving my brother at any cost, and now he wants to see how much further I can go.

"Twenty seconds." Johnny taps my shoulder to the rhythm of his count.

If I'm right, if I choose to save all those people, if I choose humanity, he will be done with me. I'll have proven that I'm not like him after all. And that means we all lose. I have no doubt that even Ben would suffer from Johnny's sick disappointment.

"Five."

A wail creeps up into my mouth—all those people!

"Two."

"Save Walker."

"Say *please.*"

"Please, Johnny. Save my brother."

He sighs happily and reaches across the control panel to tap something. "Don't forget to watch the fruits of your labor, Rain."

I tug out of his arms and step closer to the screen. Although I cannot hear the clanks of the airlock opening, I can feel it in my skull. I can see it in the terrified faces of the huddled mass in the airlock. Johnny doesn't have to tell me to watch. I wouldn't look away. I need to see what I've done.

The *clang* sounds through the crowd, reaching me only in the startled jerk of their bodies. Then the doors slide open . . . and they all go soaring, flying, tumbling one over another as they're sucked into the Void.

Johnny clears his throat and taps something. "I think there's a better view from the back window." The screen flashes to an image of space. Silver stars rushing by in the distance. The closer ones wink with brilliant light.

And even closer, the somersaulting procession of bodies in our wake.

"Now that's a hundred pieces of merchandise at over forty credits a head." Johnny's arms creep around my chest until I am the tree, and he is the choking vine. He tugs my dress so that it slips to the floor. "By my calculations, we have some seriously long nights to look forward to while you make this up to me." He's so happy, and I know why. He's finally made me into his image. Into a murderess, and a selfish, terrible being. He's won.

He squeezes me even tighter, but I can barely feel him. Two small bodies cartwheel end over end. The girls' matching blonde hair stands out like halos, and their arms stay entwined even in a frozen, horrible death. Two links in a chain, which couldn't be broken, but are lost all the same.

PART III
RED

CHAPTER
24

I lounge across Johnny's lap, my head on his shoulder. We're on the command deck, on his captain's chair, facing the very window where I truly became Johnny's Rain. I take in his musky cologne with each breath, and I have to admit that I've grown to like it.

The fact feels wrong but is true.

Johnny's fingers trick through my hair, down my side and over my hip. He'll take us to our room within the hour; his stroking is easy to predict. He's itching for my body, and in return, I'm warming up inside for him.

Two crew members stand before us. An older man wears a scrap of cloth over his eyes, and acid burns mar the skin on his forehead. The other one is younger, shifting from foot to foot.

"So, you would like to blind him because he had a part in blinding you?" Johnny asks. I can hear the smile in his voice. He hasn't had this much perverted fun since the moment he made me choose this life—the moment the Touched tumbled out of the air-lock and into oblivion.

"I couldn't have predicted that canister was going to up and explode!" the shifty one complains. "And I didn't know he was going to put his face over it at the exact moment that I lifted the lid free."

"It ain't fair that this idiot didn't look at the expiration date before ripping the lid off. Ain't fair that I've got to jump ship because I can't work no more," the blind man says.

"*Fair*?" Johnny rolls the word around in his mouth while he touches my throat. His fingers have a heat to them that I've long since grown attuned to, but still, I can't shut off his snaking touch like I did with the other men. I can't slip into that voided place of submission. Johnny has too much of me for that, and I don't even try.

When he reaches for me, I reach back.

Every time.

"And how would you like to blind him? Acid again? Or maybe a knife. Oh, I have an idea, we have some antique laser weaponry down in engineering." Johnny's fingers plug away at the com on his wrist. "I'll have Samson bring up his collection. We'll make it quite the show."

Now the blind man shifts. "I just want him to pay, Captain. I don't know about lasers, but if you could take his Void pay and give it to me or even demote him, that'd make me sleep easier."

The accused man looks like he's ready to kiss the blind one, but Johnny adjusts his narrow hips beneath me with aggravation. "So you bring this request to me, and then you back out when you hear my decision? I feel like taking both of your Void pay and leaving you both without eyes." He leans forward so that I have to hold his chest to keep from slipping off his lap. I've seen this angry twitch in him before. If I don't do something, he will have both of them flogged or worse.

"Johnny." I lift my head from his shoulder, and as I knew it would, his whole body softens.

He touches my chin like it's made of glass. "Yes?"

"Throw the idiot in lockup before he does more damage, and let the Mec heal the burns." I stare down his eyes in a way that I'm getting better and better at. "Take me to bed."

He exhales, but brings my lips in for one of his scorching kisses. Then he gets to his feet, allowing me to slide off his lap in the skimpy slip of a black dress that he makes me wear.

"What the woman wants, she gets," Johnny says. The two crew members before him are doing a terrible job of hiding their surprise at his new decision. He looks to the guilty youth first. "You will eject yourself from this ship at the next stop, which will be, ah well, that will be Leland's ship, *Stride*, in the Static Pass in only two days time."

"But Captain, I can't crew with *Stride*! That's a wanted vessel. A known slavers' shi—" The blind man elbows him into silence, and I marvel at the way the two men came to Johnny as hateful enemies only to leave as allies.

Johnny's face perks with a small smile, enjoying the youth's fear. He turns to the blind crew member. "You can see the Mec. He's down in the engine room with the other one. He may be able to help you."

Ben.

So he is alive. It had been a whole month of not daring to ask . . . of swallowing the fear that Ben's absence could very well mean his death. I thought not knowing was the worst, but now picturing him somewhere on this ship makes me ache to see him. And it *is* worse.

Johnny's fingers slide through my hair until they've found my dress, slipping beneath the material to stroke my shoulder blades. "You must have turned something over in my girl to have her bringing up the Mec. She hasn't mentioned him in weeks."

I turn from his caress. "I'm tired, Johnny. Take me to our room."

He circles my waist, splaying his hand across my belly. "Dismissed," he calls behind him as he leads me from the command deck, his touches growing more and more needy with each step.

I wonder if those men will thank me in secret ways. Do they know how close they came to catching Johnny's disturbed interest? Do they know that I will now have to drug him with my body to distract him from the idea that he almost got to watch a man blind another man?

I wonder these things, but I do not hope anymore.

Afterward, I slip out of Johnny's satiny bed and pull on the lacy nightgown that spends more time on the floor than my shoulders. Johnny's breath is even and calm as he sleeps on his stomach, one arm cascading over the side of the bed like he's too exhausted to right it.

I tiptoe to the bathroom.

It's dangerous to leave Johnny's side. He's easiest to sway when we're in constant contact. It's only when he doesn't have me near him for stretches that it becomes harder to command his focus . . . and to give myself to him so completely.

I stare into the mirror without seeing my face.

This is the price I pay for that horrible choice. My brother's life isn't worth all those Touched who were lost. And mine certainly isn't. I have to make it up to them by finishing my original plan. I have to save my brother so that at least one thing in this universe can be righted. And that means obedience to Johnny. Willingness and passion.

If I can stay in his favor, I may be able to convince him to let Walker go at the Edge. But not me. He'll never part with me, and I can't help but feel that it's exactly what I deserve. After all, my parents found each other, two redheads in a world of other colors, and Johnny and I found each other . . . two do-whatever-it-takes people in an empty universe.

It's almost a love story. Isn't it?

I slip out of the bathroom, tripping on a small disc that slides under the door. I pick it up, turning it over, just as it begins to spout gas at an alarming rate. I fling it away, the smoke already filling the room. I should call out and wake Johnny, but instead I cough twice on the vapors, tilt to my knees and tumble face first into the carpet.

I wake to a strong, terrible smell from a small bottle held right under my nose. I begin to scream, but a hand comes down over my mouth. So I bite it.

"Hell, Rain! Ow!"

"Ben?"

I sit up fast, slamming my forehead into his, and I am suddenly so dizzy that I might throw up. "What's happened?"

"You're in *Melee*. We're safe for the moment." His face is dirtier than I remember, and light brown scruff runs down the edges of his jaw. But his hair is still wild, and his eyes are the deepest blue with only a hint of their silver underneath.

I fall into hugging him, and he holds me, so solid and strong . . . and so very different from Johnny. So different that it feels wrong.

I pull away. "You have to take me back. I have to get back now!" I try to stand, but he keeps me on the bunk. "He'll lose his shit if he wakes without me. Do you have any idea what you've done?"

"He's not going to wake, Rain. He went out in his sleep. You'll be back soon, and he won't know that you were ever gone, I swear." His voice is tremulous. "Hell, I didn't think you'd be so angry to see me."

"You have no idea what you're messing with. I can't be with you!"

"You're afraid of him now," he quips. "What happened?"

"I have new priorities." I get to my feet, and this time he doesn't hold me back. "You don't know what it's like up there. You should have let me be."

"I had to see you before the Static Pass. I didn't know that you were still with him until this man came down for treatment today. He was going on and on about Johnny's 'Scarlet Siren.'"

"Scarlet Siren?"

"Yeah," he rubs the back of his neck. "Didn't strike me as a particularly flattering title either, but I knew it had to be you. I can't believe you've kept his attention this long. From what the guy was saying, it sounds like you can even influence him."

"Sometimes. And only on certain things." I cross the small space to *Melee*'s captain's chair. I drop my throbbing head against the seat and squeeze my eyes. Being with Ben has snapped me back into the real world, the world that isn't drugged with Johnny's body and lifestyle. It's suddenly so suffocating that I want to cry. "What do you want from me, Ben?"

"Wanting to see you isn't enough?" he says gruffly.

"No."

Silence grows between us like a swelling wound.

"We're going to be in the Static Pass in a matter of days. It'll be the last chance to save the Touched."

"I'm not saving anyone but my brother. So you can save your breath."

He stands as tall as he can. "What the hell happened to you? How can you be so cold?"

I get up, too. "Don't question how I survive! You don't know how I have to live! What I have to do!" I smack him so hard, and the way he takes it burns me, and then I can't stop myself from slapping him again, harder this time.

Blood red spit wells over his bottom lip, and I can't believe that I've hurt him. How could I? What's happened to me? I touch his mouth, tasting the canyon lake on Entra. I can see the shine of the moons . . . feel the *free* of the water. I pull his face against the side of mine. "I need to go. Please, don't come for me again."

His arms wind around my waist, and the embrace is so different from Johnny's needy fingers that it makes me want to stay leaning on him forever. "What did he do to you?" he asks.

I sit on the edge of the bunk. Ben sits beside me, but when he tries to take my hand, I lock my fingers in a fist. He touches the waxy white scar on my wrist from where Johnny burnt me on Entra.

"Did he heal that with my disc?" he asks. "He did a terrible job."

"He tried." I cover the scar with my hand. "I need to go back to him now. I've been away too long, and seeing you . . . it confuses me. Can you understand that?"

"Not in the slightest." He waves his hand at the door. "But you're free to go whenever. I wouldn't try to hold you prisoner."

I get up and smooth the terribly tiny nightgown over my stomach. Ben looks surprised that I'm actually going to leave. "I told you. I can't help you."

"You know he flushed like fifty Touched out the airlock after we left Entra? He wanted to punish me for trying to help them. Prove that they really are disposable and that my stunt didn't hurt him. Fifty, Rain!"

I cringe. "It was more like a hundred. But Ben, he doesn't think that what happened on Entra had anything to do with you. He thinks I planned all that by myself and that you only helped because I seduced you and made you help me. That's the only reason you're still alive."

"No way. You took the fall? Wait, how in the universe does he think *you* planned all that? You're no Mec! Hell, you don't even have any technical skills."

"Your vote of confidence is overwhelming." I cross my arms over my chest. "Johnny believes what he wants to believe, and I just let him think what he wants to think. He's no Mec either, remember? You know, you should be a bit more appreciative about the fact that you're still breathing."

"Haven't thought about it," he says. "Thanks?"

Although there is no humor, a fragment of a smile slips between us. I can't seem to help it. He gets me so angry, and it always feels so good. I run my fingers over the door release without pressing it. Every fiber of my body vibrates with warning, but I can't help myself. "Just what are you going to do?"

"I am going to sneak this"—he says while holding up his com—"into the Touched shipment when he gives them to Leland. That way the K-Force can track him using the frequency I've embedded in it. I've already sent my uncle's ship a transmission to look for it when *Stride* exits the Pass." He begins to pace. "But, for all my supposed genius, I can't get this damn thing off without Johnny's thumbprint. I was hoping that you'd help me get it. All I need is an object that he held, like a bottle or a brush."

He levels his shoulders. "But if you won't help me, I'll just have to sneak myself into the shipment and hope that they don't catch me."

"Ben, you're a freakin' Mec! You'll stick out among the Touched like an erection."

He shrugs. "Doesn't look like I have a choice. I'm on restricted quarters now. I have to stay on the lower levels and monitor the yellow girls. And Johnny rigged my com so that I get shocked if I try to rise above the crew deck. I had to trade in all my favors just to get Samson to drop that smoke bomb and bring you down here."

I let go of the door release. "You can't get on that ship. The things I hear about this Leland and *Stride* are sickening."

"All the more reason to try. Rain, if we bring down just one of these ships—*Stride* or *Imreas*—we'll have stunted the entire trade run out to the Ridges. Do you have any idea how many lives we would save? Touched lives?"

I squeeze my eyes against his words. "It's a suicidal plan."

"As bad as our idiot plan on Entra?"

"Ben." My words spring to the surface, and then stick together until I'm almost coughing to get them out. "Johnny dropped those people out of the airlock because of me."

"Because of us. That was *our* plan, Rain. It's bad enough that you took the fall. Don't take the guilt as well."

I squeeze my eyes. "You're not understanding me. Johnny gave me a choice. Well, it wasn't really a choice—it was pretty rigged, but basically he made me choose between one hundred Touched and my brother."

A sick silence fills *Melee*.

"And you chose your brother." His tone is burnt.

I risk opening an eye. Ben stares with disgust, and I turn away. "It's all a game to him. You know that. I made the best choice that I could, and now I have to live with it. I let him love me and he lets me live. That's the best that this deal can get."

He pounds his knee with a fist. "Don't believe it, Rain. Don't forget that Johnny used to make me do things, too. Terrible things, and I thought I was as damned as him. But I'm not. You're not. You want to help those people, I know you do."

I shake my head slowly. "I can't. Johnny keeps my brother in an airlock. One wrong move and he can just press a button."

"Rain, I just need an object with his print on it. A glass. Anything!"

"I can't help you." I palm the release and leave him staring after me.

I take the cargo lift up to the green level, passing the Family Room. Part of me wants to sneak in there and sleep on my mat below the wide window, but a larger part of me can't forget that every time I enter that room, someone disappears.

Scarlet Siren.

Just like the alarms on the lower decks. I really shouldn't be surprised.

I slip into Johnny's room and check for any evidence of the smoke disc, but there's nothing. Samson was good. Johnny is in the same position that I left him—arm over the side of the bed, snoring. I slip under the covers beside him.

I inch toward him, holding my hand over his bare back. The heat coming off his skin is like an electrical current, but I press myself to it all the same.

The next morning, Johnny brings me to the command deck to watch our entry into the Static Pass. He wraps his arms around my waist and holds me against the front window. "This is my favorite part," he says into my ear. "First, we have to build up enough speed so that we can coast all the way through the nebula."

The crew members shout orders at one another, revving up the engines until we're moving so fast through the Void that the ivory strings melt into a white tunnel.

"Wait for it," Johnny says, his breath rushing down my neck. "Wait . . ."

At the far end, coming closer by the heartbeat, a dense cloud of what looks just like crimson smog waits for us. I struggle to breathe as Johnny grips me tighter and tighter.

And we slam into it.

The vibrations from the roaring engines flicker out. So do the lights. Every piece of technology loses power in the Pass. Even the scarlet glow from my bracelet disappears.

Through the window, the universe has turned deep red. Not a single star penetrates the cloud, and the only way that I can tell we are still moving is the parting and swirling of the bloody hue.

The whole ship is dark. The crew members have blended into the shadows, and the command deck is one blank space. Johnny is the blackest part. Only the outline of his face picks up the fog's glow.

But Ben could see through this with his special Mec vision.

My hands tighten around Johnny's arms as I think of Ben's desperate plan to help the Touched. He probably thinks that saving this batch will be the act of goodness that cancels out all the depraved things he's done or let happen on this ship. Who knows, maybe it will.

I hope for his sake that it does.

At least his new plan is aimed at Leland. If it affected Johnny's route to the Edge and my plans for Walker, I might be tempted to stop him. Maybe. Wait, what am I thinking? What's wrong with me? I want to help Ben . . . don't I?

I do. But I can't forget that every time Ben and I work together, the death toll rises. First it was Kaya and Lo . . . then that Amanda girl as well as the three traded girls on the Entra casino. And one hundred Touched people. I remember the swirling halo of blonde hair around those two girls, probably sisters, until I feel sick.

"You're trembling," Johnny whispers into my hair. "How sweet."

A light dances into existence only a few inches from my face. I gasp, staring into the finger-long flame of the lighter that he used to burn my wrist on Entra.

"Come." He makes a fist hold in the dress material around my stomach. "It'll take a little while for us to coast to *Stride*. Enough time to enjoy the dark."

"WE'RE GOING TO CRASH!"

"Shut up." Johnny leaps from the bed, yanking his pants on while I recoil from the window. Just outside, the red nebula of the Static Pass parts to reveal a *wall* of approaching silver steel. "That's *Stride*, Rain. We're going to dock together while we coast, which means a little rubbing of elbows." He laughs just as the hulls screech and grind, followed by an abrupt snagging when the two ships lock together.

"See, we're all cozy now," he adds. Johnny gets dressed in record time. I hurry to pull on a pair of pants and a shirt, hoping he's too distracted to notice that I'm not wearing the silky, *come hither* dress he's so fond of. I roll the waist of my pants very low, avoiding the aching place on my hip where he gripped me.

"What happens now?" I ask, finger-combing my hair into loose waves.

"Business," he says. "And then some fun. Leland always has some decent liquor from the Gate, but I have to bring the girls, of course."

I stop dressing, my shirt hanging open. "You will leave me here." Johnny always leaves me when he goes out to drink on the passenger levels, and I'm surprised that I'm not more content with this arrangement. I don't really want to see *Stride* and meet this slave trader . . . do I?

"Of course you're coming, my love." He closes the buttons on my top, leaving the ones over my cleavage open for display. "I plan on showing you off, and since you're one of the few people on this ship who knows what I'm trading, I don't have to hide from you. It's actually quite refreshing." He slaps my face playfully but not so gently. "Perhaps I should be happy that you take an interest in my work. Grab the candle. You can help choose the entertainment."

Already he is acting far less like Johnny the Lover that I had become used to. He's excited and mischievous. Unpredictable.

I pick up one of the elegant candles arranged along the headboard. Slick, hot wax leaks down the side, coating my finger and stinging as it cools. "I've never seen so many candles. Isn't there some other way?"

"I told you, Rain. No power source works in the Pass. Not a single thing." Johnny leads the way to the Family Room, and we pass dozens of candles set along the walls. Their lights draw angular shadows across Johnny's body and the hall. The sudden lack of engine noise makes the corridors seem even narrower, closing us into a concrete silence.

"It's spooky."

"It's the Pass," Johnny responds without turning. He enters the Family Room, and I step through, gripping the candle. The dripping wax seals over each of my fingers like it has taken my skin for its own.

In the Family Room, candles throw strange light around the veils, but many of the girls are sitting in the center area together.

"Line up," Johnny calls. "Be quick about it. I'll take two of you this time."

Several girls exclaim, and Johnny snaps, "Just do it." He takes the candle from my hand, breaking the wax seal over my skin. I pick at the residue while he inspects the girls one at a time. What does he want them for? He said *entertainment* . . .

He finds the first one right away, a shorter blonde, who could pass for a fourteen-year-old easily. He sweeps down the line again without choosing a second. Then he turns to me. "You pick. They tend to blend together after a while."

"What are they for?" I whisper.

Johnny steps close and touches one of my curls. "They're gifts for Leland."

"But I heard that he's—"

Johnny tugs my hair. *"Just pick."*

I walk down the line, my heart limping in my chest. I close my eyes and point to the girl from the far end, the tallest in the group. She's damn near Johnny's height with razor straight, dark hair. She reminds me of Kaya a little, but that's not why I picked her. I chose her because she looks the oldest—the least afraid.

"That's it." Johnny steps back, but the candlelight continues to highlight the horror on the two chosen girls' faces. "The rest of you will be locked down until we exit the Pass. If you have a problem, you can ask Ben," he stops short, but my chest spasms at the mention of Ben's name. "If you have a problem, save it until I get back," he says and for a moment he loses his usual lordly demeanor.

"I admit it. I miss having the Mec to order around." He winks at me. *Winks.* I've never seen that behavior before, and it fills me with dread. If there's still a hidden aspect to Johnny's personality, it can't be good.

It's got to be the worst.

We exit the Family Room with the chosen girls, and Johnny hands me the candle before forcing a large deadbolt lock on the door. The girls huddle together, eyeing me as though I just stepped from their nightmares.

We take the stairs down to the docking bay where I see just how *Imreas* is connected to *Stride.* Several of the airlocks are open and sealed against mirroring airlocks on the other ship. One of the closed ones holds Walker's pod, and I push past it, not wanting Johnny's attention. I glance through the deeper dark to where I can imagine the catwalk leading to *Melee.* Is Ben nearby? Is he watching through the shadows with those amazing eyes?

I am the last to pass through the dead, empty space of the airlock. Every step brings an image of the people who knew this room as their last: Kaya, Lo, even that Amanda girl. And all those Touched . . .

The candlelight crawls along the grated floor of the airlock, and I stop when I see something—a shred of rolled-up paper. I stoop, and tug it out of the grid. This is impossible. No way.

But I don't even have to unroll the small square to recognize it. It's Lo's picture of her mom. Or what's left of it. The edges are worn so soft that it couldn't be any other piece of scrap in the universe. After all, it was kept snuggled against her skin for years.

I seal it in my palm. *Lo.* I imagine her so clearly through the shadows—her hips thrust out beneath her stretchy skirt and the pink streaks beneath her blonde hair. The neon angel who magically appeared when I could not have made it another day with Walker on my own.

And as I imagine my best friend, she shakes her head, her face clouding with anger.

I hurry my steps and run straight into the back of the tall girl. "Sorry."

"Scarlet Siren," she hisses. "Don't touch me." And she hustles to put her arms around the other girl.

"I had to choose," I whisper so low that she might not even hear me. "I have to keep him happy. I have to survive."

"Sure you do, and the cost is our existence, huh?"

Existence. I squeeze the photo in my fist and tuck it into the front of my bra. "That's a good question," I mumble just loud enough for her to hear. She cocks her head at me for a moment before passing from *Imreas*'s airlock to *Stride*'s.

Every grate and beam of *Stride* shows more age and abuse than *Imreas*'s. Rust patches catch the candlelight like spots of dried blood, and dented sections of metal indicate years of trauma. Johnny knocks on a pockmarked door, and it swings open to reveal a dozen crew members waiting.

Like the ships, the crew of *Stride* reminds me of *Imreas*'s with marked differences. They are dirty and glass-eyed, their black flight suits torn and faded like they've been in the Void for years and years.

Johnny elbows the girls toward the first crew member he

THE COLOR OF RAIN

sees. "Take them to the party room. Don't lose them. Where is my brother?"

Brother?

Leland is Johnny's brother? Nerves prickle down my back like a fleeing spider.

The crew member doesn't answer; he doesn't even look in our direction. Johnny knocks on the man's forehead, and he turns. "Tell me where Captain Leland is."

"Where Captain Leland is?" the man replies in a stiff voice. Something about his demeanor is strange—disassociated, maybe— like he's been beaten into a submissive state.

"Never mind, you waste of space. Don't know how he puts up with you." Johnny reaches back for my elbow and rips me forward, through the bowels of the murky, decrepit ship.

———◦◦◦———

We march up a steep spiral staircase, and not even the candlelight can find the end before us.

By the time we reach the top, my legs are sore and loose, and Johnny huffs a few breaths before pressing forward. We enter a command deck lit by a central tank filled with circling fish as long as my arm. The strange creatures must excrete a kind of phosphorescence, which lights the water, giving the room an eerie yellow-green glow.

The tank sheds most of its light over a waist-high command console, and leaning against it with his back to us, is a man completely dressed in white. His hair might be golden, but by the weird light, it gleams olive.

Johnny presses me into the room with a hand on my lower back.

"Lee," Johnny says.

Leland turns around. "John."

Brothers indeed. They have the same lean angles to their faces, but Leland must be at least ten years older than Johnny. "So you're bringing your girls into my command now?"

"Just this one. She's special. What do you think?"

"Little brother always needs approval."

Johnny either doesn't hear this or it doesn't bother him. I, on the other hand, am in Leland's breathing space. He lowers his face into mine so fast that I don't have a chance to pull away. Not like I could. Johnny's hand braces the back of my neck.

Leland's features are like a smoothed portrait, maybe too smooth. His eyes are brown like Johnny's except that they're flecked with gold that feels almost electric even by the dim light of the candle. My stomach churns into a tight knot, but I hold my stare for as long as he does. One of his eyes twitches a little, and he turns back to Johnny.

"She'll give you trouble," he concludes.

"I already know that much." Johnny drops his hand from my neck. "That's what I like about her. She even executed a rather elaborate coup to release my merchandise on Entra. She failed, of course, but what a game."

Leland's frown is intense in the yellow glow. "You don't get to play with my livelihood. Did you get them all back?"

"Most of them. But the only ones we lost were the too old and the too young."

"Lost?!" I say before I can stop myself. "You dumped—"
Johnny cuffs me on the back of the head so fast that I bite the
edge of my tongue.

Leland huffs, but if I'm not wrong, he's more than a little
pleased by the swiftness of Johnny's punishment. "The too old I
can do without, but the too young . . . well, you'll just have to owe
me. You know I like to keep the young ones. Head count?"

"913."

"Father wanted 1,500, John. I can't bail you out with my personal stores this time. I'll have to tell him that you ran short.
Again." *Father . . . brothers?* So the trade is not only Johnny's business but his family's business? Does Ben know that, and if he does,
why didn't he tell me?

"You work for your dad, Johnny?" I ask, my curiosity getting
the better of me.

Leland laughs. "Work? That would involve choice. Right
there, John-O?"

"Shut your mouth." Johnny moves forward like he's going to
get in Leland's face, but the blond, older brother doesn't back
down. In fact, his smile eerily grows until Johnny looks away.

"Johnny's just an errand boy with a nice suit. I bet he's duped
you into believing that he's a real self-made sort of a man."

I expect an explosion, but Johnny's shoulders hunch. He
crosses to the fish tank, laid bare, and it makes me less wary of him
for once. And more fearful of this Leland. Every hair on my body
has taken a stand against his all-white presence.

Leland pushes the candle in my hand closer to my hair. "Is
your hair red or is that a trick of the flame?"

"It's real," I say in a small voice. I clear my throat. "It's red."

"Intriguing." He glances at Johnny and then back to me. "Do you want to see the fish?"

"No."

His thin lips spread into a horrible grin. The spaces between his teeth catch too much shadow, making them look sharp. "Clearly an Earth City girl. Always awed by the universe and then too terrified of it to get any closer."

"I'm not afraid."

"Liar." He blows out the candle, and I can't stop a gasp.

"Play nice, Lee," Johnny calls. His profile walks around to the other side of the huge tank.

He's left me.

"Look for the ruby-toothed striper, John. She's a new beauty," Leland says.

I need Johnny's lighter. I need to relight this candle. I can't be here in the dark with this freak. . . .

Icy fingers caress my throat, and I freeze.

"Playing games with *my* merchandise. How rude." Even his whispered voice is frigid.

"They're people," I manage.

He chuckles, and his hand squeezes my throat. "What a drumming pulse." He gets even closer. "Tell me again that you're not afraid of me."

I don't. I can't.

"Those people are people, true enough, even if John doesn't think so. But what they *really* are is mine, little red whore." He lets go, but one finger hooks inside my shirt and caresses the edge of my breast. "I think . . . yes, I think I need to have you." His touch is as cold as something that's slithered up from a deep, wet place, and I feel terror unlike anything I've ever known.

"Yes. I will have you tonight."

CHAPTER
26

I've stopped breathing. My mouth is open, but nothing comes in or out. Leland's snaking finger digs deeper into my shirt until it's close to where I stashed Lo's mom's picture. I have to run. I have to do something—but I can't move.

A flame jumps into existence a few feet away.

Johnny holds up his lighter and knocks his brother's hand out of my shirt. He relights my candle. "Fuck, Lee. I leave for one minute."

Leland doesn't seem to be listening. "I've changed my mind, John. I like this girl. I want her."

Johnny's arm folds around me, and I've never been so thrilled to feel it tighten me to him. I tuck my own arm around his waist and squeeze his belt. "Yeah, well, don't get any ideas. I brought two others for you."

Leland breathes a long, fake-sounding sigh. "They better keep their spirits longer than the last one. She only made it five hours. Hardly worth the pursuit."

"If you want them to last, don't be so rough." Johnny strokes my hair. "They like it when you show a little tenderness."

My heart snaps back and forth in its rhythm. What will he do to those girls?

What won't he do?

———~~~~~———

Stride's common room is lined by shadowy figures. The crew member who met us at the airlock isn't the only zombie-like presence on the ship; there are dozens of them. All wearing a distant, weary look.

A large fire sits in a metal pit at the center of the room, casting orange light at the faces huddled around it. The two green girls hold each other, and Leland examines them from the other side of the flames where he lounges across an oversized chair. He seems disappointed.

He seems to have me on his mind.

I ignore the constant needling of his gaze, lying against Johnny's knees while he drinks a black, sugary-smelling liquor with his brother.

"You tell our father I won't do another run for less than sixty a head." Johnny's voice is getting wilder with each drink. "Tell him I'll find another buyer. I'll go to the Gate myself."

"You wouldn't dare," Leland responds. "You still think of *Imreas* as your passenger ship, but if you take her out of Void space to the deep outposts, you'll lose all your valued respectability. Don't pretend to be rash, John. You're too vain for that."

Gate. Deep outposts. I make a mental list to run by Ben, but then I realize that I won't be able to. I'll never have the chance if he jumps ship and hides on *Stride* before we leave the Pass.

I may never see him again.

I glance at the glass in Johnny's hand. At his wide thumb and its unique print. Ben only needs something that Johnny touched, but how would I get it to him before Ben needs to act?

"You're just like father." Johnny's voice has begun to slur. I try to take his drink from him, and he hits my hand.

Leland laughs and the sound streaks around the room like a rabid animal. "You're running your mouth because you're drinking. You need food." He snaps his fingers, and one of the shadowy forms step forward with a tray of yellow bread. He yanks on the crew member's uniform, bringing him down to eye level. "You will serve each person here from this tray," he says. "Don't step through the fire."

How ridiculously specific.

The crew member walks around the pit, approaching the girls first. The smaller one shrieks. He comes to me next, and I wait for him to lean all the way down to where I sit. What could be so scary about him?

My fingers stop over the tray while my gaze locks onto unfocused eyes. The crew member's jaw is slack and his hands shake.

"He's Touched!"

Johnny and Leland laugh together. "Don't look so shocked, Rain," Johnny says. "What would they be worth if we couldn't work them?"

"But how is he following directions? The Touched on Earth City can't manage the smallest of tasks."

Leland's eyes glint. He snaps his fingers twice this time, and another zombie-like crew member steps forward. This one is a woman—or really just a girl a few years older than me. Her hair has been shorn unevenly, and her eyes are empty, but this doesn't

275

hide the fact that she was once rather pretty.

Leland tugs her arm until she's across his lap. "They're easily manipulated. You just have to adjust their brains a tad." He takes her chin in his hand and rotates her face in the light, revealing three fingernail-sized puncture scars across her forehead.

"Adjust?"

"With this." He pulls a small pick hammer from his belt and tosses it over the flames. I fumble to catch it, and the tip pricks my palm. A bead of red swells instantly.

I seal my hand into a fist and look over the tool. Its wooden handle is stained with old blood. "You mean, you use this to . . ."

"Lobotomize them. Ingenious, isn't it? It's my own design." Leland's voice is tickled with pleasure, and Johnny laughs as he downs more of his black drink.

A sickening taste fills my mouth. I can't stand to touch the tool a second longer, and I throw the pick hammer back.

Leland catches it out of the air effortlessly. He tucks it back into his belt and then slips his hand between the missing buttons of the girl's flight suit. He caresses her chest while staring me down. "Do you want to watch me do one?" he says in a tone so low that the words feel like they only find my ears.

Do one? Does he mean lobotomize one of them or . . .

"Don't let my brother fool you, Rain. They're still worthless." Johnny is officially drunk. "You have to be so damn specific with your orders, and they work themselves to death sooo easily." He laughs like this is the crowning joke to a wonderful evening.

This is far worse than I ever imagined. Does Ben know about

this? Does anyone know that these people are not just abducted and enslaved, but tortured and warped into vacant robotic shells? How could the people who sell the Touched be okay with something this inhumane? How could anyone?

"I don't understand," I say. "How is this possible? How come no one stops you?"

Leland is pleased by my honesty. "John, have you never explained the business of this universe?"

Johnny groans. "I don't care."

"The people who own Earth City—"

"Own?"

"Don't be so naïve. The planet is owned by a corporate industry on the Gate. They take care in making things run smoothly, and there's nothing less smooth than people cutting out of work to care for ailing family members. Think of the chaos!"

I stare into the red-orange embers of the fire pit. "They're shipped away so that Earth City keeps producing." That's why they took my mom. And Jeremy. He wasn't even Touched, but he was in the way, and they took him just the same. I feel Lo's picture between my breasts. This is so much more than losing your existence. This is having it stolen.

And raped.

"Everything has a purpose in this universe, little whore," Leland adds into my silence. "Weren't you relieved to find yours between your legs?"

I clap eyes on Leland, feeling the stirring of my long numbed rage. "I'm more than Johnny's girl," I whisper. I don't know if he hears me, but Johnny's sudden snores snap the intensity of the room like a taut wire.

Leland's ravenous gaze clicks onto my body until I have to tuck myself beneath Johnny's arm. The protection works, but the dead weight of Johnny doesn't block out the looming figures of *Stride*'s lobotomized crew, nor the sound of Leland playing with his two new girls. *Ripping* sounds. Snivels and crying.

And the intermittent punctuation of his *shhh* that sends ice down my spine.

He leaves much later, taking the girls with him. I want to be relieved by his absence, but I feel nothing close to it. He'll torture them. Kill them. And not via a frozen death out the airlock . . . something much more horrid.

I picture Walker's small face, and I can't help but imagine puncture scars on his temples and a tray in his hand . . . and I begin to throw up. I stumble from beneath Johnny and heave my guts in the corner, choking on my breath until almost everything inside of me spills out. When I finish, I find the Touched girl who Leland fondled standing near me. Her eyes are dead and flat in the light from the fading fire, but she still looks like a person. A very, very lost person.

"Can you talk?" I whisper.

She doesn't move.

"Can you only follow commands?"

Still nothing. "Scratch your nose," I try, and she obeys. "Can you take me down to the airlocks?"

Nothing.

"Take me down to the airlocks," I command. She turns and leaves the room, and I snatch the first thing out of Johnny's pocket that I can find, Ben's dose rod, hoping that it has a good fingerprint.

I hurry to follow the girl. I have to hurry because the lives of Johnny's cargo depend on it . . . the souls of 913 Touched.

And one Mec.

CHAPTER
27

I leave the Touched girl in *Stride*'s rusted-out airlock.

"Wait here. Don't move. And don't tell anyone that you helped me," I command as I cross into *Imreas*. I don't like ordering her around, but there's no time for anything else. At least, for once, I don't have to worry about security alarms or cameras. All the technology on *Imreas* is as dead as the engines.

The ships and everyone onboard are like ghosts through the static fog, and I feel like a ghoul myself as I move around them. The catwalk jangles beneath me, and I steal a candle from one of the handrails, trying not to look below into the eerie shadows of the ship's unknown depths.

I find *Melee*, holding up my candle so that I can make out the door. I bang once. Twice. "Come on, Ben. You have to be in there!"

After the third knock, Ben struggles to shoulder the door open, making it click against its rails. For all the Mec's genius, *Melee* was clearly not meant to function in the Pass.

"Who's there?" he calls even though he's looking straight at me.

I hold the candle up to my face. "It's me, you idiot. Get out of the doorway."

He takes a few steps back, but his brow folds. "What are you doing here? What's going on?" He almost falls on the armrest when he backs up to sit on the captain's chair. I set my candle down on the command panel. It's the only light in the room.

I force the door closed. "I don't have a lot of time. I just snuck out of *Stride*. Damn, Ben. It's so much worse than I imagined. . . . It's a living hell. The *living* being the worst part."

He looks past me.

"Quit making that face. Are you even listening?"

"Of course I'm listening, Rain. I just can't see a damn thing!" he yells. He looks in my general direction, without really focusing on me.

"But you can see in the dark. You've got the hardware in your eyes. Why . . ." It dawns on me far too slowly. "It doesn't work in the Pass."

"Didn't you wonder why the K-Force didn't come soaring into the fog to solve this slaving crisis? That's *why* they do their business here. Mecs are as useless as paraplegics without our technology. Without our vision. I'm useless."

"Well, don't go feeling sorry for yourself. It's ugly," I say, stealing one of Lo's favorite phrases.

Something like a smile creeps up his face, but he fights it down. "What are you doing here?"

"I've come to help. You need a fingerprint. I've got something with loads of them on it."

Ben gets up and crosses the room so fast that he bumps right into me. "What do you have?" He puts his hands out, palms up. I place the dose rod in his hand and he carefully sets it on the bunk.

"It'll have to be a clear print." He fumbles to find a roll of clear tape and a small square of glass. He wraps a piece of tape around the rod and pulls it free, holding it up. "Did it work?"

Through the candlelight, I see many smudge marks. Too many. "It's a mess," I say. "There's no clear print."

He crumples it up. "Fuck! Well, there goes that long shot."

"Wait. You could take it from skin, right? I haven't washed." I mumble the last few words, ashamed.

Ben sits down and almost misses the edge of the bunk. "Hell, Rain. You'd need a spot that you knew for sure he'd pressed down on. Hard."

"Hard enough to leave a bruise?" I yank my shirt up, looking at the purple mark on my hip where he gripped me the night before . . . gripped me so hard that I haven't been able to bring my pants within three inches of it all day.

He pauses. "He bruises you with his *fingers*?"

"Don't fake surprise." I'm glad that he can't see what I'm showing him. "Will it work or won't it?"

"We can try." Ben fumbles with the tape while I step closer, tucking my shirt around my stomach. "You're going to have to help me."

I guide his hands over the spot, his fingers brushing my skin and making strange places on my body tickle in response. Below my ears, for one. The backs of my knees, for another.

"You're sure? Right there?" he asks.

"Of course I'm sure." I remember how Johnny looked through the candlelight while lying beneath me. I close my eyes and try to shake my thoughts free.

Ben smooths the tape over and over again on my hip. "What made you change your mind and want to help me?"

"He—that Leland—he *adjusts* their brains. That's how he makes them work. He lobotomizes them, Ben. Did you know?"

He cringes. "I've heard rumors of torture. I didn't know it was that bad."

"Bad doesn't come close."

"This will sting," he warns before yanking the tape away. The spot smarts, but Ben holds the plastic strip up, and through the candlelight I can see the imprint of Johnny's thumb. "Did it work?"

"Of course." I rub my hip. "Told you I was sure. I could tell you every place he's ever grabbed me. I swear the bruises fade without healing." I don't realize that I'm speaking aloud until I glance at Ben. His gaze has the kind of pity that I don't want or deserve. "But whatever. I asked for all of this, didn't I? I deserve it."

He feels for the edges of the glass plate and sticks the tape to it, smoothing it down. "You agreed to sleep with him, Rain. You did not agree to the cruelty. To the violence. As for what you deserve, well, if it was up to me . . . ah, hell, don't make me get all sappy."

I like his words, but I don't know if I can believe them.

"Let me get the glue residue." He wipes my stomach with a piece of cloth, and again, I have to turn away from his touch. A quiet sob comes through me, and I'm so lost in my nightmares that I don't know what he's doing until I feel something else.

Ben kisses my hip.

His lips are soft and cool and brief. He leans away and wipes his hands over and over with the cloth, his face bowed. "My mom used to kiss my hurts when I was a kid," he says. "I used to think that it healed them."

I tuck my shirt down and fix the waist of my pants. "My mom did that, too. And I did it for Walker."

"See? I told you we were both the same species."

"Right," I say, thankful that he can't see the way I cup my hand over the spot where he kissed me.

"So what now?" I ask.

"We see if it works." Ben seals the small glass plate into a metal frame. "I tempered the pane with an electrical current before we entered the Pass. It should give off an energy source even in this fog."

"So Mecs aren't entirely useless in the Pass?"

"I said 'should.' There's always a small chance that it'll still zap me to death," he says as though this is a little funny. "Actually, if it does work, I may have stumbled on a way to bring a power source into the Pass." His fingers fumble to line up the glass with the catch on the inner side of his com, and I help him right it. Then he places his thumb over the pane. I hold my breath, but nothing happens.

He breathes out, but then jerks, letting out a small scream.

"Ben!"

He laughs. "Just kidding."

I smack him hard. "That's not funny!"

"Then why are you laughing?"

"You're lucky I don't zap you myself."

"I'm sure you'll get the chance." His chuckle turns hollow. "It didn't work."

I push his thumb away. "Maybe you're just not lining it up right." I kneel before him and place my own thumb over Johnny's print on the glass. The com clicks and drops off his wrist, clunking on the ground. I scoop up the heavy circlet of metal. "It worked!"

"So surprised," he mocks, but his face is split with a grin. I place the com in his hand, and he opens and closes it over and over. "Okay, maybe I can't believe that it worked either." His fingers find mine, and for a moment, both of my hands hold both of his, but the hopeful look on his face makes me stand up and pace.

"So now we've got to get that thing into the Touched shipment? Wouldn't it be easier if I put it somewhere on Leland's ship myself?"

"Easier and more dangerous." Ben stands and folds his arms. "I only asked you to get the fingerprint. I take the rest of the risk myself."

"You're blind as a damn bat. Besides, I have to get back there before Johnny wakes up or Leland comes looking." I shiver. "That creepy bastard has an *interest* in me." And those two green girls . . . can I find a way to help them? "There's something else I have to do." I pick up the glass plate off the bunk. "Will this fingerprint thing work on the girls' bracelets?"

Ben's arms drop to his sides. "You want to take yours off? Johnny would know for sure that something was up, and he'd—"

"No, no. I'll keep it on. For now." I touch the silver tag on my wrist. "But I might be able to help the two girls that Leland took if I can get their bracelets off."

He shakes his head. "That sounds crazy and ill-conceived, Rain."

"Maybe." I drop the glass plate in my pocket and take the com out of Ben's hand. "But I'm doing this. I've done nothing for too long." I imagine the procession of bodies in *Imreas*'s wake, flipping through the Void. "Johnny might find out and kill me or my brother, but I won't let this happen. Not again."

I begin to push the door open, but Ben blindly grabs for my arm. He misses and gets a great handful of boob. "Hey!"

"Sorry." He holds his palms up, his face blushing beautifully. "Just stop for a moment, all right? What's your exit strategy?"

"My what?"

"How are you going to get out of all this? I mean, we'll be undocking from *Stride* in the morning. We'll be out of the Pass soon after. Then the lights and security and everything will be back on."

"And the K-Force will be tracking your com on Leland's ship, right?"

"Yes. They'll be tracking Leland. He's a higher priority than Johnny." He touches my arm for real this time. "Which means that we've got weeks before we reach the Edge. Weeks where you'll have to keep Johnny's favor. You'll have to stay with him."

"I made it this far, didn't I?" My voice wavers. *Weeks more?*

"If you get caught doing whatever you plan on doing tonight, Johnny won't hesitate to kill you this time. He may be flattered by the challenge you pose, but in the end, things have to go his way. He's a narcissist, Rain. When things really go wrong, he's going to explode."

"I know, but it's always this way, isn't it? We're always doing something crazy stupid or something that's bound to get us killed, and still I've made it through. The Edge is close now. I'm almost there."

"He's never going to let you leave this ship. With or without your brother."

Something falls inside me until I'm nailed to the metal floor of *Melee*.

"I know that. I've given up on getting away, but if I keep him happy, he'll let me get my brother off this ship."

"No, Rain." He shakes his head, his hair swaying. "You had to tell yourself that or you wouldn't have made it this far, but Johnny's not going to let you have that kind of hope. He's been forced into this life, and he's probably obsessed with you because your suffering makes his feel like less." I look away, and Ben searches for my face with his fingers. "We need to figure out how we're getting out of here."

"We," I repeat. The word tastes sweet.

He stands a little taller, and I want to touch his shoulders through his soft shirt. "Johnny might have lied back on Earth City, but I didn't. I'm going to see that your brother gets medical attention, and you deserve a new life on the Edge."

I finger the doorframe. *Exit strategy.* "So we can't just blast *Melee* through the side of *Imreas* like you wanted to before?" I'm somewhat joking, but Ben shakes his head.

"Now that *is* suicidal. Call it our 'Nothing Left to Lose' plan because I don't know for sure if *Melee*'s engines have enough juice to blast us through the hull. That was a good idea when . . . when we were going to be dead and not care about the outcome."

"Right." I almost laugh. "Well, we'll find a way. I'm Earth City street-smart, and you're a Mec. What can't we do?"

"But I'm grounded now. Without my com, I have to hide from everyone, and I won't have any access to the security and alarm system when they come back online. You'll be on your own." He pulls the dose rod out of his pocket. "Take this, at least. Do you remember the settings?"

I turn the rod over in my hand and glance over the colored markers. "The red one is adrenaline, green is knock out, yellow is that limp drug."

"Limpicilin." He grins, reminding me of his first lame joke back on the old pier beneath the spacedocks. And I can't believe we've come this far.

I flip the settings until I see a black one. Johnny's favorite color. "And what about the black?"

"Black is arsenic. That's a death shot. No med disc will bring you back after that one," he says. "Don't keep it on that setting. And *don't* use it on yourself. No matter how bad it gets. Promise me that much."

I tuck the rod into my sock, but I can't promise him anything.

His hand trails my waist until his finger hooks into my belt loop. I stare down at it for a long moment. "I want to come with you," he says. "But I'm a liability without my eyesight."

"I know." I pry his finger loose, and his hand closes into a fist. "I'll be fine."

"I hate letting you do this."

I nod, but he can't see it, so I kiss the very corner of his lips.

CHAPTER
28

I push through the blackout depths of *Imreas*. Back through the airlocks.

The Touched girl waits for me as though she never moved, not even to shuffle her feet. My fingers close around Ben's com, the thick metal still warm from his skin. I have so much to do and only an hour or so to do it.

"I need to find a place that isn't regularly used on this ship," I tell the girl.

Her eyes are glassy and unresponsive. They don't even blink. Of course she can't help me decide where to hide the com; she can only follow commands. No interpretation. No free will.

"Follow me," I say.

I pass through *Stride*'s airlock and hold my candle up. Very little reveals itself before my light, but I can tell that *Stride* was once a ship like *Imreas*. Maybe a twin ship, only whatever it has been through made it fall into disrepair.

Sliding my feet over the shadowy spots, I wait for a hole to appear and swallow me into the guts of this horrid vessel. I find one fast and grip the handrail, dragging my foot back onto safer ground. The metal bar is frayed with rust and sharp pieces snag on my palm.

"Ouch!" I yank out a metal sliver as my voice echoes traitorously.

Ouch.

ouch

I'm being an idiot. I don't know what this ship looks like out of the Pass when the lights are on and the Touched crew is moving around. I need to find a place that will be just as murky in the light as it is in this heavy dark.

The fish tank.

I spin around and run straight into the girl. "Take me to the command deck."

The spiral stairs feel even steeper without Johnny pounding the way before me. I step up and up and up, all the while shadowed by the unblinking obedience of the Touched crew member. "This is no life," I mutter just for some noise beside my own speeding breath. "And to think you came from Earth City. You're probably not much older than me."

I pause and hold the candle up to look over her face. She doesn't pause because I didn't tell her to, and she almost knocks me over. "Wait." I place a hand on her chest. "Can you talk?"

Nothing.

"Talk."

"Talk," she returns.

"Tell me your name."

"Your name," she parrots. I turn back to the stairs. Her life really isn't a life. It's a vacancy much more bottomless than the disease of the Touched.

I remember the way Leland's eyes dared mine while his hand groped about in her clothes, and I have to look away. "You've got it worse than a prostitute. You can't even give consent."

We reach the top, and I shove my candle into her hands. "Hold this and wait here . . . please." The eerie glow on the command deck leads me straight to the yellow-green fish tank. I slip toward it, watching for Leland or more zombie crew members, but find no one. I climb onto the console around the table and reach for the top of the tank.

The lid slides away, and I look down through the water, trying to estimate just where the com will fall. The sanded bottom is layered on one side by a thick, gooey filth cloud—perhaps a patch of eggs—which looks perfect for concealing the heavy metal, but that means reaching in and tossing it so that it falls at the right angle.

The strange fish swim this way and that. The largest one has black-red stripes down its sides and straw-like teeth that hook out of its rust-colored jaw. I wait for him to swim to the bottom and then lower my arm into the slimy water.

I work my hand like a pendulum as fast as I can, releasing the com so that if flips and tumbles, sinking into the vat of fish goo. "Yes!" I whisper.

"AH!"

I yank my arm out of the water, dragging the body of the red-jawed fish, its hooked teeth clamped to my forearm. I grab the ridge of its back fin and rip it away, slamming it back into the tank with a mighty splash. I slide the lid closed and jump from the console, gripping my arm.

The fish eyes me from the other side of the glass. A knowing, fishy glare.

"Sneer all you want!" I huff. "Damn fish!"

I look over the bite in the light of the tank. The spot oozes pus and blood, and I close my hand over it. I can't drip. Can't leave a trail.

I jog out of the command deck to where the girl waits with my candle. "I'm sorry, but I need some of this." The sleeves of her flight suit are already torn, and I rip a strip of fabric to make into a bandage for my bite. When I try to take the candle back, her hand doesn't open right away. "Give it to me," I say, a sudden ache pounding inside my skull.

But the flame burnt down while I was gone, and her finger burned into the wax, bad enough to raise small welts across her knuckles.

I rip another piece of her uniform to bandage her finger. "I'm sorry." My headache surges, and I grit my teeth to keep from groaning. I wonder if she can even feel pain. I squeeze her bandaged finger, and her cheek twinges.

Yes, she can feel pain. She could feel her finger scorching, but I told her to hold it. No doubt that sick Leland bastard exploits their inability to fight back. No doubt he enjoys making them suffer through their blankness.

"Take me to Leland," I manage, pulling my hair out of my eyes as we descend the spiral staircase and further into the gloom.

―――――――――

My arm burns from where that freakin' fish bit me, and my head buzzes heavily. The Touched girl leads me through the corridors of *Stride* until we come to a wide room strewn with old couches and pillows.

If it had color or life, it might resemble the Family Room.

I sneak in, drawn to the back corner where a window sheds the fog's light over a huge striped mattress—and Leland's sleeping form. I raise the candle a little higher, and its light reflects off the eyes of the two green girls.

They hunch at the far edge of the bed, holding on to each other. The smaller blonde gasps quietly, but the tall girl squeezes a hand over her lips to stop it. I wave at them, but they don't move. The tall one shakes her head back and forth. She points to Leland and draws a finger over her throat. So they think that if they move, they'll be killed. . . . They're probably right.

I pull the dose rod out of my sock and creep toward Leland. His chest is bare, revealing more muscle than his brother, but like Johnny, they both exude a striking beauty that doesn't match their darkness. Like their mother was a lovely angel, and their father was the Devil himself.

I want Leland to be worse than Johnny, but as I approach his sleeping form, I know they are more similar than different. Johnny manipulates people into obeying him and girls into sleeping with him, while Leland forces his will over the Touched who have become his slaves.

They are both a kind of rapist. Johnny is just better at hiding it.

I shake a sudden dizzy spell from my eyes and step so close to Leland that I'm standing over him. I turn the setting on the rod from green to black—the death dose—but as I lower it closer to his pale chest, the candle illuminates patches and patches of ugly scars.

They stripe his torso: a ragged, horrible chaos of long-term abuse.

My breath draws in fast. Who could have done this to him? Surely he didn't do it to himself? My mind trips over all the horror stories about Johnny's father that slip out when he's in a drunken stupor. . . .

And I lower the dose rod. Somewhere behind me, one of the girls whimpers.

My hand shakes. I can't leave him here to wake and stop us, but I can't kill him either. I don't want to be a killer. No matter what kind of monster he is. I switch the rod's setting to green and click out the needle. I have to trust that if our plan works, Leland will be caught by the K-Force as soon as his ship leaves the Static Pass. I'll let them judge him, although I'm pretty sure he won't escape death for long.

I bring the syringe to Leland's stomach and press the button. He jolts awake, snatching my wrist. One of the girls screams, and I twist and twist to get out of his icy touch. His eyes look black, but they droop until he drops back to the bed like an oily rag.

I turn back to the girls. "We have to go. He's knocked out."

The tall girl slips off the mattress, clutching her ragged clothes. "Go where? With you?! You're Johnny's Scarlet Siren!"

"Oh, shut up. You want to be rescued?" I hold my arms out. "I'm right here. But if you want to stay . . ."

The little girl gets off the bed. "Come on, Gen." She sniffles and scrubs at her face. "I'm going with her. Anywhere is better than staying here."

I cross the room to take her arm. "We have to hurry."

The tall girl called Gen takes the smaller one from me. "Where are we going?"

"Back to *Imreas*."

The Touched girl leads us through the shadowy paths of *Stride* until we reach the familiarity of the airlock. I bring out the glass plate and take the blonde girl's wrist.

Gen stops me. "What are you doing? You'll give her a shock if you try to take it off!"

"First of all," I hold up the plate, "this was made from Johnny's thumbprint by a *Mec*. And secondly, we're in the Pass. These things are dead here." I wave my own colorless bracelet in her face. "Just trust me."

Gen turns her own bracelet around on her wrist and gives a stiff nod.

I press my thumb over the glass, waiting for the clink of her bracelet's release. "You'll have to be stowaways and get off this ship the first chance you get. It'll be too hard for you to stay together, so I suggest that you split up." I drop the blonde's wristband, hearing it roll and then slip through a rust spot on the airlock floor. "Do you know the engine room?"

The girl looks from her wrist to her friend's face. "Gen?"

"Answer her," Gen says.

The small girl nods.

"Good. Go there and ask for help from the old man with the beard. He'll be gruff, but tell him that Rain sent you and that you need a place to hide. He'll help. He won't like it, but he'll help. Understand?"

She nods.

"Then go! Now!" The girl takes a few wary steps backward, and I almost shove her. Finally, she turns and runs through to *Imreas*'s airlock.

"I've got a splitting headache." I start to fall over, and Gen grabs me. I blink to clear my eyes and use the glass plate to free her from her tag. "Try to sneak onto the first passenger deck. There's a place called the Rainbow Bar. The bartender's name is Lionel, and he's got a storage room. . . ."

My mind fuzzes out of focus.

"And I should tell him that you sent me?" Gen concludes.

"Yeah. You might have to sleep with him or wait on him, but hey"—I say and then almost fall over, and she shoulders me up again—"we've done worse, right?"

I swear the ship is growing darker, and I shake the candle like that'll make it give off more light.

"You're about to pass out," she says. "What's wrong with you?"

"Don't know." I manage to get the dose rod out of my sock and hold it up to her. "Can you put this on red and shoot me? I can't seefor somereason," I slur. I should be terrified. I should be panicking, but all I want is to lie down. If I close my eyes, maybe the pain in my head will stop . . .

The shot jams through me like a knife, and I jerk back to the airlock and the tall girl with straight hair. I slip the rod back in my sock. "Thanks. Like I was saying, he has a storage room, and I've hidden some credits beneath a can on the lowest shelf. Use it to bribe someone to get both of you off this ship once we reach Edge space."

She rubs her freed wrist. "Why are you helping us?"

"Because I'm not Johnny's girl. Not really."

She backs up toward the other airlock. "Sure you're okay? What will you do?"

"You care now?" I press my aching temples and sigh. "I'm going back to him before he wakes and realizes that something's wrong. If we're lucky, Leland will stay under long after we've undocked from *Stride*."

"I should thank you." Her tall body draws a thin shadow, reminding me of Lo.

"Don't thank me." I touch Lo's picture in the front of my shirt. "Just survive."

―――〜〜〜〜〜〜――

The Touched girl takes me back to the room with the smoldering embers of the fire. I can see the outline of Johnny's sleeping form, but I can't go in.

I have one more task for this endless evening.

I lead the girl down the hallway until I find a small storage room. I shut the door behind us, remembering Lo in the storage room on the crew deck. She would tell me to do this, and I ache from wishing that she were here now to help me.

"Sit," I command, and the girl obeys. I set the candle in the center of the small space and kneel before her, her eyes staring blankly. I could tell her to stay in this spot until she died. That would save me from having to do what I know I should do, but that would also mean dying of hunger and thirst. Dying through pain.

I take the rod out of my sock and turn the setting to black. "I'm sorry, but this is best for you."

I hold the needle to her arm, but I can't press it.

"Give me your hand." I mold the rod in her fist, roll the ripped sleeve of her flight suit up and position the needle on her skin. Then I take a step back.

Press the button, I want to say, but I can't.

I kneel before her again and hold the sides of her face. She's cold, but she doesn't shiver. Her deep, wide eyes are rimmed with exhausted red lines, but she doesn't blink. I take the dose rod out of her hand and hold it to her neck. I should say something, but all my words are useless. If there's anything left of this girl in her body, she needs to know that I'm not trying to hurt her. I'm trying to set her free.

Ben's words come from the buried memory of where all this started.

"Dream of somewhere else." I take a deep breath and inject her.

She dies within seconds, and nothing changes except for the rise and fall of her chest, her eyes as glassy in death as they were during her stolen existence.

CHAPTER
29

I am kicked awake.

"Rain." Johnny's voice beats into my head. "Why are you all wet?"

I open my eyes and sit up beside the still smoldering fire. My arms and shoulders quiver, and my clothes are soaked and stuck to me in patches. "I'm sweating."

"No shit," Johnny says. "You look sick. How did you get sick?"

I push clingy strands of hair off my face. The fish bite throbs, but I pull my sleeve over the bandage instead of looking. "Maybe—maybe there is something on this ship that I've never been exposed to."

"Maybe." He frowns and squeezes his temples between two fingers. "You don't think those creatures are carrying some kind of plague, do you?" He looks over the shadows of the Touched crew members, and I swear I see him shudder. "I don't know where my brother disappeared to, but I've got a smashing hangover. With or without him, I'm getting that shipment off *Imreas* so we don't have to stay connected to this metal heap any longer."

I get to my feet and grab Johnny's arm to keep from tripping into the fire.

He shrugs me off, holding his sleeve out like it's been infected. "I really don't like sick people." He snaps his fingers at a crew member who's old enough to be his father. "Tell my brother that our business is done, and he can join me by the locks if he cares."

Good. Maybe he won't be expecting Leland to join him. Maybe we will have some luck after all. Maybe that drug hasn't worn off, and I'll never have to see that scarred creep again.

"What did you say?"

"Nothing."

He squeezes my arm. "You said, 'that scarred creep.' Did he touch you after I passed out?" I freeze. Can I really be so out of it that I don't know when I'm speaking out loud? "Did you fuck him?"

"Damn, Johnny! No!"

His grip relaxes. "You better not have."

I struggle to follow him through the chasms of the ship. Several times, I bang into a wall, making him give me dirty looks over the lighter in his hand.

A familiar crew member waits on the catwalk in *Imreas* beside a wavering line of candlelight. Johnny claps a hand on his shoulder. "Ah, Jeb, I could kiss you. Got them out and ready?"

"Yes, Captain," Jeb says. He steps aside, and I look into a sea of ghost faces lining the catwalk. They're locked together on a chain, and Jeb wastes no time in pushing them through the airlock toward *Stride*.

"You're just going to set them loose in there?" I shake so hard that I have to grip the handrail.

"They're bound. What harm could they do? Plus my brother

enjoys it when they hide. He hunts them." The candlelit catwalk swings beneath me, and I can't tell if it's my fever or the weight of the Touched marching by. So many faces.

A woman passes who could be my mother.

"Mom?" I whisper.

Johnny shoots me with his eyes. "I thought I might enjoy making you watch this, but you're really out of it, aren't you?"

I can't respond. I see the two blonde girls, skipping hand in hand in the procession. But then I blink, and they are gone. But then, they were never there. Johnny dropped them out the airlock. . . . I squeeze my eyes and peer harder at the end of the crowd. Walker shuffles among the last of them, and I reach out to touch him, but my hands fall through the empty air.

Johnny punches me in the shoulder. "That was pathetic," he says as the last of the Touched leave *Imreas*, and the airlock bangs shut. He faces the trio of crew members who handled the line of prisoners. "Get us undocked within the hour. As usual, your silence about this business *is* your paycheck. Break your silence and I sell you."

He takes me by the back of the neck and hauls me to his quarters.

The screech of metal on metal and vibrating shudders announce our undocking from *Stride*. Johnny watches at the window while his brother's ship coasts further away. "Bastard. Just like our father," he says. "Selfish bastard. I'm always too happy to see him, and he's always the same damn asshole."

I collapse on the sheets while the ceiling swings left to right. "Being rocked to sleep," I say through my fever. "Johnny, did your father do all those cuts on Leland? Looks like someone used him just to dull up a knife."

"What?" Johnny steps over, glaring down through all his dark glory.

"So scary. Johnny is a devil." I giggle.

He slaps me, and my eye socket bursts with pain. "You *were* with him! How else would you know about his scars?"

The candlelight adds a sudden harrowing depth to him, and my fear lets me focus through my aches and chills. "I didn't! I swear!"

He hits me again, his hand coming away covered in my saliva. He wipes it off on the front of my shirt. "You're a mess. Didn't think I'd ever have to say this again, but I might have to summon the Mec to take a look at you. Then we'll talk about what you did with my brother."

"You can't." I can see white, hovering spots in the dim room. "Can't summon him. Ben doesn't have his thing on."

"What?"

Even through my fever, I know the magnitude of my mistake. I push up on my elbows. "I'm hallucinating, I think. Give me a second." I stumble into the bathroom where a candle has burnt down to the very last nub of its wick. The dim light throws a shadowy halo around my gaunt face in the mirror. I splash water on my cheeks and eyes. Then I take out the dose rod from my sock. I fumble to turn it to red and give myself a shot of adrenaline.

I'm blasted by my headache as my pulse begins to pound

through me. Still, my vision clears and my brain shouts orders: *Can't rat out Ben. Can't let Johnny know about the com.*

Can't be sick.

But I am sick. I peel my sleeve back and check the fish bite. The bandage I tore from the girl's flight suit is stuck to the wound by a yellowish pus, and I run it under the water until Johnny bangs on the door.

I really must be hallucinating now because I think I see a tiny fish fall out of the faucet, dancing through the stream and down the drain. . . .

"Come out!" Johnny yells. "I'm taking you to medical before you spread some plague on this ship. Or worse—" His voice cuts out, and he bangs on the door even harder. The sound sends horrible gong-like vibrations through my skull.

"One second." I refasten the bandage and fumble to get the dose rod in my pocket. He bangs again and rattles the door. I open it and push back my sweaty hair. "I'm feeling much better."

"You look like a ghost, Rain. Your eyes are all shiny and . . . you're from Earth City!" he jerks back like I'm contagious. "Are you going Touched?"

"No!" I pull at my sweaty clothes. "I told you, I'm just sick. Going Touched is very different." The adrenaline makes me stomp in circles. "You know nothing about those people you buy and sell, do you?"

"That's not my interest." He watches me with raised eyebrows. "Leland is the one who finds them so fascinating. I'd rather push them off a cliff."

The lights flick on.

Outside the window, the crimson fog sags behind us, and the engines begin to whirl and hum through the metal skeleton of *Imreas*. But I'm hanging on Johnny's words. *Push them off a cliff?*

I cling to the edge of the bed as my first memory of Johnny overtakes me. His black-suited profile. Walker dangling over the edge of the pier, his small feet jerking in the air . . .

"That day on the pier . . . you said you were keeping him from jumping, but you were tossing him out of your way, weren't you?"

"Oh, don't look shocked. You know I can't stand those empty shells of humans. And shit, Rain, you look way worse in the light."

I face his angles. His body as lean as a knife.

"So do you," I say.

His expression goes dangerous. "If you think I won't punish you just because you're sick, you're wrong."

"Try it."

Johnny sweeps at me, knocks me into the bed quicker than I can blink. His hand strangles my neck, but I slam fists and legs and knees into him over and over. He grunts through my attack. That shot must have given my muscles some crazy strength, but the adrenaline isn't enough; I still need air.

My limbs go slack, and he lets all his weight pin me. He releases my neck and takes both of my wrists in one hand.

"Can't believe I'm enjoying this." He moves his hips to tug his pants open. "You better not get me sick."

Through the blinding halo of my fever, I feel hot tears sliding from my eyes to my hairline. "No!"

"Just when I was starting to get bored with you, you want to play the 'force me' game. Damn it, Rain, I love you." He's laughing, and his lips try to seal mine.

But I shake my head. I won't do it. I won't let him.

I won't do it ever again.

"NO!" I slam my knee into his balls, making his body double up in pain, and my hand slips to the dose rod in my pocket. "Never again!" I click the needle out and jam it into his back. It could be black—the death dose. Or adrenaline red, in which case he'll crush me with one hand. But I know which color I want it to be, and for once, the cosmos are on my side.

Johnny howls and falls to the floor. He grips his crotch, shrieking with pain. "You—you just—"

I check the setting, ready to see yellow.

It's yellow.

I stand. "That should keep things limp."

He tries to get up, but the pain keeps him on the floor. My sickness has come raging back, and I begin to slip off the bed, unable to catch myself on the satiny sheets. Johnny surges after me, and I run from the room, hearing him scream my name in a voice quivering with madness and aching and rage.

Breathing too fast, I can't get enough oxygen out of the air, and when I reach the elevator, I stumble through the doors. I have to make it down to the docking bay. To *Melee*.

Ben and I have to get off this ship.

But I've only gone a floor or two when the screeching blare of the alarm brings me to my knees. This time, for once, there's no doubt that I triggered the sirens. And now I'm trapped in the elevator . . . and the scarlet glow of my bracelet begins to flash like someone is doing something to it. Will he kill me now? Zap me?

No, he'll want to do that in person.

The siren shuts off only to be replaced by the crimson lock-down light. I struggle to get back on my feet, but a strained voice comes over a loudspeaker and glues me to the spot.

"Red tag alert. All crew ordered to capture and seize. Kill her if she resists." Johnny's voice slips into a mocking tone. *"You can hide, Rain, but now you can't run."*

"Try and stop me!" I scream at the hidden speakers. I jam my fingers into the cracks between the elevator doors. I saw that crew member shimmy out of here my first day on the ship, and if he could do it, so can I.

I strain to force the massive doors apart and resort to giving myself another adrenaline shot. My heart throbs like it wants to explode, and my muscles tense beyond their limits . . . but I get the doors open a few inches and then a foot. I'm halfway between floors, and I have to crawl up and over to get through to the next level.

But it's the first passenger level. I'm still three floors from *Melee*. . . .

I make a break for the stairs, dashing and falling down a full flight. I exit by the docking bay, wanting to run straight to *Melee*, but I can't.

I've forgotten about Walker.

I haul open the wheeling lock on Walker's airlock, slipping through the door in the moment that a pack of crew members runs down the catwalk behind me. I throw the door closed and find that I'm in my own personal hell. The airlock. Alone with Walker's pod.

I can barely make out his thin face and gray skin through the clumps of frost, but even at a distance of only a few inches, my brother has never looked so distant. So gone. "Walker," I whisper.

And that's when I hear it. The roll of the clanks.

Is Johnny *dumping* me? I run back to the door, but I can't leave Walker! I try to push his pod as the airlock doors echo a *snap*. And I freeze. And the moment seems to freeze with me. This is where I die. Walker and I together. Into the stars.

I close my eyes, listening to the last clanks, but a realization crashes over me: I don't want to die. Not now. Not with Ben still on this ship and the Touched waiting helplessly on *Stride*. I'm not finished!

But I've waited too long. The airlock is about to fly open. . . .

I turn back to the door, and I would never have rolled it open in time, except that it is already opening. I leap out, and the door bangs shut. I have just enough time to spin and see the outer doors rip open, flinging my brother's frozen prison into the Void.

Ben stands in the spot where he slammed the door behind me. "Rain . . . I'm—"

Crew members yell, cutting him off. They're coming at us down the catwalk.

His hand finds mine and we run to *Melee*. He shuts the door and locks it, and I don't know if it's been five seconds or five years but I'm on the ground. Everything has gone wobbly, like my whole existence is made out of the ghostly strings of the wormhole, and I'm only now seeing them.

Walker is gone!

A thought occurs slow and strong. There are no real colors after all, just ash against a very black universe.

"Walker is gone!"

"What in hell happened?" Ben leans over me, but his face and the ship behind him begin to shake violently along with my vision. "Rain, what's wrong with you? Are you—you're having a seizure!" Clanking and bashing echoes through the hull, and Ben shakes me. "They're going to cut their way into the ship to get at us, Rain. I need you to get up. We need to figure out what we're going to do."

"Exit strategy," I say. "Nothing left to lose."

"Are you sure?"

The banging on the hull stops and Johnny's voice calls out. "I know you're in there with your love toy, Rain. Enjoy your last moments because I'm going to crack this ship in half, slit his throat, and drown you in his blood."

"Nothing to lose," Ben agrees.

He jumps into his captain's chair, and his fingers fly over the command panel. Within seconds, the whole vessel vibrates with the sound of whirling engines. I picture the crew members jumping away from the ship, realizing that we're about to blast ourselves against the wall. Maybe Johnny fleeing for his miserable life.

I struggle to my feet and hold the back of Ben's chair. Maybe we're about to die. The least I can do is go out standing.

Ben grips the controls but doesn't move them. "I don't think I can—" He never gets to finish because I grab his hands, throwing the steering forward. The engines strain on the chain net for just a moment before we're slingshot into the side of *Imreas*. . . .

And my body explodes backward.

~~~~~~~~~~~~

"Get up, Rain!" Ben yells. "Get up! You have to see this!"

I'm nailed to the floor, but somehow, I manage to lift my head. Ben stands before the cracked front window of *Melee*, and beyond, three ship-shaped fish swim before the wink of distant stars. "Those're big fish."

"What in hell are you talking about?" Ben jabs a finger toward the corner of the windshield where the smallest fish floats on its side with a hole through its guts. "That's *Imreas*! We took out the whole lower docking level. She's a sitting duck!"

"Poor duckfish."

Ben points to the two even bigger ship-shaped fish on the other side. "And THAT is *Holmes*—my uncle's ship—right there behind *Stride*. We're saved! They'll come pick us up before they track Leland, and Johnny isn't going anywhere anytime soon."

He swings out of his chair and picks me up, squeezing me in his arms. "We've got some leaks, but we've got at least a few hours. I've already messaged *Holmes*. They should pick us up and . . . Rain"—his voice falls—"you're burning up."

"S'those damned fish," I slur. "Bitme."

Ben turns me by the shoulders. "What happened to you?"

"Should they be leaving?" I point out the windshield at the large fish that looks like *Stride*. Its engines have swollen to a brilliant blue, and it blasts away. Within seconds, the one behind it does the same.

"They left us!" Ben's voice digs into my skull like a nail. *"My uncle left us!"*

"Stupid fish." I pat his shoulder, my body collapsing inch by inch. "Poor us." My eyes close against me.

"Poor Walker."

CHAPTER
30

The Void was a dream.

But when I broke into it, I found a nightmare, and then another nightmare within the first. And then another . . .

I burn from the inside, my veins aflame, and I'm only aware of Ben's occasional yell. His mouth lowers over mine again and again, giving me breath that I do not want.

At some point, my eyes open, and I'm beneath a cascade in a white world. Water streams over me—water that hits me cool, then steams from my skin. Ben's hair drips onto my nose as he speaks meaningless words that can't beat the rush of the downpour. He looks so scared, and I want to calm him, but I slip into the dark instead.

I crack into another layer of the nightmare and find my little brother waiting. He squats on an endless black canvas, his elbows propped on his knees and his green eyes blaring. *So after all that, you still lost me*, he says.

No! I tell him, but I don't have lips to make words. Or eyes.

I'm completely without a body.

And that's because I gave it away a long, long time ago.

A constant wheeze—the sound of air leaving. It reminds me of Walker's breaths at the bottom of the pool, which were so nearly his last.

Maybe these are mine.

I open my eyes, and the noise grows louder. It's coming through the hull—the leak of our air sliding through the cracks of *Melee*. I push myself up; my head feels like it's been cracked in pieces and then glued hastily back together. Ben is asleep beside me. His cheek rests on his folded forearms on the edge of the bunk, his body curled on the floor.

I get up without disturbing him and take shaky steps until I drop in the captain's chair. Outside the cracked windshield, the Void dances, showing off its gossamer strings, and in the near distance, the profile of *Imreas* issues some kind of gas through its punctured docking bay.

We did that, I sort of remember. I rub my aching head.

We broke through. And that fish that bit me threw my body into some kind of tailspin fever. There's a new bandage on my arm along with one at my elbow. So Ben must have given me some of his special Mec blood. Is that what saved me?

I pull at the foreign bulkiness of my clothes. I'm wearing one of Ben's shirts and a pair of his pants. So he redressed me . . . but he didn't strip me of the silver bracelet. My wrist glows scarlet even though we have drifted far away from its source.

How could everything go so wrong? The Touched left in the hands of that Leland . . . Johnny trying to rape me—and then kill me? And the K-Force leaving us here to die . . . and Walker.

What have I done?

I gasp so loud that Ben wakes with a start. "I lost him, Ben! After everything, I lost him!"

He rubs his eyes with the back of one hand. "Welcome to the land of the living, Rain." He gets to his feet, shuffling as though each boot is filled with concrete. He leans against the control panel. "What do you remember?"

"My brother!"

"Out the airlock, just like you were about to be. I still can't believe I got to you in time. I was in the engine room when I heard Johnny's orders over the speakers." He shakes his head. "I've never been so scared. But I knew where I could find you. I knew you'd be with him."

I begin to cry, turning away from him so that I don't have to face his slow, hopeless sort of tone. Outside the window, the image of *Imreas* gets a little closer. But before it—only a stone's throw away—something else. Something like a rectangular box.

"Ben! It's Walker! Look! It's Walker!" I jump up. "Can we get to him?"

Ben doesn't say anything.

"You've got to have like a space suit in here. You can just send me out there and I'll try to grab him. It'll work!"

He looks away. "All the storage compartments are leaking. We're lucky we have air. For now. We can't open any doors. It'd be over in a heartbeat. Crumpled like a hollow shell."

I turn back to Walker. He's so close, but then, he's never been so unreachable. I always thought of that pod as his prison, but the truth is that it has been his casket since the moment the lid closed.

He's become a fading face. A memory like the rest of my family. My breath is stinging fast as my longing for him eclipses the way I miss my father, only to swell bigger than my body, than the Void. Than the entire known universe.

It's too much and it's all at once, and then—it's gone.

I stop crying, feeling very, very cold. Something clicks in my brain, and I can't spare one thought for my little brother. Not one. Not now. "Okay," I say stiffly. Move forward. Keep going, I tell myself. *I've got to keep going.*

"Rain, it's a shock, I know, but we tried. He knows how hard you tried."

I don't hear him; I finger my bracelet. Time to get this damned thing off. I pat my pants down, looking for the glass plate with Johnny's print, but only find Ben's deep pockets. "Where are my clothes?"

He squints at me for a long moment before pointing to the shower. I cross to the tiny bathroom, finding my clothes jumbled in a wet heap at the bottom of the shower. Clumpy bits of paper are stuck to my shirt, and it takes me a minute to realize that they're the remains of Lo's picture. So I couldn't even save that much.

I sort through my things until I find the glass plate, but it's cracked in half.

"No!"

"What?" Ben calls from where he's collapsed on the bunk.

I return to his side, looking down at him. "What happened when I got onboard? How did this break?"

He shuffles up on one elbow. "Let's see. It could have broken while you were running amok under the alarm on *Imreas*. Or when you had a *seizure* on the floor. Or when you slammed against the back wall when we broke through the side of a starship. Or—"

"Okay already."

His voice rises over mine. "Or how about when I had to hold you in the shower to keep that fever from cooking your brain?"

I blink, trying to remember the last part. "You took me in the shower?"

"And gave you CPR and restarted your heart twice and gave you about a gallon of my blood." He waves his arm at me where the crease in his elbow is now bandaged. "I've never met anyone so determined to die." He falls back on the bunk, and I sit next to him.

"Thank you." I touch his arm, wanting him to reach for me, but he doesn't.

"Yeah."

"I don't remember much after I dosed Johnny with Limpicilin."

He laughs hollowly. "Of course you did! Wow. Why else would he have gone so psychotic? Speaking of which"—he says as he pulls the dose rod from his pocket—"you *never* get one of these again. Do you have any idea how much adrenaline you shot into yourself?"

"I had to keep going," I say.

"Your heart almost exploded. And what in hell bit you? The antibodies in my blood were barely strong enough to control the poison."

"It was Leland's weird fish. I hid your com in the tank right on his command deck. I figured it would be an unlikely spot to be searched."

"It must have worked. The K-Force took off after Leland, tracking that frequency, no doubt." His voice drops to a new low. "They left us here to run out of air or become Johnny's playthings. I can't believe it. I can't."

I cross to the windshield. "But *Imreas* seems far away. Isn't that a good thing? And wouldn't it be smarter for Johnny to turn tail and run when he's fixed up?"

"You know that Johnny will come for us. He's out there right now frothing at the mouth as he watches our leaking ship." Ben shuffles out of the bunk and stretches his arms over his head. "Besides, we have no engines. We burnt them out on escape. So when he's ready, all he has to do is swing by and pick us up. If we haven't asphyxiated by then."

"So we're just waiting?" I begin to pace around the small ship. "We're just waiting for Johnny to get patched up and then that's it?"

"Pretty much." He rubs his scalp, sending his hair every which way.

"I hate waiting," I say.

"Well, what do you want me to do about it?" he asks. I finish my pace around the command area and look at his arms held out, palms up—a sort of "I give up" with a hint of an invitation. "If we wanted to be smart, we would sit still and breathe as shallowly as possible, but that might just make it so that we live long enough for him to capture us."

I shake my head. "No. We have to do something. He can't win

everything. He doesn't get to kill you and Walker. He doesn't get to have me over and over. . . ." I let the words fall. "He doesn't get to win."

His blue eyes catch on mine in such a way that I look to his mouth. His full lips. "Okay," he says slowly.

And that's all it takes.

We fly at each other like magnets. Ben kisses me hard, and my hands pull through his hair while he presses my whole body against his. This is nothing like the passion in the lake. This has gone wild. We steal each other's breath, and I tug his shirt over his head.

Outside, the wreckage of *Imreas* is just distant smoke. We ignore the ominous, wheezing leak of *Melee*'s hull, breathing recklessly. I knock Ben onto the bunk and straddle him. I know what to do, and this time I do it because I want to. Not for money or trade.

My hands trip down to his waist, but he captures them at his belt.

"Whoa," he mumbles midkiss. "Wait a second."

I don't want to stop. "Please. I need to do this for real before I die. Please." But he captures my wrists before I can open his pants, and it's too much like Johnny's grip. I rip them away, sitting up. "Don't hold me down. What's your problem?"

He rubs his face and speaks through his fingers. "I may seriously regret this later, especially considering we'll most likely be dead by tomorrow, but we should slow down."

"You're rejecting me?" I slide off him. "Because I'm a prostitute?"

"That's not . . . you're not . . ."

"I'm Johnny's girl!" I start to breathe way too hard.

"You are *not* Johnny's girl, Rain. You never were because you never gave up. Never gave in to him."

"What's this then?" I shove the scarlet bracelet in his face. "A fashion statement?"

"Hell." He sits up on the thin mattress. "I want to slow down *because* I like you. I don't want to hurt you or push you. Really, I–"

I wave my hand in his face to shut him up. "Yeah. You really like me. We've already had this conversation."

He knocks my hand away. "I fucking love you."

My spine turns to ice.

"And it feels horrible," he adds. "Like there's something manic in my body that won't be still. Kissing you is a release. A massive release, but"–he says, pointing to the bunk–"this is too much too fast. I feel like I'm crashing, and I don't want it to be this way with you. I want . . ."

I wait for whatever else he needs to say. The frozen parts of me are already melting, and I touch the soft line of his collarbone and shoulders. Johnny's body was too sharp–all angles and corners.

"I want this to be real," he finally croaks. "You feeling any of this?"

"Not exactly," I admit a little too fast. "But let me explain."

He groans and tosses himself back into the mattress. "Please, Rain, explain why I'm such a blind idiot."

I close in on his face, and my hair tumbles over one side of us. "I spent all this time teaching myself how to do this and feel nothing. And I've gotten good at it. Too good." I take a deep breath and close my eyes. "Do you remember the lake?"

"Of course I remember."

"Well, I can't really be with you without feeling that side of me kick in. Like I just have to do it. Get it over with." I'm suddenly so relieved that Ben stopped us, that I kiss him. It's slow and steady this time. It feels real. It makes my whole body tingle and swell.

I pull away, and his finger twirls around one of my curls. "All the others . . . everyone I've been with . . . they're stacked between us like a wall. Brick for brick."

His hand drops. "The others?"

"The ones I sold myself to. There are so many that I lost count, but they all blend into one burning nightmare." The words catch and jar. "So maybe I did ruin myself." A tear dares to break free, and I scrub it away. "You were right. I'm damaged."

He tugs both of my arms until I relent and lie across his chest. Another tear finds me, slipping from my cheek to his skin. "So we wait," he says. "We'll just be friends until you forget this run and all its demons. It's not like you're ever going to have to do it again."

My bracelet tag glows scarlet only inches from my face. "I'll never forget."

I'm the color of it.

"Then I'll wait until you let it go." He forces a chuckle. "Hell, I only have until tomorrow most likely."

A tiny laugh breaks from me. "True. We should be dead by then, right?"

Before he can answer, *Melee* shudders so hard that I'm almost tossed from the bunk. Ben's arms tighten around me just as another shockwave makes the metal hull screech and moan.

He pulls his shirt on as he slides into the captain's chair. Through the windshield, a great chain net closes over *Melee*. Ben presses a few things on the command panel and swivels to face me.

"Looks like Johnny couldn't wait for tomorrow."

I can't take my eyes off the view as we're hauled to our deaths.

The hulking silver of *Imreas* comes closer and closer, rimmed with the sapphire light of her mighty engines. It's the same blue that Walker and I marveled at when we sat beneath the space-docks, but now the color is promising my death.

"It's too bad we can't tell your uncle what's happening to us. Maybe he doesn't know."

"You give him too much credit. He knows that he shouldn't have left us out here. My mom is going to kill him." Ben bites his bottom lip and taps something on the glass control screen. "But you know what . . ."

"What are you doing?" I ask as Ben types things on the glass screen.

"A last call for help. Or really a screaming accusation at my uncle." He taps something final, and his fingers pause. "I sent a transmission that should reach him while he tracks down *Stride*." He points to the screen, and I lean over his shoulder to read:

TO TITAN SHIP HOLMES. ATTN: K. RYAN.
MELEE BEING RECAPTURED BY IMREAS.
PASSENGERS TO BE EXECUTED BY J. VALE.

"Lovely," I breathe. "It's like reading your own headstone."

"They need to know what's happening. It's a long shot, but maybe they can capture Johnny while he's busy torturing us to death."

"Vale?" I wonder aloud. "Johnny's last name is Vale?" The sentence sticks on my tongue. "He shouldn't have a last name. He's not human enough for that." I mean Johnny, but I'm thinking of my own lost name. Does anyone know that I'm Rain White? Am I still her after everything I've done?

Ben doesn't see my struggle. "Yeah. The malevolent Vale clan: Johnny, Leland, and their father, Errick. They make up the muscles, spine, and brain of the Touched slave trade."

"I heard Leland and Johnny talk about their father. Sounds like the devil himself. Wouldn't this Errick be the real one to go after? I mean, from what I know about Johnny, he's nothing without his father's prodding."

"He's the head, all right, and he leads a strong and untouchable band of followers. He's got a fleet of Runners under his thumb that, well, let's just say there are Runners loyal to Vale in the Void and then there is the K-Force. And the former outnumbers the latter a hundred to one."

"Damn."

"Yeah." He sighs and spins in his chair. His knees press into my legs, and I like the unyielding feel of him. "But we've helped them nab Leland. You helped them. We can die knowing that we amputated a significant limb of the Vale business."

"Victory," I mock, and he almost smiles. "What if Leland gets away?"

"We'll never know."

Something bangs and clamps, and I grip Ben's shoulders to keep my balance. The windshield has been blanked of space and stars, and now all we can see is *Imreas*'s airlock as the doors close around us.

"It'll take them about twenty minutes to hack through the door," he says.

I squeeze his shoulders. "It's not you he wants, Ben. Not really. I could go out to him, and you could stay in the ship and lock the door behind me. Maybe he'll take so long with me that your uncle will come in time for you."

He stands. "Like *hell* would I let that go down, Rain. Like *hell*."

"I know." I reach for him, and he pushes into my arms. His mouth presses my neck without really kissing, and I squeeze my eyes. I can't be responsible for Ben's death—and just maybe he'll make it back to the Edge. Maybe he'll see his mom again, and something right and good will make it through all of this. Just maybe he'll be able to recover Walker.

I can hope, can't I?

I guide his chin to my face and press my lips to his while slipping the dose rod out of his pocket. I break from him to check that it's on the knock-out setting while he whispers a sort of good-bye into my ear. When I don't respond, he pulls out of my hold.

"Rain, did you hear me?"

"If you did get free, if they came for you in time, would you try to help Walker? Maybe you could get him back."

"Of course, but what are you—"

"I'm sorry." I inject him in the thigh, and his weight crumples in my arms. I guide him into the captain's chair and turn the rod in my hand, switching the setting to black. It would be so easy to end it all right now, but I'm no coward.

Johnny will need to be distracted long enough for the K-Force to receive Ben's message and hopefully send help. I slip the dose rod back in Ben's pocket. No cheating this time. I have to do this by myself.

I have to die as slowly as possible.

—————~~~~~~~~~~—————

Melee locks behind me. The inner door of the airlock is open, and a single shadow stretches through from the catwalk.

I am here.

And *this* is happening.

For once, Johnny isn't as sharp as his shadow. His hair is uncombed and scruff lines each side of his jaw.

"*Hello, Rain.*"

But his voice is still black.

I step onto the catwalk, gripping the rail. "Looks like you've hit a rough patch, Johnny."

"Someone blew a hole in my ship. That someone is going to be hung by her own hair."

I take another step out of the airlock. I have to keep his focus on me and make sure that he forgets about Ben. "I'm surprised," I say in my best playful voice. "No crew? Passengers? I thought for sure you'd want an audience for this."

The docking bay is abandoned. On the left, the catwalk, which led to where *Melee* hung, is broken and dangling over the unknown depth of the ship's guts. Beyond it, the scraps of metal used to patch the hole make warping, uneasy sounds. Death howls.

His knuckles are strained on the guardrail, but his other hand is deep in his pocket, no doubt gripping that stone-handled knife or maybe the silver lighter.

I take another step toward him, and a disappointed look crosses his face. He cocks his head to look behind me. "Where's your Mec toy? I'll start with him."

"Dead. Didn't make it through the crash. Why do think you couldn't reach him?" It's a gamble, but I know that Johnny must have tried to attack Ben through the shocking mechanism on his com—and failed to find the signal.

His eyebrows bend. "I don't believe you. You're too calm about it."

"You know, Johnny, I'm starting to think that you never knew me. Didn't I only use him to release the Touched on Entra? And did I just use him to blast a hole through your ship or do I love him?"

I love him.

The thought hits me like a bullet, and I can barely breathe. I love Ben, and he loves me. How in the world did that happen?

I clear my throat. "You decide."

He narrows his eyes. "You don't love him. You've been with me, but then I don't think you love me either. You've been using everyone."

"Bingo," I tease. "It's almost all gone my way. I'm that good."

"Not with your crazy brother. I saw him out there, floating into oblivion. You didn't mean for that to happen during your not-so-brilliant getaway."

"I said 'almost.'" My voice falls. I really have lost my brother, but I can't quite feel it. It's like the emotion is paused inside me, waiting until I can wrap my head around it.

He smiles slickly. "I knew you'd give me a challenge even in the end. You took away everything that I could hurt you with. You *are* that good."

"Nothing to lose. Everything to gain."

He almost looks moved—and I wonder if Johnny ever loved me beyond his lust, but someone runs down the catwalk, breaking our staring contest. A boyish crew member wearing a flight suit three sizes too big carries a large welding torch over his shoulder. His beating steps slow when he sees me. "Captain, you still want me to break open the ship?"

"Maybe later," he says. "What I wanted came to me."

"So you want me to stay?" the crew member asks in a squeaky voice. "Or leave?" Johnny doesn't answer, and the boy is clueless enough not to get the picture. "Captain? What should I do?" Johnny is close to snapping again, and this boy is too close to him. But he doesn't move. "Captain?"

Johnny shoves the boy, using the weight of the welding torch to send him over the edge of the waist-high railing. He screams and falls. Horrible sounds echo up as his body breaks against the gears so far beneath us, sounds which rattle inside me and make me sway with vertigo.

My body throbs to the tune of a screaming siren, but I move closer to Johnny—within arm's reach. "Is that what you're going to do with me? How boring." I slide up so that I'm perched on the guardrail. One light shove and I'll go down just like the crew member did. "You used to have more creativity, Johnny. How *limp* you've become."

He grabs for my neck, and I don't try to stop him. He leans

me out over the drop, nothing keeping me up but his fingers around my throat. His eyes are fierce, his teeth bared, but I don't scream or fight back, and it takes the fire from him.

"Maybe you're right." He brings me back to the catwalk. "I can do better, and I wouldn't mind an audience. You made a mockery of me in front of my crew by somehow evading that alarm and destroying part of my ship." He flattens the creases out of his dress shirt. "But know this, there's no way you're getting out of this one with your heart still beating."

Johnny hauls me from one end of the crew deck to the other. He yanks me off my feet, ripping out hanks of my hair, but I've slipped deep into that voided place of submission. I would even fight the moans and cries coming from me if I didn't know how much he loves the music of my pain.

He wants the drama, the faithful cracking open of the crew doors as we pass. Their whispers and expressions feed his enthusiasm like liquor, and by the time he's dropped me by the elevator on the other side of the ship, blood runs down my forehead and the back of my neck.

Strings of red hair spot the hallway in my wake.

Johnny grins sickly. "That *was* fun. Where shall we go next? Passenger level? You still have friends there from your days as a blue tag, if I remember correctly." The elevator doors open, and I let him kick me inside.

Friends? He means my regulars, the men that I slept with. Lovely.

When we reach the floor, he jerks me to my feet and marches me across the common room. The place is empty for once, and Johnny drags me to the Rainbow Bar.

The bar is not empty. In fact, the damage to the ship and alarms and whatever else has happened while I was aboard *Melee* seem to have given Lionel his thickest crowd of drinkers yet. Still, they part for Johnny, clearing his two favorite seats by the counter. I can feel the eyes of a hundred drunken and terrified passengers like prodding fingers.

I lock eyes with a girl wearing a blue-rimmed bracelet, catching the pity in her expression before she turns back to the drink in her hand. Johnny tosses me into the chair and settles himself upon his as though it were a throne. Lionel approaches, and I read his masked surprise in the way he takes twice as long as usual to pour our drinks.

He sets the red syrupy liquid before me, but Johnny pushes it back. "Something stronger. Something strong enough to burn blue." He smiles and digs through his pocket, dropping the knife and lighter on the counter.

Lionel reaches deep into his cabinets, bringing out a dusty bottle of something as clear as water. He pours a small amount, and Johnny pounds the countertop until he doubles it.

"Lay your hand flat, Rain," he says silkily as though he's asking me to take my shirt off.

I do it. Palm down.

He flips the knife open and stabs my hand straight through.

I scream, almost knocked out from the streaking pain.

The Rainbow Bar falls silent, every eye glued to the knife

spearing my hand to the bar. Lionel's are the worst—peeled open like he's watching a gory fight to the death. He tries to mouth something to me, but I look away. I don't want him hurt because of this. He showed me a little kindness when I needed it. I stare instead at my hand, blood welling around the blade.

Johnny tastes the clear drink, and then spits a little across my hand. I seethe as the liquor hits my wound and sears up the nerves in my arm.

"Captain," I hear a familiar voice behind me, but I can't turn.

Johnny faces the speaker.

"I know this girl. If she's a problem, I'll take her off your hands. I'll buy her from you."

"You going to pay for the hole that she punched through my ship, too?" Johnny smacks his lips. The liquor he's downed must be strong as I can already see a haze in his eyes. "What's your name again?"

"Tobern. I boarded at Earth City. We played cards together on Entra." He forces a bad laugh. "You won."

Tobern. I still can't turn, but I know his thin body. He wasn't as bad as some of the others—and yet he paid for me all the same.

"Well, Tobern, here's a notion: Captain always wins." Johnny yanks the knife out of my hand, and I don't have a chance to screech before I hear the *oof* behind me.

And the thump on the floor.

Several people gasp, and a woman in the corner chants some kind of prayer.

Johnny finishes his liquor; his face twists as he swallows the burning stuff. He hauls me off my stool by the elbow. "I think we've made our point. Don't you, Rain?"

I trip on Tobern's arm. He's lying on his side across the floor. Blood seeps from a wound in his chest, and his eyes are a blank brown. Maybe he didn't deserve a medal for bravery or morality, but he didn't deserve this.

"Clean up the mess, Lionel." Johnny pounds the counter and leads me out. I glance through the crowd that has shrunk back to the edges of the room. No one dares move, not that I blame them. And as I turn one last time, I see a familiar line of razor-straight hair peeking from the storage room door. Gen, one of the girls I saved from Leland.

So she's still alive. I breathe the smallest sigh of relief. At least I did something right.

<hr />

Johnny's happily drunk by the time we make it to the command room. He drops me to the floor and collapses in his captain's chair. I look out the massive window. The strings of the Void veil the stars, and I wrap my injured hand in the bottom folds of Ben's shirt.

Are the K-Force even coming? Or am I prolonging my misery for nothing?

At some point, Johnny is going to get bored and kill me. At some point, Ben is going to wake in *Melee*, and Johnny will find him in there.

And kill him.

"I don't know what I'm going to do with you." Johnny sighs. "I'd like to hang you, but that just seems so quick. Any suggestions?"

I brush a trickle of blood from my scalp and open my mouth, but the screech of the alarm beats my words. It silences itself in record time, and a blue, blinking warning light replaces it.

Blue.

Johnny gets to his feet so fast that he stumbles. "What the—"

The command deck fills with crew members flying to posts around the room. "What's going on?" Johnny barks.

"A ship, Captain. A large ship is incoming."

The Mecs!

"It's *Stride*," someone yells.

A shock rattles through me. Not *Stride*!

Johnny collapses into his chair. "I knew my brother would come back with his tail between his legs. Father would kill him for abandoning us here with a hole in our guts."

I almost choke. We sent a call for help, and the wrong side answered . . . and if *Stride* is here, does that mean that he bested the K-Force? Could he have killed *Holmes*?

"Should we address him, Captain?" a man asks.

"No." Johnny pinches the bridge of his nose. "Let my brother come sniveling to me. Turn all that crap off, and for fuck's sake, clear out of my command. Can't you all see that I'm busy?"

The blue light turns off, and the crew members hurry to leave, several of them glancing at me as I cower on the floor before Johnny's knees.

I crawl toward him. I want to die now.

I don't want to see Leland and his crew of the damned.

Johnny seems to be having similar thoughts. He brings out his knife, flips it open, and balances it on his thigh. "I have an idea. You tore a hole in *Imreas*'s guts, so maybe I should rip a hole in yours."

Samson storms in. The old man's brown and silverish eyes dart to me, but he stares down Johnny. "Where the hell's your crew, John? We've got blasted Mecs sneaking up our ass. And what are you going to do about their request?"

"What request?"

"The bleeding transmission that's blaring through our feed!" Samson taps something on the control panel, and a stiff voice booms:

"PASSENGER SHIP *IMREAS*, YOU ARE HOLDING A MEC HOSTAGE. HAND HIM OVER OR YOUR SHIP WILL BE DESTROYED. YOU HAVE TEN MINUTES TO COMPLY."

"That came from *Stride*?" Johnny yells over it.

"*Stride* is dead." Samson manipulates the view screen until Leland's ship magnifies to take up the whole window. It leaks gas in several places and a huge gash has been ripped through the place where the engine room might have been. "There's a K-Force ship hiding behind *Stride*, and you were stupid enough to let them get into firing range."

"*Fucking K-Force?*" Johnny stands. "You're telling me that there is a K-Force ship up my ass and that it already took out my brother?"

"That's what it looks like. But they want the Mec. We give him to them, and maybe we'll have enough time to get back into the Pass. You know they won't follow." His silvery eyes glance down at where I hold my bleeding hand. "I don't know about you, but I don't want to end up in prison on the Edge for the rest of my life."

The message begins to blare all over again. "PASSENGER SHIP *IMREAS*, YOU ARE HOLDING—"

"TURN THAT OFF!" Johnny yells.

". . . HAND OVER THE MEC OR YOUR SHIP—"

"I can't!" Samson yells. "They've taken over our network!"

". . . NINE MINUTES TO COMPLY."

"What Mec?!" Johnny screams in the new silence. "You?"

Samson looks over Johnny like he might be low functioning. "Ben. In *Melee*. Down in the airlock. You brought him in yourself."

Johnny kicks me in the face, and I explode with pain. "I thought he was dead in there."

Samson's fingers fly over the control screen, reminding me too much of Ben. "No. There's a life signature. It's not moving, but it's in there. We better act fast, Johnny." Samson gazes down at where I hold my jaw. It's not broken this time, but the pain is a pitch-perfect throb that makes it hard to think. "Come on. Let's go."

I get the feeling that he's trying to hustle Johnny away from me . . . he's trying to help!

Johnny begins to leave with Samson, but then stops short. "Wait. I almost forgot." He spins around, towering down on me before he lifts me to my feet and slams his knife into my stomach.

Stars burst through my vision, and my legs crumple beneath me like some essential string was cut.

Samson shouts something, but Johnny just hauls me over his shoulder. "Now we can go."

I don't know how I've gotten back down to the docking bay, but Johnny drops me on to the catwalk, looping my arms around the guardrail so that I hold myself up.

The knife is still in me.

And Samson is gone. It's just Johnny and me.

Alone.

He checks the airlock door that contains *Melee* and taps on a tablet.

"Say good-bye to your little boyfriend, Rain." Loud, metallic clanging noises sound as the door unseals. Then *Melee* is sucked through the opening, falling into the deep of the Void. "Samson's getting our engines going. We'll take our chances back in the Pass."

My heart lurches. The K-Force will pick Ben up. He'll be safe. I did something right. And maybe, just maybe, they'll be able to save Walker. Maybe he'll live on for me. For our whole lost family.

I start to cry.

Johnny turns around, flinging the tablet over the edge so that it crashes down into the depths of the ship. I begin to slip, but he pins me against the railing.

"Finally some real tears." He fingers the wetness on my cheeks. "How about another pinch then?" he whispers. An electric pain erupts through me as he tugs the blade out of my guts. And jams it in all over again.

A black shockwave rolls through my body.

Johnny fixes my arms around the guardrail and steps back to admire his work. The pain jolting through me is like slivers of glass in my veins. I can hardly breathe, let alone keep my eyes open.

"Look at you. As docile as a baby. I bet I could even dance

with you now." He hoists me off the railing, swinging my limp body as he sways on the walkway. He even hums.

With each turn, I utter a string of moans that fill my throat with metallic-tasting blood. He stops dancing and hooks my arms around the railing once again.

Johnny runs his finger down my chin. "I want you to know that you were the best." He leans way out over the guardrail and looks down. If I could get my hand free, maybe I could push him . . . but he's too strong. Too tall. "Definitely the best. And in so many ways, I want to keep you."

"Keep me?" I say softly. Keep me? "You can't. I'm not yours." The words don't reach him, but they don't need to. They're mine, and they're real. No matter what I gave him, I kept what matters deep within me. I close my eyes and feel the edges of myself. Fine, proud, and true. I may be dying, but I'm ready.

And I'm not going alone.

I open my eyes.

Johnny is haunted and terrible, and he speaks like the center of him has been long-hollowed. "I could even keep playing this game if you hadn't taken my manhood." He slams the railing so violently that it wobbles, and my arm slips free. I slide my free hand across the blood-soaked fabric on my stomach until I reach the knife's handle.

I tug it free.

Scorching pain blinds me for such a moment that when I can see again, he's caught me. "Now, now. None of that." He knocks the knife away, and it clatters over the catwalk and down, down over the edge.

He takes me into his arms very gently. "We could have been great. Legendary. I could have really loved you," he whispers into my hair. "And there were moments when you *loved it*. Admit it."

"Yes," my words bubble with blood. And he's right. There were so many hours when I felt myself split with joy in his bed, whether or not I wanted to. There were times when I watched him sleep and realized that my life with him, for all its corruption, was the easiest I had ever known. And I'll always have to remember that I gave him my virginity. I sold it. No, he *stole* it. I almost laugh, finally knowing what that phrasing means.

I'll have to live with it all . . . for another minute, at least.

"Yes," I say again, and he sighs happily, bringing me into an even tighter hold.

My legs find the railing, and I wrap one around the bar for leverage. And then I kiss his scorching lips, tasting the terrible liquor that's still making him sway, and use my body for the best purpose I've ever used it for.

To throw us both over the edge.

His great height topples just like a skyscraper I once saw collapse on Earth City. Strong and tall, and then in a blink, rubbery and leveled. He rips at my clothes and hair without getting a real piece of me, falling beyond where I hang upside down, my one leg somehow still hooked to the guardrail.

He falls and falls.

Landing with a bone-splintering *bash* between unseen gears.

Gone.

I use the last of my strength to bring myself back onto the catwalk, to collapse on the walkway. MADE ON EARTH is stamped into the metal plate beside my face.

Okay, I close my eyes. *I'm ready.*

Footsteps hammer my consciousness and a man lifts my arm, picking me up and holding me against a wide but bony chest. He groans under my weight and smells of grease and steam. I slide an eye open and peer into a face full of sweat lines, a wild beard and otherworldly eyes. "Come on, Rain Runner. Stay awake."

"No thanks," I manage before my voice leaves me, and my heart

Stops.

32

CHAPTER

ick.

My death feels colorless—a stretch of space without stars or planets or the white ties of the Void. It's weightless and bodiless, without temperature or smell.

But there is poetry: "'And who art thou? said I to the soft-falling shower. . . . I am the Poem of the Earth, said the voice of the rain.'"

Reck'd or unreck'd . . .

It's not so bad at all.

Tick.

Except for the damn ticking.

Fingers slide across my hand, and I jerk. Something tugs, sending a sharp pain through my arm, and I open my eyes midgasp. I'm in an all-white room. Wires and tubes connect me to a panel on the wall. So I *am* alive.

"No!"

"Rain." Ben leans over me, backlit by the brilliance of the room.

"No." I cover my face. "This should be over!"

"It is," he says. "Look at me." I open one eye at a time. Ben is clean shaven and bright eyed, the blue overpowering the steel. "We're safe on *Holmes*, my uncle's ship. *Imreas* is . . . don't you remember?"

I remember the knife. Johnny falling.

"I killed him." Tears slip, and I reach for my wrist, ready to find it free of Johnny's cursed bracelet, but my fingers connect with the metal. It even still gleams with scarlet light. I hiccup a sob.

Ben takes my hand in both of his. "We can't get that off just yet. Not without possibly zapping you, but we're working on it. I'm working on it, I promise." He squeezes my hand. "You were dead, Rain. Samson brought you onboard in the hover cab just in time for the doctors to revive you, but it was close." He pauses, and I see a familiar tatty book on the bedside. My dad's favorite book. The one he read to my mother.

"That was you. You were reading to me."

"I thought you might like it." He clears his throat. "Or that it might help wake you." He hands it to me, and I squeeze the worn-soft cover and feel the flooding strength of memories. So many memories. And not just of my family, but also Lo with her wide-eyed love of "you gingers," and even Samson spouting poetry into glorious echoes as he dangled from the ceilingless engine room.

And now Ben. Ben reading to me while I cradled my own death. I glance into his eyes without seeing their color or strangeness; I only see Ben. My Ben. And all his sparks and stars.

I'm suddenly aware of how intently we're taking each other in, and I fumble for words. "I don't really know what happened. Samson was supposed to be powering up the engines. That's what Joh . . . *he* said." Johnny's name is too hard for my mouth.

"Well, Samson lied. We're towing *Imreas* and *Stride* back to the Edge. Leland is locked up. All those people are safe. You did that."

"I just followed you."

"No." He shakes his head firmly. "No. That's backward."

"Then it really is over." But as the words leave my lips, I remember why it started to begin with. I get up. "Walker!"

"Go easy." He takes my waist, and we stare at each other while he guides my hips back to the bed. Then he starts disconnecting the wires one at a time. He's halfway done before I find my voice.

"I'm sorry about dosing you."

"What you did probably saved both of our lives. Probably." He glances at me. "But that doesn't mean I liked it." He detaches the last wire from my arm.

"What about Walker?"

"We were able to recover his pod from the Void before it floated too far away. I'll take you to him." For such wonderful news, his voice is all wrong. A heavy feeling settles in my chest.

"What is it? What happened?"

"He's no worse than he was." Ben's tone reveals that he is no better either. "I wanted to have more progress by the time you woke up. You've been in a coma for weeks."

"Weeks?" I rub my arms, finding a new white scar on the back of my hand to match the burn scars left on my wrist and the crescent scar from the fish bite. I touch my stomach through the thin gown, my fingers catching on the welts from where I was stabbed. I remember the smell of metal and grease as Samson picked me up off the catwalk. "What about Samson? Will they lock him up?"

"They did arrest him at first, but since he's been helping with

Imreas's security codes, they've granted him a pardon until we reach the Edge. The courts won't go easy on him though. He helped Johnny for too long."

I slide off the bed and stand on rubbery legs.

"Walker is on a different level." Ben places a folded green uniform on the bed. "Do you need help changing? I'll close my eyes. Or I can get a woman to help you."

"No need." I reach for the shirt, but already my breath is tight and fast as though I've been running. "Maybe you *can* help. But you don't have to close your eyes. It's not like you haven't seen me naked before."

"That doesn't make it okay." His eyes are already closed, and he bunches the shirt around the neck hole to slip it over my head. "Besides, you'd be surprised how capable I am without my sight from all those runs through the Pass."

I slip the gown off my shoulders, looking at the way he holds out the shirt with his eyes sealed. I wait for him to peek or make a move, but he doesn't budge.

"Is this respect?" I joke to hide my sudden awkwardness.

"It is," he says without humor. "Like you deserve." I step toward the shirt, and he loops it over my head. My arms are stiff and slow, and he guides them through the sleeves.

"I think I got the rest," I say as I step into the pants, and Ben turns his back while I finish dressing. When I've fastened everything and braided my hair back, I lean around him and find that his eyes are still closed even though he's facing the wall.

A yearning swells in my throat, and I slip my arms around his waist, pressing my face to the hollow between his shoulder blades.

341

His shirt is so warm, and I've never realized how sweetly he smells. He holds my arms against his stomach, and I can feel the indented spot on his wrist where years of wearing a com wore the skin down to his bones.

"We'll get better, Rain," Ben says. "Every day, we'll get a little bit better."

———

We walk down a hallway as white as the room I woke in. In fact, everything is made from an opaque glassy substance, and doorways seem to yawn open when they're touched or commanded.

"This ship is so strange." I run my hand down the smooth surface. "What is this stuff called?"

"Memory glass. Although don't let the word 'glass' fool you. It's damn near impossible to break," Ben says. "Almost everything on the Edge is made out of it."

"It's beautiful." I touch the smooth hardness, remembering the surviving panes of the greenhouse. Could I imagine a whole world made out of something so precious? Unbreakable? "How do they make it so strong?"

"They smash it a few million times. Right down to the atoms until it's so pure that its molecules line up like a puzzle."

"You smash it to make it stronger?" He nods, and I love it. "I've never imagined anything like that. But how do you know where you're going? There are no signs or directions and every hallway looks the same."

"There are signs within the glasswork . . . and ads and pictures. It's a jumbled mess, if you ask me." He taps his temple.

"You need the hardware to see it."

We turn down a hallway, passing more Mecs than I ever imagined, but instead of staring at them, they openly stare at me. "Maybe they think you're the one who eats brains," Ben teases.

"One thing certainly hasn't changed. Your jokes are still pretty bad."

He takes my hand. "They're not used to seeing non-Mecs on their ship, but they're friendly."

A Mec approaches from the opposite way, resembling an older, trim-bearded Ben. His mouth is stern but his eyes have a kind glint to them. "Rain, it's good to see you up and walking. I'm Keven."

"My uncle," Ben adds. "He's been looking in on you."

Keven holds out his hand. "We owe you. Never would have brought down that son of a bitch without you, or so Ben tells it."

I release Ben's hand and shake Keven's. I find that I don't know what to say. The last thing I want to do is bring up the subject of Johnny or my status on *Imreas*, but before I can say anything, the whole ship wavers beneath my legs, and I have to grip Ben's arm to stay on my feet. My heart hammers like we're under attack. "What was that?"

"We've reached the end of the Void," Keven says. "That's what it feels like to slow down."

"We're there?" I ask. "Really?"

"Had to happen sometime." Keven claps Ben on the shoulder. "Well, I better make sure we don't crash into anything in Edge space. Keep her comfortable, Benson." He continues down the hallway, and I turn to Ben.

"Benson?"

"Yeah." His cheeks pink. "You can pretend you didn't hear that."

"Sure thing . . . Benson." I swallow a small laugh, and he knocks his elbow into mine. "He's not as harsh as you made him out to be."

Ben watches his uncle turn out of sight. "He feels guilty about almost leaving us to die. He didn't even know we were alive in *Melee* until we sent that second transmission. And he's changed. Something happened while I was gone, and I haven't sorted through it yet. He says that he thought he lost me for a while."

I remember the weeks on *Imreas* when I was Johnny's Scarlet Siren . . . the weeks I spent wondering if Johnny had actually let Ben live after our stunt on Entra, too terrified to ask. I take Ben's hand, but his fingers adjust and readjust around mine. All the while, I feel the ship moving underfoot.

Slowing.

"I have to warn you about Walker, Rain. I wasn't lying when I said that we could help him. I promise I wasn't . . . but . . ."

Ben touches the wall and a doorway slides open in the middle of the glass.

The room is more complicated than the one I woke in. Chirping machines crowd most of the free space and a control screen full of scrolling information covers one wall, but the most complicated thing is my brother lying on a bed beneath a host of wires.

His chest moves up and down.

Breathing.

CHAPTER
33

I step toward him, but the closer I am to Walker, the worse he looks. There's something very wrong in the slack lines of his face. Something more vacant than the widest eyes of the Touched.

"We unfroze him and got his circulatory system working. He needed a new heart, but that wasn't the hard part." Despite his incredible words, Ben sounds depressed. He takes most of the wires off of my brother's scalp, and I reach out for Walker without touching him.

"It didn't work," I murmur. My brother's been scrubbed clean, and his cheeks have a hint of pink in them, but he's not behind them. "He's gone."

Ben taps a few things on the control panel. "He's brain dead. We've tried everything, but there was so much damage and that disease kept stripping his neural net even when he was frozen." His eyes are rimmed with an exhausted red. "But we haven't given up."

The machines *tick* and *chirp*, and I close my eyes. "You can't remake his brain."

"Not his memories, but maybe if . . ." Ben keeps talking, but no matter what he says, I can't hear him anymore.

I sit on the foot of my brother's bed and look away. "I need some time. Please."

Ben leaves, and I curl up beside Walker's small body. He lies beneath a screen of wires while a clear tube pumps air through his neck and into his chest in a steady rhythm. Every piece of him is smaller than I remember: his nose, his chin, his bony chest.

Tears swell until I can't see him. "Why did you have to be so ready?" I touch his cheek. "Why was it so easy for you to leave?"

He answers with silence, and I close my eyes and press my face to the robotic up-and-down motion of his chest. I don't want to remember our last moment together, but like so many leaden memories, it sinks through my consciousness.

Walker on the diving board . . . *"Remember when Dad used to call me Night Bird?"*

I begin to shudder so hard that his body shakes with me. I squeeze my eyes, and my mind falls into a much older memory of being so young, kneeling by our apartment window. Behind me, Jeremy reads to himself, mouthing words. By the kitchen table, my mother cuddles Walker's wiggly baby body. He makes the worst sort of chirping noises, and I can't concentrate on my lesson.

My dad chuckles. "Night Bird. That's what we'll call the little squawker." He pinches my chin and points to the fog on the window glass. "Now, what's your letter?"

I draw an *R* into the condensation, and then add a *W*. "And that's *our* letter," I tell him.

My tears soak into the gown over Walker's chest. I know what

I have to do, but my fingers are slow to disconnect my last link to the family who made me so damn special. Still, the wires fall away one by one until he is only joined to this life through the tube at his throat.

I ache not only for Walker but also for the sense of home that lives within him—and within the memory of Jeremy, my mom and dad. I wasn't ready to lose them, but then, maybe no one ever feels ready. Maybe grief is like running the Void. You never notice that you're in it until you're coming to the end.

"Go on then, Night Bird." I detach the tube from his neck.

The last of his air slides from his lips like a tiny sigh, and I hold my brother's body, and I weep.

It's still night when I bring the sheet over Walker's head and kiss his lips through the soft material. I cried myself dry, but relief comes like a slow tide, coating my drained courage.

I twist my red bracelet, noticing for the first time that I've developed blisters beneath the metal, and some of those blisters have already hardened into calluses. "Can't run between the raindrops," I say, remembering my dad's, and ultimately Walker's, warning for me. My brother's hand slips out from beneath the sheet, and I squeeze it.

He's already growing cool.

I leave the room without having anywhere to go. Where now? What do I have left? I don't even know my way around this weird, all-white ship, but my eyes catch on a piece of paper stuck to the wall. In Ben's bold letters, it reads:

Rain →

I follow the sign, turning right. At the end of the hall, another note has me turning left. And then another right at the end of that one. The signs lead me to a wide room where several uniformed Mecs stand at posts before a variety of control stations, a command deck very unlike *Imreas*'s.

I glance around the room and find Ben's uncle beckoning to me.

"You can have a seat." Keven motions to a bench. "Benson took the cab over to *Imreas*. He said he'd meet you back here."

"He did what?" I almost shout.

Keven raises his eyebrow. "Thought it was peculiar myself. He said he needed something, but I can't figure out what. All the passengers are onboard *Holmes* until we reach the Edge, and as I understand it, they just about looted the place bare before we seized control of the ship."

I squeeze my elbows. "What could he need?"

"This," Ben says, appearing in the doorway. He tosses a small square of metal through the air. I catch it, and then almost drop it when I recognize Johnny's silver lighter. "Or I should say, I needed what was on it." Ben has a great smile on his face. He motions for me join him by the front of the room, away from his uncle and the other Mecs.

He's still grinning, but I can only think of Walker. After all I went through and all that Ben did to bring my brother back to me, I pulled the plug.

"Ben, about Walker . . ."

He smile sinks. "You said good-bye."

"I had to." I want to reach out for him, but I glance at the wall, touching the cool glass instead. The room reminds me so much of Johnny's command except for the view screen—and I find myself missing it.

"How do you have a command deck without a window?" I say and gasp.

The whole white wall listens and turns transparent, revealing the green and blue marbled surface of a beautiful planet. We're so close to it that only a hint of star-speckled black edges the screen.

"*Oh!*" I exclaim.

"The Edge," Ben says, his smile returning. He leans against the glass. "There were so many days when I thought that I would never see home again." The joyful look in his eyes tugs on me as I realize that *we're* over. If this truly is done, he will go his way, and I will have to find mine . . . whatever that may be.

"You'll go back to your family." My throat grows a little tight on the words.

"To my mom," he says. He leans up from the window. "And you're coming with me. She'll love you."

I look down, twisting the terrible scarlet bracelet. "How's that going to work, Ben? You going to say, 'This is Rain. She was a prosti–'"

"I'll say, 'This is Rain White.' No qualifiers required." He steps even closer, and I can't make myself face him. "They're granting you amnesty, Rain. It's rare, but they . . . we, I guess, are so appreciative of what you did. You'll be able to stay on the Edge, live there, and go to the university. You have choices now.

You can do anything."

I almost laugh. "I can't just start over. I wouldn't know where to begin. Without Walker, I have nothing."

"If you can't start over, start better." He holds out a small frame of glass, and it takes me a moment to figure out what it is. The thumbprint device.

I turn it over in my hand. "This was broken."

"I had a hell of a time rebuilding it. That's why I had to go back to *Imreas* for the lighter. I needed something with Johnny's print." His voice falls. "I'm sorry it took so long."

I bring the frame to the bracelet, but my fingers tremble, and I can't line up the plate with the clasp. "Can I help?" he asks, holding it over the lock but waiting for me to take the final step.

I press my thumb over the glass, and the *click* takes forever, but when it comes, the metal circlet falls to the floor.

Ben touches my blistered wrist. He digs a med disc out of his pocket. "Want me to fix that?"

"No thanks." I take the final step, closing the distance between us. "I'll just heal the old-fashioned way." I rest my head on his shoulder.

Through the window, white clouds draw wispy lines along the swirling green and blue surface of the Edge. The green reminds me of Walker's eyes, while the blue is so similar to the lights of the pulse engines high above the spacedocks on Earth City. Both colors make me smile.

Ben slips an arm around my waist, his finger twisting into my belt loop, and all the while, his words sing through my thoughts: *You have choices now. You can do anything.*

"'Reck'd or unreck'd,'" I whisper, feeling those words for the first time. "'Duly with love returns.'"

Somewhere by my feet, the silver bracelet lies where it fell, finally devoid of its stained light. I press a curl of my hair against my lips, the color no longer feeling so damning. After all, red is more than lust and blood. It is the hue of the heart and the standing proof of my unique family.

It is the signature of my hope.

ACKNOWLEDGMENTS

Thank you, thank you . . .

. . . To my husband, Christian, who enables all of my words, and my Maverick, for prodding me along in utero to write this book with not-so-gentle kicks.

. . . To my loving parents, Mark and Joan, who encourage my writing dreams, and my brothers, Conor and Evan, who give me scores to write about.

. . . To my best friends, Amy and Missy, who run up their phone bills with their support, as well as my brave and inspiring "little sister," Julie.

. . . To Karl Norton, who introduced me to Whitman, my literary gateway drug, and who then became my very first reader.

. . . To Vermont College of Fine Arts, my Hogwarts, particularly my esteemed advisors and my literary family, the Bat Poets.

. . . To three brilliant readers/writers/friends, Kelly Barson, Anna Drury, and Amy Rose Capetta, as well as Tirzah Price, for long coffee chats and blog support.

. . . To my agent, Sarah Davies, who fought for this edgy premise, and my editor, Lisa Cheng, for giving me the strength to push this story to its finest edge.

. . . And, finally, to the boy who taught my young heart to thunder and filled my universe with the most poignant rain.

My words are for you, because of you, and always in gratitude of you.